PRAISE FOR

Meg & Linus

FROM THE SWOON READS COMMUNITY

"I liked that both characters are queer, and while it is a part of the story, it's not the story itself. . . . It's delightfully refreshing."
—*Tammy Wanzer*

"What made this unique was the strong friendship between the two narrators (who were not romantically interested in each other), and how that friendship influenced their romances with their partners. It was also refreshing to have LGBT representation that was beyond stereotypes."
—*Julia Durrant*

"This adorable, warm-hearted contemporary YA is tremendously funny and full of some seriously swoony moments. . . . The world needs more diverse love stories, whether that be long-time girlfriends working through some issues, first crushes, or friendships. I really loved this story and hope everyone will get a chance to read it!"
—*Charlie*

"This book made my heart happy!"
—*GoodGothGirlReads*

"Reading [the] story was like sitting next to a mostly closed window when it is raining but the sun is still out. The sound of the rain is soothing, the earth smells amazing, a little bit of wind comes inside, just soothing and mellow and even a bit sad."
—*Lizzie*

Meg
&
Linus

HANNA NOWINSKI

Swoon
READS

Swoon Reads ✳ New York

A Swoon Reads Book

An imprint of Feiwel and Friends and Macmillan Publishing Group, LLC

MEG & LINUS. Copyright © 2017 by Hanna Nowinski. All rights reserved. Printed in the United States of America by LSC Communications, Harrisonburg, Virginia. For information, address Swoon Reads, 175 Fifth Avenue, New York, N.Y. 10010.

Our books may be purchased in bulk for promotional, educational, or business use. Please contact your local bookseller or the Macmillan Corporate and Premium Sales Department at (800) 221-7945 ext. 5442 or by e-mail at MacmillanSpecialMarkets@macmillan.com.

Library of Congress Cataloging-in-Publication Data

Names: Nowinski, Hanna, author.
Title: Meg & Linus / Hanna Nowinski.
Other titles: Meg and Linus
Description: First edition. | New York : Swoon Reads, 2017. | Summary: "Two nerdy best friends navigate high school, drama club, Star Trek fandom, and being gay"—Provided by publisher.
Identifiers: LCCN 2016011976 (print) | LCCN 2016026740 (ebook) | ISBN 9781250098603 (hardback) | ISBN 9781250098610 (Ebook)
Subjects: | CYAC: Best friends—Fiction. | Gays—Fiction. | High schools—Fiction. | Schools—Fiction.
Classification: LCC PZ7.1.N69 Me 2017 (print) | LCC PZ7.1.N69 (ebook) | DDC [Fic]—dc23
LC record available at https://lccn.loc.gov/2016011976

Book design by Liz Dresner

First Edition—2017

10 9 8 7 6 5 4 3 2 1

swoonreads.com

To everyone who enjoys liking things, to everyone who's a little bit weird, and, most importantly, to friendship

Chapter 1

"I CAN'T BELIEVE I LET you talk me into this," I say, because it's what I always say.

Sophia grins and kisses my cheek, says, "Come on. I know you secretly love the spotlight." Because it's what she always says. And she's right, I do enjoy this. Even if tonight she seems strangely sad, strangely quiet. It's not surprising. Last times are sad. Even if they involve karaoke.

"Who am I gonna sing with when you're not here anymore?" I ask, pouting at her. "My voice will go even thinner." Her face falls, and immediately I feel bad for bringing it up. "We can do Skype duets, I guess," I add quickly.

"Yeah," she says. "Yeah, I guess we—" She lowers her eyes, doesn't finish the sentence.

Summer break is almost over, and in just a few days she will be moving away while I am staying here, starting my senior year of high school.

I want to do something epic with Sophia before she goes. Something we can remember until we see each other again. Of course I'll visit her once she's settled in at college, and she'll be back for Thanksgiving at the latest, but before all that, I want to do something special. Just the two of us.

However, tonight, we're out for karaoke with most of her recently graduated drama club friends. Their last karaoke night together before they're all moving away. Special in its own way, but not quite what I was thinking of.

I'll come up with something. I'm sure of it. But first of all, Sophia and I are up next for our traditional duet—I always agree to this even if I'm really not much of a singer. It's fun, though, and I like singing, even if I don't hit all the right notes and my voice sounds almost embarrassingly thin. Sophia is really good, though.

She stares down at our joined hands and I give her fingers a tiny, reassuring squeeze. I guess she's finally getting nervous about college and moving out and growing up. I would be, too, if I were her.

I'm going to miss her so much.

Onstage, the boy with the blue streaks in his hair who's been bravely battling his way through Celine Dion's "My Heart Will Go On" for the past few minutes is finishing up, and next to me, Sophia tugs at my hand. I turn my head to look at her, and she smiles. "Our turn," she says. And, oh god, I love her voice, even when she's just using it for speaking.

"Let's do this," I say, leaning in to kiss her quickly. I don't let go of her hand as we walk up to the stage to punch our song selection into the machine. We don't have to discuss this; we always sing "Something Stupid" together. It's our song, at least for karaoke. Listening to it as a recorded version, on the other hand, is another story. It's our favorite (completely good-natured) argument. Because Sophia loves the Frank and Nancy Sinatra version while I will defend Robbie Williams and Nicole Kidman to the death.

But today we're just singing, no discussions, just my thin and wobbly voice and her strong and soulful one, and I've been looking forward to this all day, ever since we decided to come here tonight.

We've done this duet so many times we even have choreography. It's choppy and awkward but also kind of awesome, because it's silly and fun and we came up with it together.

The music starts and the first verse is mine, so I stretch my hand out for her to take as I start singing.

I can tell from the moment she takes over that something is . . . off. I can't really put my finger on what it is, though. Her voice is as beautiful as ever and she doesn't miss a step of our weird dance, but . . . I don't even know.

We dance and we sing and she smiles at me, but there's still that sadness in her eyes when she looks at me. And I'm not sure what's wrong. Is this still about leaving? Is this because this is our last duet for possibly months?

We finish up to the applause of her drama club friends and the other random people scattered throughout the room before stepping off the stage together.

She starts heading back in the direction of our table immediately, but I stop, holding her back, her hand still firmly in mine. "Sophia."

"Hmm?" She turns, looks at me, and I can't look past that sadness in her eyes anymore. It seems to only get more pronounced the more time passes. "What's up?"

"I was just going to ask you the same thing."

She shakes her head. "What? No, everything's okay."

"Are you sure?" I ask, because I'm not. Not at all.

"Yeah, of course. Do you want another soda?" She changes the topic.

I'm not convinced. I know her. I know she's lying to me, but I don't want to press the issue. Not here, not now. And anyway, if this is about her leaving, I'm still working on coming up with one last big date, some big gesture, something special to celebrate her before she leaves. Once I come up with it, maybe that will help to cheer her up. At least I hope so. "No, thanks," I say. "I'm good."

I let her tug me back to the table, sit down in my chair beside her, but no matter how hard I try to ignore it, I can't stop this feeling of worry gnawing away at my insides.

Other people from our group take the stage one by one, all of them recent graduates using this night to celebrate their newfound freedom. I'm the only one not yet graduated in this particular group of people, and I'm really glad she asked me to come along tonight. There is so little time left before she leaves. We're trying to make the most of it.

I lean my head on her shoulder and she threads her fingers through mine and together we watch the stage while our friends sing. Slowly, I can feel the worst of the tension leaving her shoulders as she relaxes against me.

"You should sing us another one," I suggest quietly, shifting a little closer to her. Singing calms her a lot of the time. Maybe it would help.

"Maybe." She sighs. "You want to sing it with me?"

I lift my head from her shoulder. "No, I want to hear you." I attempt a smile. "I love your voice."

"You know I love yours, too," she says and smiles, the first real smile I've seen from her all evening.

I laugh and close my eyes when she kisses me, and maybe it will all be okay. I know she's sad. I am sad, too. But no matter how much to-night feels like a good-bye, I know it isn't one, not really. It's just the beginning of things changing. We can handle that, together. I know we can.

She comes over the next day—an afternoon date at my house while Mom is at work. We're going to hang out in the backyard and enjoy the nice summer weather.

"Hey," she greets me as I open the door for her.

"Hi," I greet back and lean in to kiss her hello before stepping back to let her walk past me into the house.

I'm going to miss her so much. But things are looking a lot better in the bright light of day, as they usually do. It's just one year. One year until I graduate, too, and then I can follow after her. If I get into her college. But my grades are good, I have all the extracurriculars I need, I think my chances are pretty solid to actually make this. And we can do one year, can't we? I know it's possible.

"You want some lemonade?" I ask, walking up behind her to wrap my arms around her waist as she's toeing off her shoes by the stairs.

"Sure," she agrees, and I press my face into her wild dark curls for a second before pulling back to walk ahead into the kitchen.

"Are you excited yet about leaving?" I ask, getting the pitcher from the fridge and pulling two glasses from the cupboard. Ignoring it isn't going to make it easier. And I remember how excited she was when she was accepted into her dream college. We celebrated for days. With a cake and lemonade picnic in her backyard, and then we went to all of our favorite places around town (our favorite coffee shop, the movie theater, our corner in the park, and many others) and took pictures of her visiting these places for the first time as an (almost) college student.

Maybe she is just in a bit of a funk because it's all finally starting to get real? I'm going to have to do my best to cheer her up. It sucks for me that I have to stay behind, but I want her to be excited about college. I want her to have a great time there until I can finally join her.

I hear her socked feet padding across the floor toward the kitchen table, and turn my head when she needs longer than usual to respond. She flickers a smile at me when I give her a questioning look, shrugs her shoulders a little.

"Yeah. Sure. I am."

And I get it. It's scary. The first time living away from home, in a strange new place with strange new people, of course she's nervous. But I know she's going to be fine once she gets there. Sophia makes friends so easily, everybody loves her. As they should. She's perfect.

"Call me when you get lonely," I tell her and offer a smile, and she does smile back at me, but doesn't say anything. "Hey. Are you okay?" I ask.

She stares down at her hands and shrugs again and I close the distance between us to give her a hug. She hugs me back tightly and I can feel how tense she is, and there's the worry creeping back in, even in the bright light of day. Sophia is usually the most cheerful person I know. Something is just—wrong.

"Do you want to sit outside?" I ask, pulling back far enough to look at her. It's a beautiful day, maybe the sun will help cheer her up. "Even if I'll be covered in freckles tomorrow, I don't care. The weather looks like it will totally be worth it."

She nods. "You're the best! And yeah! Sounds good," she agrees. "Thanks."

"Okay." I nod and fill our glasses with ice while she puts some cookies on a plate for us.

Sunshine, sugary-sweet lemonade, and cookies. I'm going to make her feel better somehow. I don't want her to be sad about leaving, even if I am a little sad myself. But this is a good thing for her, and I want her to be able to enjoy it. And it's only a year. We can do a year. It's going to be so worth it once I graduate and follow after her.

So I lead her out onto the back porch where we sit down on the steps side by side with our cookies and our ice-cold lemonade and I take her hand as we watch the sunlight play on the grass and wait for her to talk to me about whatever it is that's on her mind.

I'm here for her. I know she knows that.

"I've been thinking." I finally break the silence when I can't take it anymore. "You know, my grades are okay—"

"Says the girl who's most likely going to be class valedictorian," Sophia interrupts, bumping our shoulders together.

I squeeze her fingers a little, laughing. "Well, anyway, I should probably add some more artsy extracurriculars to my application, shouldn't I?"

Sophia frowns. "Why?"

It's my turn to shrug. "Just so I have them. To round out my application? If we want to be back in the same place next year—I know your college really likes—"

"Actually," she says, "about that. I wanted—um."

"What?"

"I wanted to talk to you."

"About what?"

"College." She bites her lip, looks straight ahead, doesn't meet my eyes. "My college. Just—are you sure that's actually where you want to go? Isn't that—I don't know. Is that the best idea? For you?"

I open and close my mouth, looking for the right words, and I don't get it. We have talked about this so many times; every time in the past I discussed my plans to apply to her college for next year she never said anything to make me believe she didn't think it was a good idea. "Of course it's a good idea," I finally settle on. "Why wouldn't it be a good idea? You're there!"

"Yeah, but. Is that the only reason you want to go there?" she asks.

I shake my head. "Of course not. I mean—well, it is a really good school. You know it is. You're going there. And—I thought we wanted this? I mean, we talked about this. So many times. You never said—"

"You talked about it," she points out. "I didn't."

"You don't want us to go to the same college?" My stomach suddenly feels hollow and my palms are cold and sweaty. What is happening?

"I didn't say that," Sophia says. "I just meant—do you really and honestly think that this is a good idea? Because you have to be sure. This is a really big decision. You can't just go where I go."

"Why not?" I want to know. "And, yeah, I know it's a big decision. That's why we've talked it through so many times. You're my girlfriend. It makes sense for us to be together. Doesn't it?"

She still doesn't look at me, but slowly, very slowly, pulls her hand away from mine, folds her fingers in her lap as she stares down at the ground. "Maybe it doesn't," she says, and I can feel the words sinking like bricks into my stomach; this can't be happening.

"What are you saying?"

And she finally turns her head, finally looks at me, and I'm looking right into her face as she says the words I never expected to hear in a million years.

"Maybe we should break up before I leave."

. . . This was not the kind of epic event I wanted to happen before she leaves. Not at all.

Chapter 2

Linus

I REALLY LIKE COFFEE. A lot. Coffee is important to me. There is nothing better than a nice cup of coffee to start a morning or to get you through a busy afternoon.

The good thing is that my parents also love coffee. I don't know, maybe it's genetic or something. In any case, for any of this to make sense it is important to know that as a result we have a really, really good coffeemaker at home. A really good one. I love that coffeemaker. It's the best thing about my mornings.

And yet, this summer I have spent a really large number of days having my coffee at the coffee shop down the road from my high school instead.

I've only started doing that this summer. Hanging out there. By myself. Getting some reading done, or even just playing games on my phone. This is a new thing for me. Not because I usually only go out with large groups of people, but because I usually prefer the quiet of home. And my best friend, Meg, was busy a lot of the time this summer, so we met up less than we normally do.

As a result, my summer has been rather lonely, but that's okay. I have honestly enjoyed all this time to myself; I've read so much and I've even gotten a bit of a tan from sitting in the backyard with my books when I wasn't hanging out here in the coffee shop. (Mostly I just freckled, though.) And some days I did hang out with my friend, but I probably turned down her invitations to hang out more often than she did mine.

You see, I had a very good reason for hanging out alone at this coffee shop so many afternoons.

His name is Danny and he is absolutely and ridiculously perfect, with his dark hair styled upward to look spiky and his soulful brown eyes and his cute smile. He also has really nice arms.

He's a barista here, he's new, and I think he's my age. I don't know anything more about him because I don't have the faintest idea how I would even start a conversation, but I like just sitting here and drinking my coffee and being in the same room with him. Is that creepy? I don't want it to be creepy. I know nothing would ever happen between us, even if I could somehow find the courage to say anything to him, anything more than is required for ordering a cup of coffee, or sometimes, when I'm feeling adventurous, a coffee and a piece of chocolate cake.

But yeah. I mean, he's probably not even gay. Chances are that after his shifts he goes to meet up with his perfect, witty, attractive girlfriend to go on wonderfully romantic and entirely straight dates with her.

And even on the off chance that he's gay or maybe bi, he certainly wouldn't be interested in an awkward chubby little dude like me.

But still, I like going to the coffee shop when he's working. And I like being able to simply look up from my book or my phone to see him standing there behind the counter with his spiky hair. Before this summer, I didn't even know I had a thing for spiky hair, but apparently I do.

Also, he's always really nice to me, during all those non-conversations we have. He smiles at me every time I order my coffee from him. He probably smiles at everyone, I guess it's in the job description, but . . . I don't know. I still like it. It makes me feel good. Although I know he must smile like that at everyone, a smile is nice, you know? Being smiled at is nice. And if it's done by someone you think you really, really like, it's even better.

My official excuse for going is the caramel macchiato. Which is seriously delicious. Some days I just buy one and leave. I don't want to seem weird by hanging out here by myself all the time.

Today I'm in luck and he's working, standing by the register and taking orders. I almost like it better when he's making drinks because it means I don't have to talk to him directly. I'm not so good at that.

It's already quite crowded when I enter, mostly older people who are probably picking up their post-lunch-break coffees at this time. Anyone my age is probably hanging out with other people instead of stalking innocent baristas at their summer jobs.

"Hi," Danny says when it's finally my turn, smiling at me just as friendly and professionally as he always does.

"Uh, hey," I say, wondering if he's starting to maybe recognize me after I've been coming here pretty much all summer. But I doubt it. This is a popular place and there must be hundreds of people coming through here all the time. "I'd like a large caramel macchiato, please."

He nods, and his grin is a little crooked. "Coming right up."

I pay and step aside to make room for the next person, but of course I've chosen the exact moment there's a lull in the previously busy stream of customers, which means it's suddenly just me standing awkwardly at the counter with Danny the barista who doesn't know I like him.

I quickly pretend to be checking my phone even though I haven't received a text in more than four hours.

Luckily, there's no need to endure small talk, as Danny rarely ever engages in that, either. The other baristas here usually have comments ready about the weather or some news item or just something nice and easy to pass the time. It always makes me a little uncomfortable, which is most likely the opposite of what they're trying to achieve.

Well, my social weirdness is hardly their fault.

But Danny is mostly silent, which I like. He almost seems a little shy. Like me. At least we have that in common. I like having something in common with him, even if it's just the inability to chat with strangers.

I finally have to lower my phone because there's just nothing on it to look at, and I feel silly just flipping through my apps without any purpose—usually I at least have some messages from my friend Meg, but she's been quiet lately. She's probably busy saying good-bye to her girlfriend, Sophia, who's going off to college this summer.

When I look up from my phone, Danny is standing there with a rag wiping at a piece of counter that already looks spotless. I can't help but swoon a little at his obvious attempt to look busy. It's just a little hint of him being at least a little bit awkward, too, like me. But it feels like a connection. Just a little something we have in common.

The girl working with him that day finally pushes my drink across the counter, smiling at me. "Here you go."

"Thank you," I say, reaching for the tall cup.

"And have a nice day," she adds.

"Yeah, uh—you, too," I say back, flickering my eyes over at Danny for the briefest second. He looks up and his smile is polite but still unbelievably cute. I turn on my heels and find a table, the last one that's free, and hurry over to sit down and get out my book so I can finally really look busy and feel a little less embarrassed.

Only because I'm me and a smooth retreat would have been way too much to ask for, I trip over my own feet just as I reach my seat and bump into the table, which wobbles precariously as I try to steady myself and promptly knock the sugar dispenser to the floor when my hand slips on the tabletop.

I bite my lip to hold back the curse—no need to draw even more attention to myself—and drop my bag, put my coffee on the table. Miraculously, only a little spilled over the sides and mostly soaked my hand and sleeve. I know how to protect my coffee even if I don't always manage to protect my dignity.

I drop to my knees and pick up the dispenser, which has, of course, burst open upon impact with the floor, spilling sugar everywhere, and start to rather stupidly brush at the mess on the floor, not really knowing what to do with it.

And of course it's Danny who suddenly appears next to me, kneeling right there beside me with a hand brush and dustpan. "It's okay, here, let me," he says, and starts brushing the sugar into a neat pile.

"I can do that, it's all my fault, I can—I'm so sorry, I can just—" I stammer and hold out my hand for the brush, my face burning; I know I probably look as red as an overripe tomato by now.

"It's okay, really," he says, quickly and effectively scooping up the sugar pile with his dustpan. "No harm done."

"I didn't mean to," I promise. "I just tripped, I'm so sorry, I can help, I—"

"Already done," he says, and smiles at me. "No big deal."

"I'm so sorry," I repeat dumbly.

"You didn't trip on purpose," he says, and gets up, actually holding out a hand for me. "Did you?"

I shake my head and take his hand and oh god my palms are probably gross and sweaty and I blush even more, but he helps me to my feet without even losing his smile. "No," I promise.

He nods, and lets go of my hand. "Enjoy your coffee."

"I'm really sorry."

"I know. And it's really okay," he repeats in his usual friendly voice, and walks away.

I sit down and take a few deep breaths and slowly, slowly, my heartbeat returns to normal. And, okay. Maybe it wasn't such a big deal. But he touched my hand.

That just now may have looked like nothing to an outside observer, but it was actually quite a good interaction for us. And yes, I know it doesn't mean a thing and he's already forgotten the clumsy, round-faced little weirdo who never manages to say enough to make a lasting impression unless he trips over something. But I'm still happy with it. If this is the most I can ever get anyway, this was really good. And now I have delicious coffee to make my afternoon even better.

I wait until I can be sure no one's looking at me anymore before I send off a short text to Meg. I'm not expecting a quick response, but reaching out to her still makes me feel better. She doesn't even know about Danny specifically, but she knows there's a cute barista, and she knows me; she'll understand how much this means to me.

I'm looking forward to school starting again (yes, I'm being serious—I like school, okay?), but if I'm being honest, I am really going to miss my afternoons here at the coffee shop. I'm going to miss being smiled at by the cute barista who is most likely straight and forgets my face every time I turn my back.

But I really am pretty sure that he is about my age; maybe I'll see him around school when it starts. I can't remember seeing him there before, and I certainly would remember him if he went there. But maybe he's new in town? Or maybe he's just here for the summer and I'll never see him again once the summer ends. I hate that thought.

But for now, I'm enjoying my coffee and the occasional smile from this boy I don't know, and yes, it has been a pretty good summer. I really cannot complain.

Chapter 3

THIS MIGHT BE THE FIRST year since I started school that I'm not excited, and it's all Sophia's fault.

I sit in my car and stare at the school building looming tall and gray before me. Dozens of students are weaving around one another, multi-colored blurs providing lively chaos against the drab backdrop of the scene. I watch them clumping into random circles, dissipating, bumping into one another all across the wide steps leading up to the main entrance. There's an elegance to it, an excited energy that has never failed to draw me in until now.

Only this time, the usual excitement I've been looking forward to all summer is impossible to summon, because whoever invented girlfriends clearly didn't think this all the way through, all of these emotions that come with a breakup. I'm angry at her for leaving me, but more than that I just miss her so much I can't breathe sometimes, and it hurts.

And now my last first day of high school ever is ruined, and I'm not going to get it back. Just as I'm not going to get her back. It's never going to be perfect the way I wanted it. It's just . . . all ruined. All of it.

I sigh, push my glasses up on my nose, and reach across the seat for my book bag. Might as well get this over with, because being newly single is still no excuse for missing class.

I open the car door and am immediately greeted with the hum and chatter all around, the busyness of a first school day. Yup, the world is still here and still loud and still probably mostly ignoring me, which is actually kind of the way I like it. Maybe my classes will manage to cheer me up at least.

I'm not even halfway across the parking lot when I hear hurried footsteps off to my side.

"Meg! Hey, Meg, wait up!"

I even manage a grin as I turn to greet him, take in the familiar sight of the round little guy in too-short pants and a sweater vest and neatly parted blond hair, smiling eyes sparkling with excitement as usual as he scurries over.

"Linus! I see you survived the rest of the summer!"

He shrugs, bumps our shoulders together as he starts walking next to me. "I called you last week. Like, five hundred times. Didn't you get any of my texts? Seriously, where have you been these past few days? Is everything okay?"

"I'm sorry. I was . . . busy." I feel bad. I know he must have been lonely this summer while I was hanging out with Sophia all the time, trying to make the most of our last days together. And then I dropped off the face of the planet completely once she walked out of my house that day. I just couldn't bear to face him and tell him what had happened. I barely even talked to my mom for days. It would have been like reliving the breakup all over again and I wasn't ready for that. But I feel bad for vanishing without a trace like that.

He deserves a better best friend.

"I thought you had disappeared! Or left the country! Or maybe found a way to graduate a year early and go off to college with Sophia—"

"Yeah, no." I laugh, and it comes out a lot more bitter than I had intended. "That sounds completely realistic."

"Hey!" He grins at me. "You might be the only person at this school who is actually smarter than I am. If anyone found a way into college early—"

"So not what I meant," I say, but being called smart by Linus, who is kind of a genius, is really flattering. I'm not about to turn down a compliment like that.

"Meg?" he asks, and stops walking, and when I turn to him he looks worried. "Really, is everything okay?"

I give up, shoulders slumping, and hang my head to stare at the dark ground of the parking lot beneath my feet. Sometimes it just really sucks having a best friend who actually knows you. "Not really?"

"What happened?"

I brush my hair from my face and can't quite make myself look up at him. I haven't actually told anyone other than my mom—telling people will just make it real—but Linus is my best friend and it's not like he isn't going to find out sooner or later.

"Sophia dumped me."

He stares at me as if I've been speaking Elvish. Except, he'd probably have understood that. "Um. Excuse me?"

"Look, it's not really hard to understand at all: Sophia broke up with me. It's really a very simple concept. We were together. Now we're not. Do you need me to write it down for you?" I wince a little, shocked at myself for talking to him this way. I have no idea what's wrong with me today. But because Linus is the sweetest person alive, he doesn't turn on his heel and walk away from me like I would have deserved. Instead, he looks really worried and takes a careful step closer to me.

"No, I did understand the words," he says, still blinking at me as if he's not quite sure he's getting it right. "They're just not really making much sense. Did you say Sophia dumped you?"

I nod, tightly grabbing onto the strap of my book bag. "Yup." I'm holding myself so tense that my shoulders are starting to hurt from it, but I can't help it; I feel weird and I really could use some sign of sympathy. Maybe a best-friend hug, just something to make this morning suck a little less.

Instead, Linus frowns some more and I'm starting to worry that his face may actually get stuck like this and it'll be all my fault. "Are you sure?"

I groan, roll my eyes at him. "Oh my god, Linus, she was my girlfriend, yes I'm sure! Can I maybe have a little sympathy here? I mean, like, what, I'd go and make this up? I don't—"

"Oh no," he says, face falling, taking a tentative step closer. "Oh no, oh, Meg, I am so, so sorry, that is horrible, oh my god—"

And then I finally get my hug, and suddenly it's a little difficult not to get overly emotional in the middle of the parking lot. Linus is a good hugger, and not just because he's soft. His sweater vest smells like fabric softener and he hugs like hugging is very serious business that you have to get exactly right.

"Thank you," I say, voice muffled by the fabric of his shirt, so I hope he can't hear the amount of sadness in my voice.

"I can't believe it," he says, and hugs me tighter. "Honestly, this goes against everything I believe. I feel like we must have sidestepped into an alternate timeline."

I nod against his shoulder and close my eyes for a second. This is more like the reaction I was hoping for.

"Hey, are you okay?" Linus asks, giving me a worried look as he pulls back.

I smile at him, because it's not his fault this last first day of school is the worst first day of school ever. And because I've known he's been on my side since the day freshman year when those hockey players snatched my phone out of my hand and threw it in the Dumpster, and he climbed in with me into that smelly grossness to help me retrieve it. "I will be okay," I promise.

Countless movies and books promise me that it's the truth, even if I can't quite see it yet. But I guess sometimes you just have to hang in there until you can.

"Do you want to come over after school and watch really sad movies and have way too much sugar?" Linus asks.

I take his arm as we're walking side by side, lean my head on his shoulder. "Yes. Please. That sounds really good."

Chapter 4

Linus

I WALK HER TO HER physics class even though she tells me I don't have to.

"Really, this is ridiculous," she says. "I can find my own way."

"I'm here for emotional support," I insist. "You know. 'You're not alone' and all that."

"That's sweet, but I'm not going to have a breakdown in the middle of a crowded hallway," she promises. "Also, I'm not sure that's how emotional support works."

"I know," I say. "But we can't go for coffee right now because class is about to start, so this will have to do until then."

She bumps her shoulder into mine, which I know means thank you. I wish we actually could go for coffee right now. I'm worried about her. But instead I walk her all the way up to her classroom door and hug her quickly before turning around to hurry back down the hallway. I have to run in order to not be late for history now. But when your best friend just got dumped you sometimes have to risk being a few seconds late to class, even if it's the very first class of your final year of high school. But Ms. Rodriguez likes me. I know her because she ran the Model UN last year and also enlisted me as a tutor for some of her students. So I'm hopeful that I won't get in trouble for almost being late and won't be labeled the "late guy" for the rest of the semester.

I'm not a teacher's pet or a nerd. I just genuinely like my classes and I want to do well.

. . . Okay, so I am a bit of a nerd.

Or a massive nerd, actually, if we are being quite honest here. I don't really see what's wrong with that. It just means that I like things that are considered lame by the people who get to decide what's cool and what's not cool. But just the fact that they think that astronomy club and debate team are lame doesn't make it true. Why should their opinions matter more than mine?

Meg and I met through an extracurricular, actually. It was during the brief time our school had an LGBTQ club.

I know that it doesn't make sense to a lot of people, our friendship; apparently gay guys and lesbians have nothing in common, right? At least if all friendship is solely based on talking about what kinds of body parts you like on other people. I can safely say that I have never had a friend with whom I bonded solely on the basis of appreciating other people's body parts.

It was *Star Trek*, actually, that brought us together. Because that first afternoon, Meg showed up wearing a T-shirt with a large Spock on the front along with the words LIVE LONG AND PROSPER. And I guess I stared a bit. Not to be rude, I just . . . hadn't really met too many people before who got the awesomeness of *Star Trek*.

Anyway, once we were done for that afternoon and getting ready to leave, she glared at me from her seat and asked, "Didn't you say you were gay? Because you might want to rethink that since you're sort of staring at my boobs, you know?" I kind of stammered out an apology, probably blushing redder than a fire truck, and explained to her that I was just a huge, huge *Star Trek* fan. And she believed me and somehow we walked out together and kept talking and I was mostly just really incredibly glad that she didn't hate me for looking at her T-shirt all afternoon.

The club was disbanded after just a few weeks due to "lack of interest," but it went on long enough for the two of us to connect and stay in touch. So I guess some good came of it, after all.

I like Meg. I like our friendship, but not only because we'll never, ever fight about a guy or a girl. We're opposites only in the obvious ways: She likes girls; I like boys. She is tall and skinny, and I am short and, um, rather portly. But I fail to see how any of that matters.

There are lots of reasons why we get along. It's because Meg likes quiet afternoons with coffee and books as much as I do. She's also one of the only people I know, other than my parents, who understands exactly how wonderful *Star Trek* really is. The old *Star Trek*. Not the new movies. Of course I appreciate Chris Pine as much as the next person, but I also appreciate Gene Roddenberry's vision; the man was a genius.

Meg and I also share a similar taste in music and she is honestly the best study buddy I have ever had in my life (and also the only one). That time my chem lab partner bailed on me when we were supposed to prepare a presentation together, she spent a week helping me out with my project every afternoon even though she had her own to work on. We've always just partnered up with each other since then if that was at all possible.

I know we'll most likely be competing for the spot of class valedictorian. She's the smartest person I've ever met. But I guess that's a bridge we will cross when we come to it.

To be honest, the news of Meg and Sophia breaking up really, genuinely freaks me out. You know that *Doctor Who* episode "Doomsday," when Rose and Ten are forever separated because she gets sucked into a parallel universe? This shocks me even more than that episode did, and I still can't watch that one without crying.

I don't have any romantic experience of my own to speak of, so I'm not an expert when it comes to relationships. But Meg Montgomery and Sophia Jones just made sense together.

They weren't weirdly symbiotic the way you see with couples sometimes—you know, those couples who can't walk two steps without linking their fingers; those couples who are not even holding hands, just doing this weird tangly thing with their fingers. Those couples who will insist on kissing each other noisily all the time and who can't sit in chairs next to each other like normal people but are always kind of on top of each other. Those couples that make you kind of uncomfortable all the time and who you won't hang out with as a single person because it will just make you horribly, horribly depressed.

Well, Meg and Sophia were not like that. It was more like . . . Sophia would go over to Meg's on an afternoon and Meg would help her with her pre-calc homework, and during their homework breaks Sophia would teach Meg the fox-trot or salsa because Sophia was really into dancing. And I know Meg had fun learning to dance even though she never even thought about it before Sophia came along. They complemented each other. Isn't that what all of us want?

They talked about the kind of puppy they wanted to adopt once they were married and living together. That's how serious they were about their relationship.

They never showed each other off. Maybe it's the lesbian thing and the fact that people kind of react to that whenever they see it. Like, two girls holding hands or kissing each other in the hallways of a public school? Either they'll gather an audience of male perverts who'll try to talk them into a sexy pillow fight (which is seriously just a weird thing to do; do they actually think they carry pillows in their backpacks? Or that they'll start having sex right in front of them if they just ask nicely enough or shout it at them loudly enough?) or they'll have people make rude comments about them. It's pretty much always one of the two.

But I don't think it was that. Not just that.

Their relationship was never about the world. It was about them.

I just really honestly cannot believe that they broke up.

If not even they could make it work, that doesn't make me feel very hopeful about the future.

And really, hope is pretty much all I have; my own romantic life hasn't been all that exciting lately.

That sounds misleading. What I mean to say is, my romantic life has been nonexistent, the same way it has been my entire life previous to this vaguely undefined *lately.*

I know that most people probably don't have half as many relationships in high school as TV makes us believe they do, and I shouldn't be worried, and I shouldn't let it get me down.

But the thing is, I'm a seventeen-year-old boy who has never had a boyfriend and while I do have many other things in my life that make me happy, I just really . . . want one.

I know I would be so good at it, at being someone's boyfriend. If I could just have a chance to prove it!

There was a guy for a little while whom I met over the Internet, and I'm not going to tell you how because you'll laugh, but I don't know, we just connected somehow and started e-mailing and IM-ing a bit and we exchanged pictures and he was really cute and really nice and maybe if he hadn't been living in Portugal, which is awfully far from here, we might have given it a shot. But in the end, we just started talking less and I know he has a boyfriend now, and maybe that's for the best.

It isn't like I was in love with him or anything anyway. And I know that for a fact because I do have a pretty good idea what being in love feels like after my summer of hanging out at that coffee shop, even if I don't have a chance with Danny. I doubt he even remembers me.

But he's just so cute.

He's also in the hallway right in front of me, I realize all of a sudden, and it's enough to almost make me trip over my feet. He's standing right there, talking to a girl I recognize immediately as the president of the drama club, and I stop in my tracks as I see him shaking hands with her as she waves her clipboard at him and points down the hall toward the bulletin board, and he nods. Is he thinking about signing up for drama club? That just seems so . . . fitting. He looks good enough to be an actor, and he's shy enough that I have no trouble believing he's probably really sensitive, too.

I know that I don't have a shot with him. People like Danny don't go for short and nerdy guys who prefer working in the library over gym class and get excited about *Star Trek* reruns. Well, guys like Danny probably don't go for other guys at all. But I can dream, right?

At least I realize, as I slide into my chair just as the bell rings, that apparently we have first-period history together this year. He's right behind me through the door and slides into the chair two seats over to my left. So there is something good about this morning after all, something to maybe help me calm my nerves after Meg's shocking news this morning.

I'm going to sit in history class and steal subtle glances at his beautiful brown-skinned profile and pine away in peace. I am really good at pining. It's one of my strongest talents.

Chapter 5

PHYSICS CLASS DOES A LOT to calm me down.

I like science and math, I like numbers; I always have. And being able to focus on something that makes sense to me definitely helps distract me from all the things that currently don't make much sense at all. Like the fact that I no longer have a girlfriend.

You know what the really frustrating thing is about all of this, though?

I can't even really blame Sophia for ending things between us.

I mean, it sucks. I am not going to pretend that I'm not heartbroken, because I am. I was so sure that Sophia and I were going to last; I had already sort of planned our wedding. I could picture it quite clearly: Sophia's dark skin against a beautiful white dress. Sunflowers as decoration, and Linus was going to be my best man, of course. We were going to write our own vows, and I was going to talk about how I'd known she was the one since I was sixteen, and it would have made everyone cry.

Maybe I should have waited to think about all of that until we were actually engaged. I see that now. And it's not like I had actual plans. More like . . . daydreams, I guess. But hey, I was really certain that it was going to happen! I had no reason at all to believe otherwise, since the few times I made comments like "I want this cake at our wedding" or "Do you think this should be our first dance at the wedding reception" or something along those lines, Sophia laughed and hugged me and agreed with me!

But through all of my heartache, I do know that she had a point in saying that long-distance almost never works and that it probably would have been really hard, maintaining our relationship with both of us being in different states.

What I don't get is that it would have been only for a year. She wasn't willing to give it a shot for one year?

The difference between us, I guess, is that I would have been willing to try. She wasn't. And even though I don't want to miss her after she broke my heart, I still do. I miss everything about her, down to the way she used to drum out weird rhythms with her pen against her books when we were doing homework together. It used to drive me up the wall. Now I just want it back so badly.

And really, when it comes down to it, she did this so we'd both be free to do whatever we wanted if either of us met someone new.

But what if I don't want to meet someone new?

I know, I know. I'm seventeen. How can I possibly know what I want to do with the entire rest of my life, let alone who I want to be with?

Well, I mean, I guess you have to know Sophia to understand this. She's one of a kind. There is no one like her. You can't know Sophia and not be in love with her. She's kind, beautiful, smart, funny . . . and so, so talented.

She taught herself to play the guitar when she was a kid, and just two years ago she started with clarinet and got so good so fast she even made it into the school orchestra that same year. She always had big roles in the school plays, but she never bragged about it, instead helped everyone else out, running lines with them and making friends. She's been doing ballet since she was very young, and she's so graceful, even when she's just walking, but she has no problem getting silly and just jumping around the room like a crazy person when her favorite song comes on the radio. She gets excited so easily and she loves everything and everyone, and everything and everyone loves her back.

She is just one of those people who make the sun rise in every room they enter. She makes people happy.

She always made me happy.

So yes, I get why she broke up with me, and at the same time I don't get it at all. I don't want to meet anyone new. I'd rather still be her girl-friend even though we can't see each other every day than not be her girlfriend and not even be able to call or text her. Things being as they are, I'm not even able to think of her and imagine how great it will be the next time we do get to see each other. She won't be coming back now to have a glass of lemonade with me on the back porch, our shoulders leaning together as we look out over the small patch of grass Mom calls a garden and just talking about everything and nothing like we used to. It's not going to happen. It's never going to happen ever again. And I don't know how to handle it.

I'd rather have a little bit of her than nothing at all.

But, as with every interpersonal relationship, it's not just my choice who we are together, or if we are anything together at all.

I don't even know why I didn't tell Linus sooner. I know he would have been there for me. I guess I didn't want to ruin his summer? And also, I didn't want it to be real, and as soon as you have to admit something to other people, that's when it starts feeling real. And I just . . . couldn't.

At least this is the one positive thing to come out of this whole mess: I'll get to spend more time with Linus now. I know I had been a bit neglectful of him in the months leading up to Sophia's graduation.

I wanted to soak up as much time as possible with her.

I miss it now, those last few weeks of the summer when everything was still perfect. I miss her playing with my fingers when we were watching a movie together. I miss walking up behind her to bury my face in her curly hair when she was making coffee. I miss her singing to me in the car when we were driving somewhere together. I miss *her*.

In retrospect, it seems like it was a good choice spending so much time with her this summer, seeing as how our time together was so limited. Even if I didn't know it then.

Once class ends, I make sure to pack up my things as quickly as I can and hurry out before anyone can get the idea to approach and talk to me. I am not in the mood for small talk today.

I have English next, which is at the other end of the building, but since I left in such a rush I have time to stop by the bulletin board near the lockers where the sign-up sheets for all kinds of extracurriculars are already up. I haven't put too much thought into what I want to do this year yet, but I kind of feel like maybe trying something new. Something I haven't done before. Something a little unexpected. Not cheerleading, though. I admire everyone who can do it, but I'm really not athletic or bendy enough for that. That rules out yoga club, too. And definitely not marching band, because (a) I don't play an instrument, and (b) their uniforms are red. I don't look good in red, thanks to my stupid orangey hair.

But I'm not going to make a decision right now anyway, and not even all the sign-up sheets are up yet, and also I'm gonna be late for English if I don't get going.

I turn around and almost collide with a guy standing there staring at the drama club sheet.

"Oh," I say. "So sorry."

"It's okay," he says, smiles, and I smile back, staring impolitely for just another second before he's the first to hurry off. I know this kid. Well, I don't know him. But he's one of the baristas at Linus's favorite coffee shop, I am sure of it. Average height, spiky hair. Kind of cute, for a guy. I know Linus has had a crush on one of the baristas there all summer and this might just be the guy. He fits Linus's description perfectly, vague as that had been. His name is Danny, according to the last name scribbled onto the drama club sign-up sheet. Danny Singh.

Well, I think I've figured out what club Linus and I should join.

Chapter 6

Linus

MEG IS ALREADY SITTING IN our usual back corner of the cafeteria by the time I manage to get my own lunch.

I walk over to her, drop into the seat opposite hers. It's weird that it's just us this year; usually Sophia was always here with us. Her absence feels strange to me now, not only because I'm used to having her around but also because I'm not sure I should mention that I miss her. I don't want to upset Meg.

When I sit down, she looks up from the book she has propped open against a pile of other books and frowns at me, hand pushing at an errant lock of red hair that has escaped from her ponytail. "You're late!"

I shrug. "Sorry. Had to stop by my locker."

It's not exactly the entire truth. Well, I did have to go by my locker to get rid of my disgustingly heavy physics book. But I would have been here faster if I hadn't spent an extra few minutes pretending to sort through some papers while I was really very secretly watching Danny talking to someone a few lockers down. He is just so cute when he talks, waving his hands around wildly when he gets excited about something.

"I'm sorry," she says, and sighs. "I didn't mean to be rude or anything. I guess I just have separation anxiety after—you know."

I smile and try to look as reassuring as I can manage. "You know I wouldn't leave you without a heartfelt text message consisting of at least one hundred characters and a really vague emoticon."

She puts a hand over her heart. "Stop it, you're too good to me! You're going to make me cry!"

"Maybe I would even slip a note in your locker."

"As long as you didn't write me a poem."

"Not even if it's a really moving one about the power of friendship and the optimistically idealistic message that no matter where we are in the world, we'll always totally be besties for life, exclamation point, smiley face, less-than-three?"

She laughs. "Especially not if it's anything like that."

I sigh deeply and shake my head at her. "Your strange aversion to poetry is really baffling. What happened to you as a kid that makes you reject beautiful, emotional word imagery?"

She rolls her eyes at me and kicks me under the table. "Shut your face and eat your lunch before it gets cold."

"I'll actually have to open my face for that, though," I point out.

"Besides, I am not categorically against poetry per se," she tells me. "I just like it better when it's set to music."

I nod. "That's what we call a 'song' among experts."

"Smarty-pants."

"I'm just trying to help!"

"By the way," she says, "have you given any thought to your extracurriculars for this year? Because I thought we could maybe sign up for something together."

"I like that idea." I take a sip of my soda and consider all the clubs at this school, and then I catch a glimpse of familiar spiky black hair a few tables over, right in the middle of the usual drama club crowd, and I can't control the way my face heats up. It just makes me wish I was a little less fair-skinned so that not everyone could see me blush all the time. "I was thinking of maybe trying something new this year," I blurt out before I can stop myself.

Meg squints at me and I know she can see the way my face has turned red. I'm just hoping she'll let it go.

"New?" she asks. "Like what, for example? Drama club?"

I pretend to think about it, even though that was exactly what I was going to suggest. She must have seen me glancing over at the drama club lunch table just now. I nod slowly so that I won't seem too excited about this. "Yeah, why not? That could be interesting."

She stares at me for a bit and I try to keep my face as blank as possible so that she won't guess at my true motivation. Which she can't, because she doesn't know about Danny. Well, she knows there's a guy. She even knows where he works because I can't help it, he's so cute, I couldn't keep it all inside all summer, I had to mention him to her eventually. Repeatedly. But . . . it's not like it matters. Nothing's going to happen with him anyway.

I know I should tell her I want to join drama club because of him. I feel weird not telling her. But I do know that I have set my sights way too high with this, so . . . I guess it's going to stay my little secret.

Of course, just at that moment I hear him laughing over at his table with the people I assume are his new friends, and my eyes have already darted in his direction before I can stop myself. Have I mentioned yet that he has a really cute smile? Because he has. It's the kind of smile you don't want to miss seeing, because it's like Lembas bread—one tiny morsel of it can sustain you for quite a while.

I quickly look back at my lunch tray as soon as I realize what I've been doing, but it's too late—Meg has already turned her head to see what captured my attention and when she looks back at me, there's this little gleam in her eyes that rarely means anything good.

To make matters worse, I can feel myself blushing quite furiously.

"I see," she says, sounding very smug about it.

"No you don't," I try, but she just smirks widely.

"He's cute."

"I really hadn't noticed."

The way she is able to raise one eyebrow almost to her hairline has always been slightly frightening to me, and it's even worse when that look is directed at me.

"Meg—" I start, but she interrupts me.

"Can it. Is this the coffee shop guy? He's joining drama club, and you know it, don't you? He's sitting with them. And I saw him signing the sign-up sheet this morning. Your secret plot has been revealed."

"There is no secret," I assure her. "Please, just let it go? Maybe joining this particular club isn't such a great idea after all."

"No, we should totally join the drama club," she says. "Trying new things is good. And it would give you the perfect excuse to talk to him."

That makes me laugh. "Like he'd be interested in talking to me."

She frowns at me. "What's that supposed to mean?"

I shrug. "I'm kind of chubby and a bit boring and he is, like, really good-looking and probably has a million friends—"

"Okay, what does his number of friends have to do with anything?" she asks, confused. "And he's a drama geek; they're not exactly popular, either, are they? Plus, he's the new kid. How could he already be popular? He's definitely not popular yet! He'll be happy to make new friends!"

"He's more popular than we are. Plus, those drama club kids are actually pretty cool. Aren't they?"

"Sophia was in drama club," Meg reminds me. "And she still dated me. For two years."

"All right, but—"

"Also, you're cute as a button," she continues. "He'd be lucky to have you!"

"I'm not—"

"And since when are you boring? When have you ever been boring?"

"My idea of a perfect Friday night is rewatching *Firefly* and then reading until I fall asleep on the couch."

"So?"

"I own not only a pair of *Star Trek* pajamas but also Batman pajamas."

"Which are both awesome."

"The Batman pajamas have a cape attached to them."

"Even more awesome!"

"I actually like going to class."

She groans and throws both hands up in frustration. "Because you actually like most things! You're one of the most passionate and intelligent people I have ever met in my life—how is that a bad thing?"

I stare sullenly at my pasta that's slowly getting cold and scowl just to prove her wrong, even if all the nice things she is saying about me just make me want to get up and hug her. "Meg, can you honestly see someone like him even looking at someone like me? If he even likes guys, which I doubt he does!"

She is quiet for a moment, and when I look up to check her face, she is just watching me, eyes narrowed.

"Okay," she says slowly, biting her lip, obviously thinking this through. "True, we don't know if he's gay. And it's not like we can just ask him. And he's new, isn't he? So there probably isn't anyone else we can ask about him; no one will know him well enough yet. . . . But, anyway, Linus, my point is: If he is . . . of course I could see him being interested in you. Why wouldn't I? You two would be adorable together."

I lower my eyes back to my lunch and finally pick up my fork and I don't even know why we're talking about me all of a sudden.

"Weren't we discussing extracurricular activities?" I remind her. "Because one thing I am completely serious about is astronomy club— it's just so much fun!"

She sighs. "I know you're changing the topic on purpose," she says. "And we're not done discussing this. But okay. We can talk about astronomy club, too."

"Thank you," I tell her, and I know I have won this round. Meg has a lot of opinions about extracurricular activities, and we both have a lot of opinions about astronomy club. This could take all day.

Chapter 7

Meg

AN IDEA'S STARTED TO TAKE shape in my head ever since lunch with Linus earlier today.

He thinks I forgot about the coffee shop guy he was looking at and blushing about redder than my mom's favorite nail polish, before he distracted me with talk of extracurricular activities. And I let him think that he had succeeded in distracting me, because I do have an idea forming, and that idea is going to become a plan. A secret plan.

I think it's perfect. Well, it's going to be, once I figure out all the details.

You see, Linus is my best friend in the world, but for someone as awesome as he is, he has a spectacularly low opinion of himself when it comes to romantic things.

I guess part of it is due to the fact that he's gay and, I don't know, it's just difficult to tell if someone else is queer or not, most of the time. Especially at our age. And it's not as simple as walking up to someone and asking them. First of all, that requires a lot of confidence. But also, and even more important, doing that could mean accidentally outing them, which you don't want to do. Or they might be offended, which I personally don't understand at all—people assume I'm straight sometimes and I don't yell at them. But really, very few people our age are out (and I understand why—there are some real jerks at our school), and as a result, the dating pool is more of a dating . . . puddle. Very small. That's why I felt so lucky to find Sophia.

But I know that Linus mostly assumes no one will like him anyway because he's not the traditional Popular Guy Type, and movies and books lead us to believe that that is who you need to be if you want to be successful and have a lot of friends. So many teen movies are only about the poor, misunderstood, stereotypical nerds who just need the perfect makeover before people decide to finally notice their existence. Just pluck your eyebrows and change your sweaters and lose ten pounds and suddenly that asshole who was shallow enough to never look at you before will fall madly in love with you. Like that is what matters.

Why are you only allowed to be happy if you look like you stepped right off the cover of a magazine? Not that there is anything wrong with looking like that, but can we stop making people feel like they have to if they want people to like them?

When I first met Sophia I was fifteen and I was awkward. But, come on. Honestly! Who isn't awkward at fifteen?

Well, Sophia wasn't very awkward in my eyes. But when you listen to her talk about that time, she didn't really see herself as especially pretty or elegant, either.

Still, she was perfect to me. All wild curls and graceful movement when she was walking down the halls.

Then one day I had to stay late in the library for a study group, and when I was walking out I just happened to walk past the classroom the choir uses to rehearse. They'd apparently just finished rehearsal and she came barreling out of the room carrying a tall stack of sheet music right when I turned the corner.

I have no idea why she tripped, but she did, and the whole stack went toppling over, paper flying everywhere, and, you know what? Being polite really pays off. She cursed and dropped to her knees to start gathering up the scattered sheets, and I hurried over and just knelt down beside her and said, "Here, let me help you."

And she smiled at me and thanked me and together we picked up every piece of paper and restacked it while I tried not to freak out too much, because I'd seen her around school occasionally, and I had always thought she was beautiful, and now I was kneeling next to her on a dirty high school floor.

"Thank you so much," she'd said when I finally handed her the pile of only slightly creased paper I had collected.

"Not a problem."

She had sighed. "Now I just need to get these all in the right order again. And there goes my lazy afternoon."

To this day I don't know where I got the courage, but before I could think too much I'd already asked, "Do you need a hand with that?"

We'd spent maybe fifteen minutes getting the sheet music into its proper order again and then another half hour just talking because apparently the choir was doing a tribute to Queen and I'm such a huge Freddie fan. She tried to get me to join, but I'm not a good singer so I had to decline. Then she sang me a few bars of "A Kind of Magic" and "It's a Hard Life" and made me promise to come to their concert in November. I'd promised and we'd walked out to the parking lot together.

After that she'd always smiled at me when we passed each other in the hallway, and sometimes she stopped by my locker when she saw me there and we chatted a bit. It took me three weeks to realize she was flirting with me, because nobody had ever done that before. Once I started to suspect that that was what she was doing, I did my best to flirt back, and when she asked me out a month after the Choir Room Incident I was so happy I could have proposed to her on the spot.

But yeah, the point is, I didn't dress very well and I had a terrible haircut and I didn't even have many friends. But Sophia liked me anyway.

Call me crazy, but I have always believed that if someone ignores you when you're wearing a reindeer sweater and clunky sandals, they have no business suddenly liking you just because you come floating down a ridiculously wide staircase in a ball gown and with your glasses exchanged for contact lenses.

I mean, listen. Not all of us can wear contact lenses. I can't. My eyes are too dry. They just go all red and itchy when I put lenses in them. It's the very opposite of attractive. Makes me look like a weird zombie demon. And if I ditch the lenses and the glasses completely—well. The truth is, I'm blind as a bat. I'd come down those stairs in a heap of ball gown and glass slippers.

Anyway, there is a point to this rant, and it is as follows:

Linus is not a Popular Guy Type. But he is wonderful. He's a real catch. He's smart. As in, genius level of smartness. He has the absolutely greatest sense of humor of anyone I have ever met. He's kind. He's the most loyal friend you could imagine.

So he's not super skinny. He's not tall. He has kind of a round face and he's more than a bit . . . rotund, but that's just how he looks. That's just Linus, and he looks good.

Besides. It's not like the guy he was checking out looks like he jumped off a magazine cover. Sure, he has some serious hair game going on, and he's taller than Linus, and he seemed nice enough when I bumped into him by the bulletin board. But he also looks a little too skinny, almost on the lanky side. Also, I've seen him walking toward the lockers after lunch and he is definitely not unawkward; I distinctly remember him slouching along the school hallway as if he had grown too fast and didn't quite dare stand up straight all the way just yet for fear of finding out he was afraid of heights.

Well, anyway. My mind is made up more and more the longer I keep thinking about this, the plan already starting to take shape in my head.

I'm going to set them up with each other.

Before the first half of this school year is over, Linus will have gone on a date with Danny Singh, Mystery Guy.

Chapter 8

Linus

WE NEVER GET MUCH HOMEWORK the first day back after the summer, so I only have a few things to take care of once I get home and then the afternoon is all mine. While that is most definitely an exciting prospect, I did just have an entire summer off and I don't really know what to do with myself.

I try watching TV, but there's nothing on and I don't feel like re-watching any of my box sets. I try reading a little, but I'm feeling restless and can't focus on the book, so after I realize I've read the same sentence ten times, I put the book down.

My parents always come home late these days—work keeps them busy.

Meg should be here soon, though. And then we can play video games or hang out at the park or go for coffee (maybe Danny will be working?). Or just stay in and watch something, since I don't know how she feels about going out today; I know she usually prefers to do quiet things when she's sad.

She hasn't seemed too sad, though. Which worries me a bit, if I'm being honest.

I can't keep my thoughts from continually returning to the entire Sophia Situation.

I get up from my seat on the couch and walk into the kitchen to make myself a cup of coffee that I am going to enjoy in my solitude while I wait for Meg to get here. It's hard feeling sorry for myself for having a slightly boring evening when Meg has been sitting at home these past few days all by herself doing whatever it is people do who just got dumped.

I know that I have to do something.

I know Meg and Sophia. I know that whatever happened between them, it probably can be fixed. And they're my friends—I don't want them to be unhappy.

If I could just find out what happened . . . maybe I could fix it? Or at least help them figure it out.

But I cannot ask Meg about this. I wanted to ask more about the circumstances of their breakup a few times during the day, but every time she just got this hurt look in her eyes and changed the topic. And I really don't want to upset her, even if I do think she is deflecting a bit. She does that. It's usually not a good sign.

Maybe this is my own lack of romantic experience talking, but I swear, I do believe that they don't want to be broken up. I know Meg doesn't. And if I know Sophia at all, she's probably sitting in her dorm room at college crying into her pillow because she misses Meg.

Okay, maybe not. But I really did think that they were the real deal. And maybe I just need to understand it for myself. I just have to be really careful about it because I don't want to upset either of them and they probably don't need a creepy friend poking around in their business when they just want to move on.

So I fill the coffeemaker, press the button. Nothing cheers Meg up like coffee, so I'll have it ready for her when she gets here. After this summer, coffee has some awfully good associations for me, too, and I already was a fan to begin with. Once the coffeemaker is gurgling away merrily on the counter, I go back to the living room to retrieve my laptop and carry it back into the kitchen, where I sit down at the table.

If I can't fix my friends' relationship, I can at least check social media, where people share everything no one wants to know about completely freely. Maybe spending a few minutes reading about what other people had for breakfast will make me feel less lonely. Who knows?

The smell of coffee filling our tiny kitchen, I make myself comfortable in my chair and click to a new tab in my browser.

I have barely opened my timeline and scrolled through just the first few posts (picture of a cat, a weird poem, a guy from astronomy club is buying a croissant at his favorite bakery, another picture of a cat), when the chat window interrupts my solitary socializing.

I sigh deeply and take a look in the bottom right corner, then promptly suck in a breath, holding it in, trying not to panic.

Because.

What do I do what do I do what do I do?

It's Sophia.

Talking to me.

Via chat.

Her message contains no greeting, no pleasantries, nothing I could easily respond to should I choose that that was the right course of action in this particular situation.

What it says is, quite simply:

How is she?

And I sit there, fingers hovering over the keyboard, and I don't know what to do, until there's a knock at the kitchen window and Meg is smiling at me through the glass. I slam the lid of my laptop shut, and I swear I can feel my heart leap its way right into my throat.

At least this afternoon suddenly isn't boring anymore.

Chapter 9

Meg

LINUS LOOKS LIKE A STARTLED puppy as he stares at me through the kitchen window and it makes me laugh out loud even if that's a bit mean.

I make my way over to the front door and he lets me in, still looking weirdly guilty. Who knows what he was doing on his laptop. But hey, he knew I was coming over this afternoon.

"I smell coffee," I say in lieu of a greeting.

"Of course you do," he answers, laughing nervously. "What kind of a friend do you think I am?"

He looks like the kind of friend who's currently hiding something or being embarrassed about something. I narrow my eyes at him and tilt my head, but he just keeps avoiding my eyes and bouncing on his feet and I decide to take pity on him and not make him tell me what's going on. "Backyard?" I ask instead. "The weather is beautiful."

"Sure." He seems relieved. "We can make an episode list for our *Star Trek* rewatch."

I clap my hands together excitedly. "Yes! Go grab a notepad and a pen; I'll get the coffee."

"Meet you outside," he agrees, and almost falls over his own feet as he scurries for the stairs.

I shake my head at him fondly and walk off in the direction of his kitchen at a far more dignified pace. I know his kitchen as well as my own by now, so I quickly get two mugs and fill them for us, then carry them out through the living room, careful not to spill anything onto his parents' carpet. I have to set them down on the small end table next to the back door, on top of a stack of magazines, to nudge the door open.

It's beautiful outside. Sunny and warm, birds singing, the air full of that late-summer smell of cut grass and wet leaves and earth. It's such a lovely afternoon and it makes my chest ache because Sophia always used to drag me outside when the weather was like this. Just to walk around or get ice cream or go for a swim. She would have loved this day.

She probably is loving this day, if it's the same weather in her college town. I just won't get to hear about it.

"Okay, we're all set." Linus shows up behind me, legal pad and pen clutched to his chest. "Let the list making begin!"

"Yay!" I hand him his mug and he takes a sip immediately before walking past me toward the wooden set of garden furniture on the far end of the porch, setting down his writing utensils and pulling out one of the chairs for himself.

I follow and sit down across from him, force a smile onto my face. "Do we go chronologically or are we just randomly brainstorming first?"

He makes a thoughtful face and taps the end of the pen against his pursed lips. "Uh—random at first? Because strictly chronological is difficult anyway with the *Deep Space Nine* and *Next Generation* overlap."

"True." I nod. "In that case, *Next Generation*: 'Inner Light.' Season five."

He wrinkles his nose at me. "Really?"

I reach out and tap the paper impatiently with my index finger. "Yes. Random brainstorming. Write it down. I like that episode."

"Okay, fine." He sighs, but he does write it down. His handwriting is neat, small letters, slanted just a little to the right. "This means I'll make you sit through that *Voyager* episode where the Doc daydreams about being a hero."

I groan. "I knew it. But yeah, okay. I guess that's fair."

I drink my coffee while Linus gets out his phone to look up the title of that episode—not even nerds like us know all of the titles by heart. I'm still sad, but I'm really glad Linus just lets me be distracted. Unlike my mom, who wants to "talk" about it all the time. Sometimes I really just want to remember that I still do have things worth getting up for in the morning. Like hanging out with my best friend.

Chapter 10

Linus

WE TAKE TURNS ADDING EPISODES to the list, and I think it's really coming along nicely. It'll take us quite a while to watch everything on the list, especially since our time during the school year is limited, what with homework and all that. But it's nice, having something constant to look forward to whenever we have some downtime.

The longer we're sitting here discussing episodes, the more Meg's smile starts looking real. It makes me happy to see her smile. And it helps me forget about the message from Sophia I got earlier. I know I have to respond to that eventually—it would be rude not to—but I don't even want to think about it right now.

"You know, you claim you like the social commentary and yet here you are adding every cracky episode ever made to the list. Maybe you should rethink what kind of a fan you really want to be," Meg says, rolling her eyes at me.

"What? They're funny!" I huff out a breath. "Don't tell me you don't like the funny ones; you know I've heard you laugh at some of this stuff before."

She leans back in her chair, grin challenging. "So your thesis is that entertainment has a higher value than things that make you think and possibly encourage you to learn new things?"

I laugh out loud at that. We've had this argument many times. Well. It's not really an argument; we pretty much agree. But it's still fun. "No," I answer. "I'm saying that they can be the same thing. And that entertainment has value separate from any possible thought-provoking content, because making people laugh or offering them an escape from reality can be as valuable as making them smarter or more informed."

"Yes, but can't intellectual stimulation also be an escape?" She smirks at me.

"Sure it can, but that doesn't mean funny stuff can't."

Meg thinks for a second. "Art is just as important as medical research and politics? That's what it comes down to, isn't it?"

"I'd say it does." I tilt my coffee cup to check if it's really empty. "In the . . . big picture. Whatever that is. Hey, do you want another—?" I wave my cup at her.

She nods, grabs her own cup to follow me into the kitchen. "Always."

"I think we have cookies somewhere," I tell her, sliding the back door open. "Unless Dad ate all of them for breakfast again."

"Chocolate chip?" Meg asks.

I give her a stern look over my shoulder. "Do you even need to ask?"

"Hey, a few weeks ago you suddenly had Oreos. I'm still confused about that."

"Yeah, I don't know what that was about," I admit. "I think Dad got confused when he went shopping. Mom specifically put 'chocolate chip cookies' on the next shopping list and underlined it five times for good measure."

"I don't understand your mom's strange aversion to Oreos." Meg sighs. "But at least I can count on the contents of your cookie cupboard to provide some stability in my life. Well, most of the time anyway."

I grin and shake my head at her and lead the way into the kitchen to get our refills. "Oh, do we include the movies in the rewatch?" I ask.

She considers it for a moment. "We could. If we watch them on the weekends."

"Well, it's not like I have other plans on a Saturday," I tell her, and she laughs and pats my shoulder.

"That's okay. I don't, either. Well, not anymore. At least we have our friends from Starfleet, right?"

I bite my lip, mentally kicking myself for bringing up weekend plans. I didn't want to remind her of Sophia. But we'll go right back to our list-making once we have our coffee. I can't fix this for her, but I can make sure to offer distraction and copious amounts of caffeine until she's ready to finally talk about what happened.

Chapter 11

Meg

I GET HOME JUST AROUND dinnertime after hanging out with Linus all afternoon. I'm feeling mostly okay. Spending some time being distracted really helped.

Since I have the entire evening to myself now that my girlfriend is not only living several hours away but is also, you know, no longer my girlfriend, I decide that the best way to spend my time is to watch movies.

I like movies. And also, I know that this year at school is going to take a turn for the busy and exhausting very, very soon, what with all the homework and clubs and extra studying I have to find time for. I am a firm believer in taking your breaks when they present themselves, before things get crazy all on their own again.

Besides, if I actually want to help Linus approach that guy he likes, I should probably educate myself on all the ways of setting people up romantically. And what's better than a good and completely unrealistic movie plot to give me ideas?

I start with *The Parent Trap* because that movie is delightful and it's also on Netflix and I also feel that it might have the best material for helping me to come up with a plan to throw two people together.

So Linus and Danny Singh, Mystery Guy, are not my parents. And I definitely don't want my parents back together—we're all better off with them divorced. But I think the basic concept of setting two people up to spend time together can be applied to different levels and degrees of relation and acquaintances.

Which reminds me, halfway into the movie, that I don't really know anything about him. If I want to set him up with my best friend, I should probably find out a few things about him first. I'm almost one hundred percent sure he's a transfer student because I've never seen him around before today, but just in case I decide to check.

I pause the movie and go get last year's yearbook from my room—if he was at our school last year I'm guessing he's a senior like Linus and me or maybe a junior, but no younger than that. He shouldn't be too hard to find.

I unpause the movie once I'm back in the living room, drop into my spot on the couch, and prop my feet up on the coffee table (Mom's still at work so she can't yell at me for it) before I open the yearbook, its spine resting between my knees.

I start flipping through the pages, hoping to spot something that could help me, but after about twenty seconds I land on page twenty-three, which has a really huge group photo of last year's drama club, and in the middle of that picture is Sophia. I snap the book shut and drop it to the floor in a sudden burst of anger. Does everything always have to remind me of her? Why won't she leave me alone? Isn't it enough that she already called twice this week? I haven't even been able to make myself pick up the phone.

Maybe it's because it's only been two weeks, but I really don't want to be reminded of her right now. Which kind of makes me think that signing up for drama club with Linus might not be the best idea. Sophia lived for drama club. It's not going to be easy, having to pretend like it doesn't get to me at all.

The front door opens and closes and I drop my feet from the coffee table in a smooth, practiced reflex.

"Meg?" my mom calls, and I pause the movie again, frowning at the digital clock on the DVD player as she enters the living room, still in her summer blazer and with her heavy purse hanging over her shoulder.

"Mom? You're late. Like, crazy late!"

"I know. Crazy day. I'm not even finished yet, but people were insisting on eating canned tuna in the office so I decided to take the rest of my work home for the day. It's just mostly reading anyway."

"I want to be able to do that at school." I let out a dreamy sigh. "If I could just take my work home with me whenever people decide that French class is the perfect place to start spitball attacks on each other—"

"Doesn't that ever go out of style?" Mom slips her blazer off, throws it over the back of a nearby chair. For some reason, our living room is full of random chairs. Some are used for sitting, but even more seem to be Mom's idea of interior design. Some are used as stands for our various potted plants. Some are even functioning as makeshift bookshelves.

"Guess not." I shrug. "It's gross."

Mom walks over and sits down next to me on the couch. "It's spit-soaked paper, yeah, it's gross! What are we watching?"

"We?" I shove her a little, grinning. "Mom, you have to work! You can't get fired—you need to support me in the lifestyle I am accustomed to!"

She squints at the screen. "Is that *The Parent Trap*?"

"Excellent eye."

"Also, they're not firing me, they need me."

"Of course they do," I agree, and pick up the remote to unpause the movie.

My mother works at the Museum of Archaeology, which is awesome because on more than one occasion she's brought me along to work and I could visit the exhibition without paying, and usually I can even bring a friend. Linus loves the museum. Sophia used to love it, too.

But then, Sophia also used to love me.

I stare through the movie on the screen and suddenly feel miserable again.

Mom looks at the yearbook on the floor, then back up at me. "Meg?" she asks.

"Yeah?"

"Are you okay?"

I swallow heavily and nod. Second time I've been asked that today. I don't like that people have to ask me this. "Yeah."

"You don't have to be okay, you know? Not right now."

I nod again. "Thank you. I know."

She's quiet for a little while and we just watch the movie. I know that she's, in all likelihood, not done asking me if I'm okay and she's not done trying to get me to "talk," whatever good that is supposed to do. But I appreciate the fact that, for now at least, we can just sit here and be silent.

"If you want to, we can have pancakes for dinner," she suggests.

And I wipe my nose on my sleeve and laugh even though I don't want to. "I'd like that. Thanks, Mom."

She hugs me from the side and kisses my hair and it's nice to know that at least I'm not alone. "Anytime, Meggie."

If I get pancakes for dinner, I'll even let her use the hated nickname.

Chapter 12

Linus

WHAT IS THE PROTOCOL FOR chatting with your best friend's ex-girlfriend, specifically if you still, through no fault of your own, don't have any real details about their breakup?

I want to be there for Meg. She's my friend. But here's where it gets complicated: So is Sophia.

So, Sophia is not my best friend the way Meg is. But I do feel loyalty toward her, too, and I still really don't know what the hell happened between them and I am really very well aware of the fact that it is none of my business and that I should respectfully keep out of it.

Which I had every intention of doing earlier this afternoon when I decided that I wouldn't pry and just take care of my friend instead.

Now Meg has gone home and I'm sitting here with my laptop, trying to decide what to do about Sophia's message. Because I have to do something, but I simply have no idea what.

My hands are a little sweaty and my stomach feels weird; I don't want to do the wrong thing and make matters worse. But here I am staring at my laptop screen and there is Sophia's message, still just there, still just staring back at me, prompting me to respond in some way. I don't want to be rude!

The question is: Which is ruder? Ignoring Sophia's message or talking to her when Meg doesn't even talk about her?

I bite my lip and think, and it's not like Meg told me I have to hate Sophia now or that I can't talk to her. I don't think even Meg hates Sophia. She's just upset. And Meg knows that I'm friends with Sophia, too.

And how can I ignore a message like that?

How is she?

Is this what it feels like when your parents get divorced and you feel like you have to pick a side? But no, that seems overly dramatic and inappropriate as a comparison.

I make up my mind and type out my reply, hoping to everything I don't particularly believe in that I'm not doing anything wrong.

Sorry for the late response. She's okay.

Sophia, apparently still online even though it took me hours to write back, responds within seconds.

No problem. Are you sure? You don't have to spare my feelings. I know she probably hates me.

I think about it, and decide to go with the truth.

She didn't say much about what happened between you guys. And I don't know how much I should tell you, because I don't want to upset her.

It takes a while before Sophia replies this time, and I'm just hoping I wasn't too rude.

I get that, she writes. *I don't want you to betray her trust. It's enough that I hurt her by dumping her.*

I hesitate for only a moment, but I need to ask this. I'm sorry. I'm only human. I'm weak.

What did you do?

Again, there's a few seconds' pause before her reply comes through.

It's complicated. I was worried she was making rash decisions about college. For me. Also I didn't want us to have to live through a year's separation feeling like we were tied down by someone who was never there.

Oh. I shake my head, and the thing is, I get it. Kind of. I don't understand it fully, but I don't have to.

That makes sense, I write back.

No it doesn't, she writes immediately. *I made a mistake, I know that now.*

Well. I slump back in my seat and don't really know what to say to that.

I'm sorry, I type.

It's my own stupid fault, comes her reply.

I can't pretend to be an expert on whose fault anything is. But all the same, this makes my heart hurt. I don't want them to be unhappy. Either of them.

Have you tried talking to her? I ask.

She won't take my calls.

Is there anything I can do?

For a while, nothing happens. Then she writes:

I know you're already there for her. And it's really not my place to ask you for anything else.

You can still always ask, I promise her. *I'll listen!*

Thank you, she writes. *I have to go right now. But actually . . . if you're sure you don't mind, can I ask you for one little favor first?*

Just told you that you could!

Can you give her a hug from me? Don't tell her it's from me, though.

I swallow, and maybe this is a bit like watching your parents get divorced. In a very quiet, very quick divorce, with both of them clearly still in love with each other.

She loves hugs, I write back.

Yeah. I know.

Not a problem, I promise. *Consider it done.*

She responds with a simple <3 and I close my laptop and then close my eyes for a moment.

What a mess. And I have no idea how to really help either of them.

Chapter 13

AFTER I GOT ABSOLUTELY NOWHERE with my Danny Singh, Mystery Guy, research last evening, I am already thinking of different ways to find out more about him today so that I can determine whether or not he's right for Linus. And then, when I walk into my second-period math class, there he is right there in the second row, chewing his bottom lip and looking a bit nervous.

I really am quite certain that he is a new transfer—the more I think about it, the more I'm convinced that I have never seen him around before.

I get confirmation for this when our teacher walks into the room and Danny immediately hurries up to the front to hand her a slip of paper and explain with a lot of hand-waving and smiling how sorry he is for missing class yesterday. Apparently he had a doctor's appointment.

Ms. Gilbert sends him back to his seat with an answering smile and a pat on the back, and he sits down, looking significantly less nervous.

I keep sneaking glances at him all during class to figure out how good of an idea it is to simply approach him after class and introduce myself. It seems the easiest way to get him and Linus closer together. I can befriend him and introduce them. He would look adorable next to Linus. They can fall madly in love and get their picture-perfect happy ending and thank me in their self-written wedding vows for getting them together in the first place.

So as soon as class ends I make sure to keep a close eye on him, ready to hurry out or hang back depending on what he is going to do.

What he does is get out of his seat and walk back up to the front to approach the teacher.

I pack away my things slowly, drop a few papers on the floor deliberately so I can pick them back up while looking not at all as if I'm eavesdropping on the conversation at the front of the classroom.

"Danny," Ms. Gilbert is saying, "how may I help you?"

Danny shrugs. "It's, uh. I don't mean to cause any trouble, but—some of the stuff you mentioned today . . . I don't think we covered that in my last school. I'm afraid I'm not quite—I mean—"

"Do you think you need to be placed in an easier class?" Ms. Gilbert asks patiently. "Because it's not too late for that."

"Oh," he says. "I don't know about that. It's more like—do you maybe—could you by any chance point me in the direction of someone who can tell me what was covered last semester, and I'm sure I can catch up on anything I missed—or, I don't know—"

"I'm sure that can be arranged if you just stop by toward the end of the day," Ms. Gilbert assures him. "I'll have a list of topics for you, and I have a few names of students you could ask for tutoring. If that helps."

"Yes! Thank you so much," Danny says (politely, he's polite; I file that away as one more thing that simply makes him perfect for Linus) and I put the rest of my things away and slowly walk from the room while waiting for them to finish their conversation and for him to gather his own things and follow after me.

Now I really have an idea, and it's a brilliant one, if I do say so myself.

I wait outside the door pretending to be going through my bag until he walks right past me, and I quickly skip after him before he can get away, shout out just a little too loudly, "Danny!"

He jumps a little, turns, stares at me wide-eyed. "Huh?" he says eloquently.

I clear my throat, lower my voice to a slightly saner volume. "Sorry, sorry, I—um. Hi. I'm Meg."

"Danny," he answers dumbly, then winces. "Obviously you know that already."

"Yeah, I'm sorry about that," I say quickly. "I didn't mean to eavesdrop just now," I lie. "I just couldn't help but overhear. You're looking for a math tutor?"

He nods, looking a little embarrassed. "Yeah, uh. It's just—"

"Oh no, I get it," I assure him. "You're new, right?"

"Second day." He sighs. "My other classes were okay, but apparently my last school was kind of behind in math."

"You want to catch up?"

He nods again. "If I can find anyone to help me out."

"Well, you're in luck." I smile at him.

"Are you a tutor?"

"Oh." I shake my head. "No. I mean, usually yes, but right now I have so many other commitments—anyway, my friend Linus is a fantastic tutor and I happen to know that he is still available, and you should totally ask him!"

Danny looks a bit suspicious, which I guess is understandable after being stopped in the middle of a hallway at a new school by a strange girl who yells out your name as if you're old friends. "Thanks," he says. "But Ms. Gilbert said she'd give me some names; maybe I should wait for—"

I wave a hand at him impatiently. "His name will be on that list, I can guarantee it. But you should ask him as soon as possible before someone else does. Everyone knows he's a great tutor. He really is the best; if you're serious about catching up, you're definitely going to want his help!"

Danny hesitates and I'm afraid I may have overdone it a little, but then he smiles and shrugs. "Okay. That sounds like it's worth a shot. Thank you. Who is your friend?"

I quickly show him a picture of Linus on my phone and explain the way to his locker, and Danny nods along and definitely looks interested.

"You can find him at his locker after last period," I say. "He'll be there. Or I'll tell him to find you. Whoever runs into the other first, then." I grin.

Danny looks a little red in the face, but he's probably still just embarrassed about needing a tutor. I have to try to get Linus to approach him first, I decide. Just to make sure this will work.

"Thank you," he says. "I really appreciate your help!"

"Not a problem," I promise. "I'll see you around, okay?"

He looks grateful, and I guess being new at a place as big as this must be kind of scary. I make a mental note to keep my eyes out for him from now on regardless of whether he talks to Linus. I'm sure he could use some friends. And also, the more I talk to him, the better the chances of him and Linus connecting. I offer a parting smile before walking away. Now I just have to find Linus to convince him of the brilliance of my plan. In a way that won't make him realize it is something that I planned.

Sometimes, all you need is just a little bit of luck.

Luck, and really good ears, and a kind of psychic best-friend radar that allows you to locate your best friend even if he is currently busy hiding out under the stairs behind the cafeteria, waiting for the merry band of people in sports jerseys to pass so that he can make his way to English.

Those Sports Jerseys are a bunch of assholes who kind of take offense to the fact that Linus is good at math and does his homework, as well as to the fact that he's gay, as if that has anything to do with them. Funnily enough, they also insist on criticizing him for not looking like the athletic type—which is, frankly, just a bit mind-boggling. That especially was something that used to really set off Sophia whenever she heard it.

It is usually not the smartest thing in the world to engage these jerks by talking back to them, but I will never forget the day Sophia walked up to them, hands on her hips and that disdainful look on her face she used to get when people were just being irrationally stupid in her presence, and told them, "For a bunch of straight guys who think it's so weird for men to check out other men, you sure spend a lot of time staring at his ass, don't you think?"

When we got out into the parking lot after school that day, we found that they had egged her car, but it was still totally worth it for the looks on their faces. And Linus and I helped her clean it later and then went out for pizza, so it was a pretty good day, all things considered.

But now I am thinking about Sophia again, which I don't really want to be doing. Still, maybe details like this will help explain why I don't want to dwell on any of this—life is different enough without her, without me constantly reminding myself of just how different it really is.

I thread my way through the Sports Jerseys, who are still hanging out outside the cafeteria—for all I know, they have forgotten their way to their next class and are just waiting around until one of them remembers how to use language and ask for directions.

For some reason they've never been as mean to me as they have been to Linus. It's not like they're nice to me—they've said some pretty horrific stuff, and more than once one of them has offered to do things that would supposedly turn me straight, according to their promises.

And, for the record, it's not just the boys. It's a lot of girls, too. Like Lizzie Harris in math class last year, sitting behind me with her friends before the teacher arrived and declaring loudly, "Well, you know, some people just have to turn lesbian when they realize no guy in his right mind would ever look at them twice."

I try not to react to this kind of comment, but it hurts.

At least that kind of insult is better than some guy walking up to you when all you're doing is talking to your girlfriend and suddenly you're being told that "Okay, so that black chick is hot, but you know she's not actually a dude, right? But I have some friends who would totally volunteer to show you what you're missing out on," punctuated with a wink, a laugh, and a shoulder-bump.

It just boggles the mind the more you think about it.

Because (1) I am perfectly happy not being straight, and (2) yeah, sure, if I wanted to magically discover the greatness of being straight I'd do it by making out with one of those idiots; I'm sure that would totally show me the light.

I will just never understand how some people honestly believe that making another person feel severely uncomfortable is the best way to win them over. I guess it starts by telling little girls that boys only pull their pigtails because they like them.

I tend to turn and walk away when they start, and they never follow me. I know not everyone is that lucky. (What a weird word to use in this context; I'm lucky that I'm only getting harassed a little. Yay!) Sophia used to snark back at them. I usually used to find Sophia and tell her about what happened and most of the time that helped me feel better. This year so far they have left me alone, but I'm not counting on the peace to last. At least I've built up a certain tolerance to it, and it's only ever been verbal harassment for me, plus those few times they've stolen my things and tossed them into Dumpsters or flushed them down the toilet. And it really is all kinds of messed up that I can count myself lucky it's not been worse than this.

Anyway. Sorry for the weird tangent, it's just those Sports Jerseys. They make me uncomfortable.

Linus is pretending to be reading something on his phone but looks up when I approach him.

"Hey, what's up?"

I grin at him. "Danny Singh—you know, the new kid? He's looking for a math tutor!"

He blinks at me. ". . . Okay?"

"And you're really good at math."

"Yeah, I know."

"So . . . ?"

"So, what?"

I heave a sigh and roll my eyes to the ceiling. Which is really dirty, ew. Public schools, man. "Linus, you're one of the smartest people I know—how are you not connecting the dots here?"

He is still looking at me like I have suddenly grown a second head. "Meg, I get it, I do, but even you can see how this is a really bad idea, can't you?"

That just makes me frown. "No, I don't," I admit. "Why is it a bad idea?"

". . . Because."

"Have I ever told you I really admire your eloquence? You should be the president's speechwriter."

"Ha-ha. Very funny."

"Look." I take his arm as the Sports Jerseys finally dissolve their misshapen human circle and wander off, and I start steering him in the direction of his English classroom down the hall. "He needs someone to help him with math. You are good at both math and explaining things. And then there's the added bonus that you'd get to spend time with him. How can you not think this is a good idea?"

He groans. "Because that means I will have to talk to him!"

I nod. "That would not only be unavoidable but also a rather beneficial side effect of this arrangement. Yes."

"What if I completely embarrass myself?"

"Like, how?"

He shrugs. "Failing to utter a single word, sweating profusely, and then passing out. Or what if I suddenly forget how English works and start speaking only in Klingon?"

It's my turn to blink at him, feeling just a little hurt. "Did you learn Klingon over the summer without telling me?"

He laughs, pats my hand. "I wouldn't do that to you. It was just an example."

"A bad one, in that case." I shake my head at him, bump our shoulders together in a gesture I hope is encouraging. "I promise you that it won't be as bad as you think it will be. Okay?"

"What if he asks me for help, and I tutor him and just end up embarrassing myself? Or if he decides he doesn't want me to tutor him after all?"

I tilt my head at him. "I'm pretty sure that won't happen. He's new here, right? He doesn't know anyone."

"Just indulge me here. It might be a disaster, you know?"

"Okay." I pinch the bridge of my nose, take a long breath. "So . . .

on the off chance that something goes wrong, which it won't—you'll come straight to me and I'll buy you a whole chocolate cake and we'll come up with a new game plan."

"It will be embarrassing."

"Or it might lead to something really amazing," I point out. "You won't know until you try!"

"You sound like a badly written greeting card with one of those kittens on the front that give you a thumbs-up or whatever," he says.

But I know that I at least got him thinking about it.

Chapter 14

Linus

I AM NOT USUALLY SOMEONE who worries excessively. Or at least I don't think I am. Most of the time I'm pretty happy, actually.

There is some bad stuff sometimes, but I think everyone has things like that occasionally. Like that time I was twelve and thought my parents would be getting a divorce. The parents of a kid in my neighborhood had just gotten divorced a year before and suddenly Mom and Dad were fighting all the time. For all of one week. As it turns out, even people who are married sometimes get pretty mad at each other, especially when one of them forgets to lock the car and it gets stolen. (Dad still feels bad about that, even if Mom forgave him years ago.)

Then there was that afternoon last year when I borrowed Meg's car and it broke down by the side of the road and while I was waiting for help, I imagined all the ways I could have broken it and how mad Meg was going to be at me and I started speculating how much it would cost to have it fixed up and how many tutoring sessions I was going to have to give to pay for it. I was so relieved I nearly cried when Meg was not mad and it turned out that it was only a faulty fuel gauge and I had merely run out of gas. (And actually the afternoon got pretty awesome later because Meg and I watched the *Firefly* episode "Out of Gas" and ate cookies, and don't most things usually eventually work out okay?)

Of course I worried when my grandma was in the hospital for days and they couldn't find out what was wrong with her. And of course I worried when Mom lost her job and couldn't find a new one for a few months. But who wouldn't worry about these things?

My point is, I may seem like a worrier to you at first glance because I'm awkward and I do a lot of things that involve a lot of thinking. Many people get thinking and worrying all mixed up; they are not the same thing and they don't always have a lot to do with each other. But I really am not a worrier.

I'm also not traditionally shy, despite the fact that so many people think I should be, because I'm good with numbers and I'm a little short and I'm a little chubby. I'm not usually shy, but I'm awkward and I'm really bad at small talk.

Maybe "selectively shy" is a good way to describe my approach to social situations. Like, I have no problem walking up to most people and starting a conversation. I get along with the school librarians, I always have a chat with the checkout people at the grocery store, and I'm on a first-name basis with most of the bus drivers from all the times I couldn't get a ride home with anyone and didn't feel much like walking.

The only problem is that I have absolutely no idea what to say when I meet people I really want to have a conversation with. I have a tendency to panic.

Like that time I was out looking at colleges with my dad and we ran into Alan Tudyk. In a sandwich shop. To this day I have no idea what he was doing there. Well, he was probably buying a sandwich. And I didn't even recognize him at first, because who expects that to happen? But then my dad was like, "Hey, isn't that the dude from that show you forced me to watch?" And, well, yeah, it was him.

I mean, I wouldn't have gone up to him even if my legs hadn't decided to go all weird and wobbly all of a sudden. Because, seriously, let the guy buy a sandwich in peace. But my point is that a normal person could have made the conscious decision to leave him alone instead of turning really pale and then blushing tomato red and then being unable to utter more than one-syllable words for the next fifteen minutes.

So, talking to Danny? Agreeing to tutor him? It could be a massive disaster of previously undiscovered proportions. There is absolutely no telling what might happen if I attempt this.

And yet, the thought doesn't leave me alone all through bio class—it is almost too good to be true. And it's not like I expect anything, I don't really want anything from him, I just . . . oh god no, I couldn't do it. It's too weird.

I just hope that Meg isn't going to be disappointed. I'm still feeling a little bit guilty about talking to Sophia behind her back. I should really tell her about it as soon as possible before it gets too weird. Because if I wait too long, it will just look like I didn't want to tell her.

I always find that not letting things pile up all around you until they overwhelm you is the best secret to avoid excessive worrying.

Not letting things pile up, however, doesn't do a whole lot to calm your nerves when you're standing by your locker after last period to put some things away, and someone clears his throat next to you, and when you look up it's the guy you've been thinking about all day.

It's Danny. Standing right there next to me. He waves one hand in an awkward wave and looks a little embarrassed.

"Hi," he says.

I stare at him, can't even remember how to blink, opening and closing my mouth dumbly. How do words work again?

"Uhh," I manage after a long moment of silence.

"Linus, right?" Danny asks, flickers a little smile at me, and I forcefully pull myself out of my shocked stupor.

"Linus," I repeat. "Me. I mean. That's me. I'm Linus." I wince, wishing the floor would open up and swallow me whole.

"I'm Danny," he tells me.

"I know," I reply immediately, and resist the urge to bury my face in my hands.

He looks surprised, but not in a bad way, and I'd probably take that as a good sign if I weren't having so much trouble breathing properly. My palms are tingling.

"You do?" he asks.

"Well . . ." I panic a little, because how do I make this sound as non-creepy as possible? "From the coffee shop," I make myself explain. "Um. I mean, I was there a lot, and . . . and you were there a lot, too. . . . Because you work there, of course. And you wore a name tag. But you know that. I'm—sorry." I snap my mouth shut, and I can feel my face burning from my ears all the way down to my neck.

"Yeah, I remember you," he says, and I can't quite read the tone in his voice.

"Cool," I say lamely.

He takes a breath. "I'm sorry to just—um." He bites his lip, his right hand fiddling with the hem of his left sleeve. "I don't mean to be weird, but I heard that you're kind of good at math and that you tutor occasionally? Because—uh. I'm new here and I was just—looking. Um. For a tutor. If you do that kind of thing."

I know I have to become a more active participant in this conversation, so for some reason I choose to nod vigorously. I probably look deranged. "Yes. I'm a math. I mean a tutor. I mean, I do. Tutor math. Sometimes." I suck in a sharp breath, wishing I could just faint in peace or at least press my overheated face to the nice cold lockers to cool down a little. I can hear the sound of my own heartbeat and I'm feeling a little woozy.

"I'm only asking because I could use some help and I was wondering if you're, um. Free. Sometime. Just—whenever. I'm flexible." He lowers his eyes. "With my schedule, I mean."

I laugh and it sounds shrill even to my own ears. "No, sure, of course," I hasten to assure him. "I'm free. I mean, I have, uh, stuff. To do. Sometimes. But yes. I can do it. When I don't have stuff, I mean. Which is not all the time, I'm mostly, uh . . . free. No problem."

His face lights up with delight. "Seriously? That's wonderful!"

"Yes," I say. "Um, I mean. Yes, I can do it . . . Friday?"

"Friday is great," he agrees.

"I like Fridays," I say just for the sake of saying something.

He laughs. "Friday afternoon, then?"

I nod again, making my head move a little more slowly this time. I feel dizzy enough as it is. "Sure."

"Okay." He smiles, waits a moment. "I'll find you tomorrow and we'll work out the details?"

"Okay," I agree.

He waits another moment, then gives me a little wave before he turns and walks away.

I slump back against the locker next to mine and bite back the whimper rising in my chest, trying to get my breathing back under control.

What the hell just happened?

Chapter 15

I DON'T SHARE A LOT of classes with Linus so I haven't seen him in several hours by the time I spot him approaching across the parking lot after school.

We have plans to hang out and keep each other company this afternoon, and I'm looking forward to it because it's one more opportunity to maybe talk him into getting his nerve up to offer his tutoring magic to that Danny guy. I just firmly believe that Danny would like him if they ever got to know each other.

And honestly, I'm really proud of the way I'm handling this little project. It proves that I really am okay even without a girlfriend. I was a little afraid it would affect me negatively, but look at me handling school and taking care of my friend all at the same time! So maybe I'm meddling a bit, but it's for the best. I may have to get a little creative with those two, maybe resort to some crazier plans, but hey, when did I ever say I was a completely sane person? At least this is only marginally crazy—it's not like I'm locking them in an elevator together or anything.

Anyway, I push myself off the car door I'm leaning against once I see Linus walking toward me, and I immediately know that something has happened.

Because for one thing, he's not so much walking as wobbling his way across the parking lot, his face as white as a freshly bleached sheet, his eyes wide and pretty much unblinking as his mouth hangs almost comically open.

"Linus?" I ask carefully, quickly checking him over for obvious injuries in case the Sports Jerseys got to him. "Is everything okay?"

He says something that sounds mostly like "Uhhhhrrrrgh" and I frown at him, raising a hand to touch the back of his hair.

"Did you hit your head or something? Do you need me to take you to the nurse?"

"Nahh-ahh," he says, and stands very still, chest heaving with too-deep breaths as if he's hyperventilating, and just stares at me with those big, round eyes.

"Okay, you're freaking me out a little," I admit, not sure if I should call for help or make him sit down first.

"He—I—" Linus provides helpfully.

At least he's almost using words again, and I take that as a good sign. "Who?" I ask.

He shakes his head, breathes too fast, opens and closes his mouth before he says, voice higher than usual, "Danny."

That sounds promising, but I still need more information. "Danny?" I prompt him.

"He." Linus swallows again, breathes audibly, shakes his head, flails his hands around a little. "He talked to me."

"Oh!" I can feel my mood lifting almost immediately. "That's nice! How did that happen?"

Linus turns away, bends over with his hands on his knees, and pants at the asphalt of our high school parking lot. "I'm going to throw up. Oh my god."

"No, don't do that," I tell him. "Tell me what he said instead!"

"Oh my god oh my god oh my god," Linus breathes, wheezing a little, and I put a comforting hand on his back.

"What did he say? Do you want to sit down? Do you need some water?"

"Sit," he says, and immediately flumps down right there in the parking lot on the summer-warm asphalt.

I think we could have found a better place to sit, since my car is right there behind me and it has seats that are clean and everything, but I'm a good friend so I just shrug and sit down next to him if sitting right here is what he prefers.

"Was it bad?" I have to ask. "Because you kind of look like you might pass out."

He seems to think about it for a second, then shakes his head. "It wasn't that bad," he says. "It could have been better. I didn't know what to say, but I think I managed to keep it sort of together until I made it outside and away from him."

"Then what's with the major freak-out right now?"

"He asked me to tutor him."

"Oh my god!" I squeal, slapping my hands over my face so enthusiastically I almost knock off my glasses. "Seriously? That's wonderful!" It's all going according to plan, exactly the way I wanted, and I do a little internal happy dance.

"Yes, I'm delighted," Linus says, but his face looks as if someone had just told him that Gene Roddenberry had come back to life for an hour and he'd only just missed the chance to speak with him.

"Then why the long face?" I ask, playfully punching him in the arm. "Hey! This is a good thing, isn't it?"

He barks out a high-pitched laugh, eyes still too wide. "Oh, is it? Is that why I'm sitting in the parking lot completely freaking out about it? Because this was just like a minute-long conversation in a crowded hallway; what do you think is going to happen to me once I really have to talk to him in actual sentences that convey actual meaning?" He waves his hands helplessly. "I'll probably die."

"You are not going to die." I roll my eyes at him, then scramble to my feet before offering him a hand up. "You're going to be fine."

He takes my hand, his own a little clammy, and lets me pull him to his feet. "I guess I'll have to tutor him in the library. A public place sounds a lot less stressful. I'll need exit strategies in case things go south. And the library calms me."

"Excellent idea," I assure him, happy to see that the color is already returning to his face. That's just Linus for you. He's never upset for very long.

"And maybe I'll prepare cue cards with light conversational topics so I don't instead go off on a thirty-minute tangent on the influence that social media has had on our generation when I attempt small talk."

"Sure," I say, gently pushing him toward the passenger-side door of my car.

We'll have to have a talk about the cue cards, because I may have a mild case of social awkwardness as well, but even I know that's kind of a weird idea. But for now I have to get him to my house so I can feed him some coffee and get him to sit down somewhere that was actually meant for sitting.

"Now get in the car already. We have coffee to make and then we're going to discuss what you're going to wear to your first study date!"

He winces. "Can we call it a tutoring session, please?"

"Whatever." I roll my eyes at him, start walking around the car. "We can call it whatever you like as long as I get to pick your shirt."

"Sometimes," he says, and opens his door, "I don't even know why I'm friends with you."

I laugh and finally get behind the wheel so we can get started on our well-deserved afternoon of not doing anything in particular.

Chapter 16

Linus

SO, I DON'T REALLY KNOW what happened. Like, I do know that I was standing by my locker putting away some things and minding my own business when Danny suddenly appeared next to me. I also know that despite my knees suddenly feeling completely unsuitable for supporting the entire rest of my body above them, I somehow managed to stay standing. And I also know that I didn't do anything so embarrassing and irredeemable that he turned on his heels and walked away from me, never to be seen again.

What I don't understand is how he showed up next to my locker in the first place. Here is a list of all the times in my life cute boys have approached me to start a conversation with me before today:

1. Never

. . .

That's it. That's the list. It has literally never happened to me before, and when I was eating my cereal this morning I honestly didn't expect that today would be the day of all days when I would finally be able to put an actual name on that list.

It's not like people haven't approached me for help with schoolwork before. I have done this tutoring thing a few times already, because I do have really good grades and once you've tutored one person, word kind of gets around.

And the thing is that sometimes when people just want to have a reason to talk to that cute girl who always has the answers in bio, they'll ask her for homework help. But when your grades are actually slipping and you do care about that kind of thing, you go and find the school nerd to help you out.

And I know that is what happened here; I am not the cute girl Danny wanted to get closer to. Because first of all, I'm not a girl (and Danny might not be gay), and second of all, I'm not cute.

Well. I am maybe a little bit cute. But not in the way that makes people want to date me. Just in the short, funny, round-faced dude kind of way.

So, yes, I know why Danny approached me and I know that this does not at all qualify as an event big enough to make it onto the potential list of Hot Guys Who Have Talked To Me. But I can tell you, my knees did not care about that fact in that particular situation, and neither did my pulse, which insisted on simulating me passing the twelve-mile mark at a marathon in the middle of the hottest day in August. (At least I imagine I'd feel something like that, should I ever pass the twelve-mile mark at a marathon. Which is unlikely.)

Anyway. People asking me to tutor them is definitely something that has happened before. Not like, a dozen times, but it's also not something that surprises me when it happens.

And yet. And yet!

It's Danny! Whatever his reasons for asking me when he could have just as well asked Meg or someone else who has good grades in math—well, I don't really care. To be quite honest, all I care about right now is being able to acquire a certain level of cool that will allow me to act like a normal and sane person when me meet up for the first time this Friday. That leaves me just about three days to fundamentally change my entire personality. Totally possible, right?

"Hey, are you okay?" Meg asks, and I realize we have stopped in front of her house and she's getting out of the car while I'm still sitting there with my seat belt on, staring dumbly ahead.

"Oh my god," I say. "Sorry. Totally drifted off, I don't even know what happened."

She smirks. "I might have kind of an idea, actually."

I can feel myself blush furiously and quickly get out of the car, mumbling, "I'm sure I have no idea what you're talking about!"

She's walking up to the door to unlock it, grins back at me. "Yeah, you do."

"You're making too big a deal out of this!"

She groans, pushes the door open, and I follow her inside to toe off my shoes by the entrance. "Why are you being difficult about this? This is a good thing!"

"It just doesn't mean anything," I remind her.

"You don't know that it doesn't!"

"You don't know that it does!"

She pouts, blinking at me from under her lashes. "So you won't even try to flirt with him?"

I sigh. "Meg, I wouldn't know where to start!"

"I can help you with that!"

"Please don't!"

"Okay, then just . . . isn't there anything I can do?"

I shake my head. "Why is this so important to you?"

She shrugs. "I just care about you."

I think about it, then lower my head. "I'm just not sure this is a good idea. He's new, he just needs some help, and I—"

"You are helping him," she cuts me off, and I follow her into the kitchen, where she hands me a bottle of water from the fridge. "That doesn't mean you have to completely discard any possibility of it turning into more eventually."

I lean back against the kitchen counter and open my water, take a slow sip from the bottle. I know she means it when she says that she just wants to help, and I guess it can't hurt to just approach this situation with an open mind. Even if I know it won't lead to anything. And I guess she needs a little distraction. I can do this for her, as long as it doesn't get too out of hand.

"Okay," I say slowly, sighing internally. The things you do for friendship. "If I let you dress me for the tutoring session and promise you that you can come straight over afterward and we'll dissect everything that was said between us—would that make you happy?"

She bounces a little on her feet, nods excitedly. "Oh my god! Yes! That would make me very happy! Thank you!"

"Okay, then."

For a moment, she looks concerned. "Are you sure? I mean, I know I can be a bit pushy, but . . . I don't want to make you do anything you're not comfortable with."

"No, actually, I think I'd like your help," I admit, and find that, well, yes, maybe I do. "Just don't make me dress up in anything embarrassing?"

She rolls her eyes at me. "Just hide everything you don't want to be wearing before you let me have a look at your closet."

These are the moments when I think that she definitely deserves to win the spot of class valedictorian over me.

Chapter 17

Meg

IF I'M BEING HONEST, THE more time passes, the more annoyed I get at myself. Because there are still days like today when I wake up already thinking about Sophia, and every time that happens it ruins my entire day. I'm really ready to finally be done with this.

But, I remind myself as I gloomily stare down into my coffee cup over breakfast Friday morning, it's not even been three weeks now. I don't think three weeks is enough time to get over a breakup like this one. Maybe I'll just have to wait this one out.

"Good morning," Mom says, entering the kitchen already dressed for work.

"Morning," I say back, unable to sound too enthusiastic about the beginning of this day.

Mom kisses my hair in passing and rubs my shoulder as she heads for the coffeemaker. "You look sad."

I keep staring at my coffee and shrug. "Whatever."

"No, not whatever." Mom gets her coffee, sits down across from me at the small kitchen table, ducks her head to catch my eyes. "Are you okay?"

I shake my head, sigh. Because . . . this morning, I'm not. It sort of comes in waves. "Not particularly."

She nods. "You know," she says, "you haven't even done any real wallowing yet. Maybe you're finally ready?"

I shake my head emphatically. "No! I'm not. I'm not going to do that. I'm not going to go through any stages of grief or whatever. It happened, and now I have things to do regardless. It's senior year, I have to—"

"Meggie," Mom says, sounding concerned. "You're allowed to be sad, you know? I'm worried about you."

"Yeah, well, moping around isn't going to magically convince her that we're better off together," I point out.

"No," Mom admits. "But it'll make you feel better."

"No, it won't," I insist.

"You were hurt. You have to allow yourself some time to heal."

"I'm fine!"

"No," she says. "You're not. You miss her. And that's okay. You're probably angry. And that's okay, too. I mean, I miss her, too. I liked her. And I liked how happy she made you."

"I don't want to talk about it anymore," I say firmly. "Can we just not talk about it anymore?"

She sighs. "I'm not going to make you talk to me if that makes you uncomfortable," Mom promises. "But I think that you should talk to someone. I don't know. Linus, maybe?"

I laugh. "He doesn't need this. He has his own stuff."

Mom gives me a worried look. "I'm sure he'd be there for you if you told him how you feel."

"I feel like I want another cup of coffee," I say. "That's really all I want right now."

"You and your coffee. Is there a twelve-step program for that?" Mom says it in a joking voice, but her face is serious. She gives me a long look, then smiles at me. "Hey, if you want, I can call in sick today and we can go shoe shopping? What do you say?"

"Mom, I have school!"

"You're also going through stuff, it's the beginning of the school year, and you haven't missed a day since you had the flu in third grade. You can afford it."

"It's a tempting offer," I say. "But Linus has his first tutoring session today with that guy he likes and I have to be there for him or he's going to vibrate out of his skin. I've never seen him this nervous before." I can't help but grin a little. The thought of Linus maybe possibly finally getting a boyfriend and the romance he deserves is enough to cheer me up a little.

She grins back. "That sounds serious!"

"I hope it is! They'd be really cute together!"

"Well, okay." Mom nods at me, smiles. "Go to school and be awesome. But we're going to take a day off next week or the week after. You pick the day. It doesn't matter when. And we're going to go shopping and have some food that's really bad for us and maybe watch some incredibly bad movies. Just us. You deserve a day off. All right?"

"Thank you," I say, and finally drink my coffee. I actually like the idea. And maybe Mom is right, maybe I do need just a few hours to actually slow down a bit and do something nice.

I am still feeling a bit shaken, after all.

Chapter 18

Linus

IT'S FRIDAY.

This is not unexpected. I learned the days of the week quite a while ago, thank you! And yet I am so entirely unprepared, it's not even funny. I am not even remotely ready and at the same time I am really, really looking forward to it.

You don't have to tell me that I am entirely and completely overreacting and probably making it a hundred million times worse by building it up in my head like this. But seriously, try being in my head for a bit. I can't really help it.

I have changed my clothes three times this morning and in the end I have at least stuck with the shirt Meg suggested I should wear. It's a good shirt. But I've changed pretty much everything else and I haven't done that thing with my hair that she suggested. If I show up looking too radically different, he might notice and realize that I am noticing him and it might all get terribly, terribly awkward and weird and I don't want that.

In fact, now that the initial shock has worn off, it occurs to me that if I just act normal and don't do anything weird like making a move on him, whatever that would even entail, we could even maybe become friends. Maybe. It's not completely impossible. He just seems really nice and maybe if I can manage to not be too awkward . . .

In any case, even if it's just tutoring, I'm pretty sure that this could be a lot of fun.

I enjoy tutoring. I like explaining things and helping others understand them; it makes me feel useful and needed and I guess I just like helping people.

And also, I just like people.

People sometimes seem to assume that just because you like learning about things, you don't like being around people. But you can like books and people at the same time! You can like as many things as you want! You're even allowed to be good at sports and good at math, if you're so inclined! You can be a great oboist and an excellent car mechanic! You can love cartoons and Shakespeare! You can even like all of the old *Star Trek* series and the reboot, and I will totally judge you for it. But that's just my taste and you can feel free to disagree with me. We don't all have to like the same things.

The day flies by, which is both good and unnerving. Good because this way I can't drive myself insane with worry. Not so good because suddenly it's the end of last period and I can't put it off any longer. I'm going to meet up with Danny, the cutest guy in this entire school.

"Do you want me to wait for you after school so we can go have coffee, or do you just want to come over once you're done here?" Meg asks, suddenly showing up next to my locker.

I look up at her, startled out of my thoughts. "You don't have to wait," I tell her. "I'll just take the bus over after tutoring and you better have the coffee ready when I get there! I'll probably need it!"

She salutes, grins at me. "No problem. You'll even get a cookie. Text me when you leave here?"

"Sure."

"Well, then." She pats my shoulder, looks almost as excited as I feel. "Go be charming. You can do this! I believe in you!"

"I know I can do this," I point out. "I've tutored math before."

She rolls her eyes at me. "Not what I meant!"

"Go home," I say, and playfully nudge her shoulder. "I've got this."

"I know you do," she says, and turns to go.

And I take a deep breath and close my locker and turn for the library.

I can do this. No big deal. It's just tutoring.

Chapter 19

Meg

I WISH I COULD SNEAK into the library and spy on Linus and Danny, but I'm not creepy, so I don't do that. It might distract me from my weird mood, though.

All day long, I haven't been able to pull myself out of this funk I am in. I'm sad and irritable and a little miffed that Linus didn't really seem to need me at all today—I could have accepted Mom's offer of taking the day off and going shopping instead.

And now I am being unfair. Linus didn't ask me to come to school today. That was my decision. And also, I do know that he was probably a lot more nervous than he let on.

I drive myself home and let myself into the silent, empty house. I think I'll have at least an hour until Linus comes over. Probably longer.

Maybe he won't come over at all. Maybe I was right all along and they'll hit it off right away. Danny will fall madly in love with Linus and they'll extend the tutoring session into a date and really all I ask is that I can be best woman at the wedding. Maybe that will put me in a better mood. Because right now, I'm just lonely and bored.

Coming home from school is pretty much the same routine every day: I walk in the door, take off my shoes, and put them on the shoe rack. I put my book bag down by the stairs that lead up to the second floor and walk through into the kitchen, to start a fresh pot of coffee and put away the remaining dishes from breakfast. Mom and I are usually in a bit of a hurry in the morning and only manage to put the milk and anything else that is perishable back in the fridge.

Only today when I enter the usually empty kitchen, Mom is already in it and just closing the dishwasher, turning around when she hears me.

"What are you doing here?" I ask.

"And a good afternoon to you, too, my favorite daughter," she says.

"Did you make coffee?" I ask a little greedily at the sight of the full pot still in the machine.

"Yeah, I needed a jolt of caffeine before getting back to work. The renovations on the second floor at the museum got so loud I couldn't hear myself think in there," Mom says. "So I brought the rest of my work home with me."

"I really am so jealous that you can just do that," I tell her, and walk over to the cupboard to get a mug and treat myself to my first afternoon coffee of the day.

I own a variety of mugs for my afternoon coffee: I have a TARDIS mug, two different *Star Trek* mugs, a Yoda mug, one with Shakespeare quotes, and a *Firefly* mug. Today, I choose Shakespeare.

"Quiche for dinner?" Mom asks.

I nod. "Linus might be here, too."

"No problem."

Usually, Mom and I make dinner together and then pick something to watch that Mom ends up ignoring a lot of the time because she's busy reading over some things she brought home from the museum.

It doesn't bother me because it means she doesn't complain when I put on *The Mummy* for the third time in a week. Which she shouldn't be doing anyway, because it started out as her favorite movie. Even though she denies it and, in her capacity as resident archaeologist, dutifully complains about its many historical inaccuracies, I know she still secretly loves it.

It's not unusual for me to watch a movie three times a week. I have this thing where I need to watch a movie that I enjoyed over and over again. A lot of people find that annoying. Linus makes fun of me for it, in that kind way that he has for making fun of people that means you can never be mad at him for it. Sophia used to tease me about it, too, but then she'd sit down and watch *Pirates of the Caribbean* for the fifth time with me anyway, despite her complaint that she already knows the entire dialogue by heart. That's love for you! Or . . . at least it was love.

But remembering these things makes me sad, so I'm not going to dwell on them.

I don't know, I guess I just always thought that if you found someone who's willing to put up with all your crazy just to make you happy, it must be the real thing.

But I'm starting to dwell on it now, so I should go do something else.

"I have homework," I tell Mom. Time for some distraction by some indisputable facts about ionic compounds, courtesy of Mr. Mahoney's chemistry assignment.

"Don't forget your coffee," she says. "I should get back to work, too."

I have a few more assignments to get through after chem and I only have an hour today, after all, because after that Linus will come over and we will analyze his "date" with Danny.

I know, I know. He insists that it isn't a date. And maybe it's not. In fact, he's probably right and this is really just a tutoring appointment. But at least one of us should be happy, so I'll make sure those two crazy lovebirds will get it together eventually.

I know Linus gets lonely. Even if he never ever complains about it. Linus rarely ever complains about anything.

When Sophia and I were together, we made sure to include him as often as possible. Still, he must have felt like a third wheel so many times. I mean, I feel like I'm having abandonment issues today and he is, as he keeps insisting, not even on a date.

I take my coffee and my bag upstairs and sit down at my desk, where I continue to sit for minutes and just stare moodily down at my chem homework. Honestly, I usually enjoy this. I like studying, it's interesting, and chemistry has always held a certain appeal for me. Today, however, it just doesn't do anything for me at all, no matter how much I try to focus and be excited about it.

I have actually considered chemistry as a major for college. But I have considered twenty other things as well. History is fascinating. But would I want to focus on languages? Or maybe archaeology, like Mom? I also love math, though, and lately I have been really into astrophysics. But I'd also like to help people directly, and being a doctor sounds like something that I might really, really want to be doing with my life. On the other hand, imagine working in a museum and getting to translate ancient scrolls that no one has looked at in sometimes thousands of years? Isn't that just the coolest thing ever? Even if—or maybe because—in real life, mummies don't come back to life. But then imagine working in a lab and getting to work on the future instead of studying the past!

I wish I knew what to do with my life. I sometimes really envy the people who do.

Like Sophia. And I am not saying that getting there was easy for her; she put a lot of thought into it as well. Entire nights we stayed up on the phone together, talking it over and over and over and over. . . .

But, I don't know, the moment she finally settled on music therapy, it just seemed right. To both of us: to her, who chose a path for her life, and to me, who loved her and wanted her to be happy and fulfilled.

She could have been anything she wanted to be. But the thought of her actively working with and helping people and making their lives better by using something she loved so much—I just know that she is going to be amazing.

And I am thinking about her again and what the hell, why can't I stop? This just isn't fair. My homework is still lying abandoned before me and this is clearly not the best possible use of my afternoon.

I wonder when all of this will finally stop hurting so much.

With a sigh, I turn back to my chem assignment. If I can just shut off this tiny, annoying part of my mind for thirty minutes, maybe something grounded in fact will help me take my mind off all this pointless moping.

Chapter 20

Linus

WE HAVE AGREED TO STUDY together in the library but, it occurs to me as I walk down the hall, we forgot to specify exactly where we would meet.

So I am faced with a rather interesting dilemma all of a sudden: Do I go in and wait for him there, or is it politer to wait out here for him?

Usually when I'm tutoring people I just start on my own homework in the library until they feel it's time to show up. But. Is Danny going to be late? I don't know!

This is absolutely not a big deal and it's not a complicated decision to make, but it suddenly seems like one. Which means I remain standing outside the glass doors to the library like an idiot, clutching the strap of my book bag and shifting my weight from one foot to the other before I think: What if he is in there already? I am, after all, only five minutes early. And I don't know how he feels about punctuality; he may be in there right now sitting at a table already and waiting for me to show up.

But, I continue my speculation, let's say he really is already in there. Would it seem overeager to walk in five minutes early, or would it just seem professional, or would it seem like maybe I am just five minutes early because I didn't keep waiting out in the hall like a moron until it was exactly the right second to walk in?

While I am still pondering this and trying to make up my mind, a voice speaks up right behind me.

"Oh, good, you're here already!"

Dignified as I usually am, I let out a squeak and jump approximately five feet high before landing back on my feet, face burning and one hand pressed over my pounding heart.

"Danny! Hi! I—um. Didn't see you there! Um." Well, I think, wincing, good thing I keep my eloquence even after nearly leaving my own body with fright.

He cringes, lowers his head a little, rubs the back of his neck with one hand. "Sorry. I didn't mean to scare you."

"It's okay," I assure him quickly. "I only almost died. No harm done!"

"Good," he says.

"Uh," I continue, trying desperately to avoid any awkward silences. "So. Ready to, uh. Make sense of some numbers?"

He nods and gestures for me to go ahead through the large glass doors. "Yeah, sure!" he says. "Looking forward to it!"

So, I know he is totally exaggerating, but it still makes me blush that he's being so nice to me. I turn away quickly to hide my face and in my rush to escape almost miss the door handle and narrowly avoid an embarrassing collision between the glass door and my face. I really need to get a grip on myself and I know it, but something about him just seems to deactivate all the clumsiness inhibitors in my system. And I don't have too many of those on a good day.

We find a table near a window and I drop into my chair, a little surprised when he immediately sits down next to me instead of across.

Sitting next to each other makes tutoring a lot easier since we don't have to read our notes and textbooks upside down. However, I have found that most people like the table as a barrier between us. Don't sit too close to the gay nerd—people might see!

Danny does not seem to have any of those concerns as he pulls up his chair and drops his bag under the seat, props his head up on his hand, one elbow on the table, and looks at me with a small grin. Well, he is new. He probably doesn't know that I'm gay and that people might judge him for wanting to sit near me.

I grin back because I don't know what else to do right now.

"Okay, then," Danny says. "Here we are! Teach me, oh wise one!"

That makes me laugh, loud enough it immediately makes me look around for the librarian. I like Ms. Carter and I don't want her to be angry with me.

"I'll do my best," I promise him. "So, is there anything in particular you need help with? Or just like, you know . . . homework?" I wave my hands in a wide circle around the last word to encompass the vast universe that is math.

He shrugs, looks away, and blushes a little. "It is—pretty much everything, yeah. I—I think it's just that we didn't cover any of this at my old school, you know? I just need to catch up and math is not—it's just not my favorite. My grades are good, but this stuff just gives me a headache. I mean, what even is a secant line? You know." He looks almost apologetic, as if insulting math is going to be insulting to me personally. "I just look at all this and it's like my brain just sort of rejects it? It's really frustrating and it doesn't help my GPA."

I nod and try not to swoon visibly and of course he has good grades, of course; he is, after all, just ridiculously perfect in every way.

"It's from Latin, *secare*," I say, "which means 'to cut.' It's a straight line between two points on a curve."

He blinks at me. "Excuse me?"

"A, um. A secant line. Your question."

He laughs. "Right. Thank you! I assume it's all good for something?"

"I promise you that it is."

"I guess I have no choice but to believe you."

"Maybe just show me what you've been having trouble with in class and we'll start there?" I suggest.

"Sounds good," he agrees, and bends down to dig through his bag.

I only stare at the elegant curve of his back for a few seconds, until I realize what I'm doing. Then I quickly avert my eyes because I am not a creep. But from what I can tell, he does indeed have a very nice back. Not as broad and wide-shouldered as those Sports Jerseys. Just nicely shaped and as lovely as the entire rest of him.

I get a pen and notepad from my own bag and hope he couldn't, like, feel me looking.

"So, you kind of like math, then, huh?" Danny asks, still busy searching through his bag.

It's my turn to shrug. "Kind of, yes. I find it interesting. And sort of soothing sometimes."

He sits back up, puts his things down on the table, and lifts an eyebrow at me. "Soothing? Really? How so?"

I think about it for a moment, trying to find the right words. "I guess," I try to explain, "it's the satisfaction of seeing individual things coming together in a way that makes sense. Like, having a set problem in front of you and arranging it all into a clean and definite solution. It's like making sense of things, you know? Bringing a sense of order into something that otherwise seems chaotic." I blush, lowering my head. "And now I'm babbling. I'm sorry."

He shakes his head quickly. "No, no, you're not babbling at all. I totally get it!" He bounces in his seat a little. "I mean, not about the numbers obviously; they still scare me. But I kind of feel that way about words, so . . ."

"Oh, yes, you're in drama club, right?" I ask, then realize that it might be weird to know this much about him and quickly add: "Uh, I just saw you talking to some of the drama club people the other day when I was thinking about signing up myself."

"Oh," he says. "You should. And yeah, I am. I always did drama club at my last school and it's really fun."

"My friend Meg's girlfriend used to be in drama club," I say. "She always loved it."

He frowns. "She isn't in it anymore?"

"She graduated," I explain. "She also broke up with Meg," I add, because apparently I really feel like oversharing today. I just can't stop saying random things. "So she's really her ex-girlfriend now. That's going to take some getting used to."

"I'm sorry. That sucks for your friend," he says, and we both go quiet for a while, not sure what to say.

"So," I finally speak up. "Um. Math?"

"Yes," he says. "That's what we're here for, isn't it?"

"Absolutely," I agree, nodding probably way too enthusiastically. "We're here for the numbers!"

"So you can convince me they're cool," he agrees, and smiles widely, showing all of his teeth, which just makes me blush again.

"I will do my best to infect you with as much of my nerdy numbers-appreciation as possible," I promise solemnly.

His smile fades. "Hey, don't say that like it's a bad thing."

"Uh, what?"

"The nerdy thing. It's not a bad thing to like stuff."

"No, I know, I—" I shake my head at him, a bit taken aback. "I didn't mean it like that. I just—I don't know."

"I mean," Danny says, "I totally fail to understand why you like this stuff, but hey, I'm a drama geek. That's not really very conventionally cool, either, I guess. So, whatever, right?"

I have to think about that for a moment. Drama club actually sounds pretty cool to me, if I'm being honest.

"Well, I guess once you're a famous actor and an international superstar, it's going to start being pretty cool," I argue.

"And when you invent a new kind of spaceship that finally gets humans to Mars, that won't be cool?" He smirks at me.

"I don't even know yet if I want to go into engineering or—" I start, then break off when I realize that it had probably been a joke. "No, I see what you mean. Not many people see it like that, though."

"Well, that's their problem." He looks at me with his head tilted to the side, cheek propped up on one hand.

I don't know what to say to that because I don't know what he means, so I say nothing and instead lower my eyes again because being looked at for so long is a little weird and makes me feel a little self-conscious.

Finally, he clears his throat and says, "And anyway, I don't think I even want to go into acting."

"Oh?" I contribute articulately.

He shakes his head, bites his lip, looks a little embarrassed. "I—I like to write," he admits.

"That's awesome," I answer. "Like, novels?"

He nods. "Short stories, mostly. I've been working on a novel for a while. And I wrote a play over the summer."

"That's really cool," I assure him.

"I don't even know if my stuff is any good."

"Have you ever let anyone read it?"

He shakes his head. "A few people, yes. But it's just on the Internet, uh, no one I actually, um. I don't know if it's any good. But it's fun, you know?"

"Having fun and doing things you enjoy is important," I confirm and smile in a way I hope is encouraging. "And one day when you're the world's next J. K. Rowling or Joss Whedon, I'll point at your picture in a magazine and tell my grandkids, 'I tutored him when we were young!' I just know it!"

Danny smiles, eyebrows drawn together. "So, either you are not as good at math as you said you were, or you just described a scenario in which you age twice as quickly as I do? Or why exactly do you have grandkids when I'm thirty?"

I laugh. "Oh, you mean to get famous young; you didn't tell me that. I'm sorry. I'll reset the parameters according to your specifications."

"You're a dork!" Danny laughs, but it sounds as if he really means it in a nice way.

Or maybe that is just wishful thinking on my part.

But either way, I am definitely enjoying this a lot!

Chapter 21

Meg

HE'S SMILING WHEN I OPEN the door for him, which I'm choosing to see as a good sign. Even if Linus is, quite frankly, usually smiling. Sometimes I wonder what it's like living inside his head; I know how high his expectations are that he sets for himself, how much anxiety that gives him. And yet he is always putting on a smile and seems so optimistic most of the time. Except when it comes to finding a boyfriend, apparently.

"How did it go?" I ask.

He shrugs, looking just a little smug. "Not bad! Not bad at all!"

"So, it was a date after all?" I prod, because it doesn't look like he's going to volunteer any more information on his own.

Instead of confirming what I assume to be fact, his eyebrows draw together and he looks very confused. "No! Of course not! I'm tutoring him. You know that."

"Are you quite sure about that?" I close the door behind him as he walks past me to take off his shoes by the stairs.

"Of course I am sure—I was there!"

"Well, you are maybe not the best person to judge this kind of thing!"

He rolls his eyes, straightens up from putting his shoes away, and puts both his hands on my shoulders. "Listen carefully, Meg," he says, looking me in the eyes. "You have to stop this!"

"Stop what?" I ask sullenly. "I'm not doing anything!"

"Yes, you are!" He sighs. "And it's insane. I am tutoring Danny. And I need you to stop reading anything else into it. Because it's weird and not true."

"He asked you to tutor him," I point out.

"Yes. I know that. Thank you."

"He could have asked anyone, but he asked you!"

At that, he merely lifts an eyebrow at me, tilting his head to the side. "Yes?"

I throw up my hands in frustration and sigh loudly. "There are so many people he could have asked, Linus! Are you aware of that? He could have asked me. He could have asked one of the people who actually advertised tutoring on the bulletin board. Or one of the other people on Ms. Gilbert's list. But he asked you. He specifically came looking for you!"

"Coincidence," he says. "Perhaps I was the first nerd he ran into that day. Or maybe he knows someone I have tutored before and that's how he decided to ask me."

"Or maybe," I insist, "he likes you and that's why he came looking for you!" I'm not ready to give up on this idea yet. If there's even the slightest chance that I could be right about this, it means that Linus could be happy. And I really want him to be happy.

"Why is this so important to you?" he wants to know. "Because you have to admit that it is just a little weird for you to be so preoccupied with my love life."

"I don't know. You're my best friend. Isn't that reason enough?" I lift my shoulders, and there is quite simply no way I could explain this in actual words. "And I'm not preoccupied with your love life. I just happen to be a good judge of character and I'm telling you, he likes you!"

He nods, pauses, smiles down at his own socked feet. "Okay. Well. Do I get my cookie now? I believe you promised me a cookie in exchange for me entertaining you with all the boring details of my afternoon."

"Yes. And I'll make coffee. Right." I smile back, pretending to drop the subject. I'm just going to listen and draw my own conclusions. And then I can decide upon an appropriate course of action once he's gone home this evening.

In the kitchen, Linus is putting some cookies on a plate while I'm refilling the coffeemaker.

"So, are we still joining drama club or what?" I quickly change the subject. And honestly, it's the perfect plan. Since it seems like Linus is not going to take the initiative in becoming friends-and-hopefully-more with Danny, it is imperative that we create common ground between them in some other way. I like this idea more than ever. They'll have a neutral place to hang out and spend more time together, on top of tutoring. At this rate, I'll have them engaged by Christmas.

"I don't know," he says. "What would we be doing in drama club?"

I turn to lean my butt against the counter and look at him. "Well, what does everyone else do in drama club? Acting and stuff, I guess. Sophia said they also always had people who just did stuff like lights and costumes."

"I don't know anything about any of that," he points out.

"Does it really matter what we do?" I ask. "It might be fun. Sophia loved it. I'm sure it's fun."

"It might be," he admits. "I'm not saying that I don't want to."

"Then what are you saying? It was your idea, you know? You suggested this in the first place."

He looks at me suspiciously. "Yes, I remember. And I do kind of want to. I think it sounds fun. But are you only pushing for this so hard so that I am going to have to hang out with Danny? Or do you want to join because it used to be Sophia's favorite club?"

I don't really know how to answer that because I don't know the answer. So I say nothing. The truth is, yes, I do want to see Linus and Danny together. But . . . I don't know, it does feel like holding on to a part of my ex-girlfriend at the same time and somehow that seems even more pathetic than playing matchmaker for my best friend so I don't want to think about it.

"Hey," he says. "Maybe you really should try talking to Sophia."

"No." There. At least that is something I have an immediate response to.

"Why not?"

Now I'm starting to get angry and I don't like it. "What could she possibly have to say to me that she hasn't said already?"

"You'll have to listen to her to find that out."

"No, thank you! I believe she has already said everything she ever needed to say to me. I don't know what else there could be at this point."

"I bet that she's really sorry for everything."

"Oh, well." I snort. "If she's sorry, I guess that makes it all okay, then."

"Of course it doesn't," he says. "But maybe you'd at least understand why it happened."

"No," I repeat, and shake my head firmly. Because the truth is, I am wondering what happened. And I am wondering if maybe there had been anything I could have done in order to prevent it from happening. But more than that, I am terrified. I am terrified of asking her what went wrong and finding out that we were never actually as happy as I wanted us to be. I am terrified of finding out that it was all only ever in my head. I am terrified to learn that she never really loved me at all.

I don't want the last two years of my life to have been nothing but a lie. So, no. I do want to know, but I don't want to know. If that makes sense at all.

"Do you at least want to talk to me about it?" he offers. "You know I'm always here for you, don't you?"

I do know that. I know he loves me and that I can talk to him about anything and he would never hurt me. But this—I am just not ready. Maybe I'll never be ready. You don't just get over someone like Sophia.

"What I want," I say, "is to hear more about your exciting afternoon!"

"It really wasn't what you want it to be, you know that, right?" he asks.

"I know that you want to talk about it, though, right?" I ask back. "You just spent an afternoon with the guy you're in love with and you're probably dying to talk about it."

He blushes. "I wouldn't say 'love.' I barely know him."

"But you do want to talk about him."

He groans, hides his face behind his hands to hide his grin. "God, yes, I really do."

"I knew it!" I laugh triumphantly, then check on the coffeemaker. "Coffee's ready anyway. Grab the cookies; I'll bring the mugs."

He nods and walks ahead into the living room.

So, it seems that he does indeed need my help with the whole Danny situation. Because he does like him. And, I mean, okay. Maybe I am wrong. Who knows? I can't be sure that it's mutual and I can't know that this will work out. But what's life without a little risk? I'm never going to do anything to hurt him. I wouldn't do that. I'm just going to observe and push when necessary.

He looks at me when I walk through with the coffee in my hands. "You are still thinking about me and Danny, aren't you?"

I shake my head emphatically. "Of course not! Whatever gives you that idea?"

He sighs. "Okay," he says plaintively. "I can't stop you from being insane. But the minute you start writing fan fiction about us, you can find a new best friend. And good luck finding someone who won't mind your running commentary on *Deep Space Nine* episodes."

I try not to look too excited as I'm trying to figure out their ship name. I can't believe I have overlooked this detail so far. I need a good portmanteau for the two! Lanny? Dinus? Dannus? I'll have to give this some more thought.

"Oh god, you are actually thinking about this now, aren't you?" he asks, horrified.

I laugh. "Relax. You know I'm not much of a writer." It's true. I tried my hand at fan fiction once, but it wasn't pretty.

"Danny is a writer," Linus says quietly, and his mouth does that twitchy thing it does when he tries too hard to keep the smile from splitting his face in half.

"Oh, is he?" I say, and file this information away for later. Maybe I can use it.

Look, I said it before and I'll say it again: I'm not going to do anything crazy. I'm not going to lock them in a supply closet at school or abandon them in the woods with only each other for company. But if I manage to—create certain opportunities for them, that's not something you could really call "interfering," is it?

And that is all I am going to do. I swear it. I'm going to create opportunities. And if nothing happens, that's fine. I'll admit that I was wrong and let it go. But if I am right . . .

Well, I really do want to be the best woman at their wedding.

Chapter 22

Linus

MEG TEXTS ME EARLY ON Monday morning that she's not coming to school.

Everything okay? I text back, frowning into my coffee.

I'm okay, she replies. *But Mom has this idea that I should take a day off for self-care or whatever after being dumped.*

She's not wrong, you know, I tell her.

I don't know about that. But she's taking me shopping, so who am I to argue?

I grin and shake my head. *You should absolutely not argue with that, I agree!*

I know, right?

Buy lots of nice things! I text her, and drain the rest of my coffee.

We usually only carpool if we're planning to hang out together later, so it's not like I've been counting on her this morning. I'm not really on her way to school and usually it's easier if Mom or Dad drops me off on their way to work and I always manage to get home somehow—one of them picks me up or I take the bus or sometimes, if I don't have anything else to do that afternoon, I walk. It takes a while, but I don't mind. Sometimes I get to borrow one of my parents' cars. I don't have one of my own.

Today I was supposed to get a lift from Dad anyway. Mom's gonna come by this afternoon to pick me up. She only has a half day at work today.

I grab my things and walk back into the kitchen, where Dad is still very engrossed in his newspaper. Does anyone else still read actual newspapers on actual paper? It seems incredibly old-fashioned to me. And not the smartest choice environmentally, either, when you can just as easily get the news on your tablet computer or your phone. But Dad doesn't like reading on his phone.

"Dad?" I say, and he looks up, startled.

"Huh?"

"Ready to leave? I don't want to be late!"

"Oh." He pushes his glasses up on his nose and blinks at me. "Right. Of course."

"I have the keys," I tell him, dangling them in front of his face, because I know he tends to forget them.

He gets up, takes them, and ruffles my hair in response. "Thanks, kiddo. Okay, let's go!"

I follow him out the door and try not to roll my eyes at him too obviously while I try to flatten my hair again, which had been perfect before he messed it up. I love my dad, but I swear he'd forget his own head sometimes if it wasn't firmly attached to his neck.

School without Meg is pretty boring. Since we don't have many classes together it's not like we usually keep each other company all through the day. But I'm used to knowing that I have someone to run into in the halls and have lunch with.

As per her texted instructions, I at least walk by the bulletin board and put both our names on the sign-up sheet for drama club. I'm actually really starting to look forward to this club even if I'm sure that I'm a pretty terrible actor. I've never tried it, though, so who knows. And the way I see it, you don't have to be good at something to enjoy it. My dad plays the clarinet and he loves it dearly. It's the sole reason we spent that summer three years ago sound-proofing the basement, because to the rest of the world his "music" is mostly torturous minutes of endless screeching. But he has fun with it.

The club meets for the first time Tuesday, so we're just in time to sign up, too.

"Hey, you've really decided to join, too. Awesome," a voice says behind me. A very welcome voice.

"Hi, Danny," I say, and turn to smile at him. "Yeah, I mean, I'm not even very clear on the specifics yet, like, what it even really is you do, but I'm excited to try it!"

"It is very exciting," he assures me. "I'm glad you decided to sign up!"

"So am I," I say, and keep smiling, and don't really know what to say next so I just keep babbling. "I mean, I'm definitely not in this for, like, a big part or whatever. I don't think I want that. I probably wouldn't be very good at it. I was thinking more of easing my way in slowly, you know? Something insignificant. Do you think there will be any parts for people who tend to stumble over their own feet a lot? Or, if there's nothing else I'd also totally be up for just being in charge of lights or whatever. Unless that's really complicated, too—I don't know anything about lighting now that I think of it, but I'm generally a pretty fast learner—"

"Oh no, we'll definitely get you up onstage," he interrupts, grinning widely at me. "Trust me. It's fun! And I'll help you. You know, if you need help at all. But—just—you can count on me."

"Thank you," I say. He's so nice.

"So, listen," he continues, hiking his bag higher up on his shoulder. "I'm actually really glad I ran into you, because I have a question for you. Or—it's, um, more like a favor, I guess. And you can absolutely say no, I just—"

"Danny," I cut him off, and I cannot contain a grin; he is adorable when he starts rambling. "What is it?"

"Right, um." He laughs, rubs the back of his neck. "I was just wondering—I know we're supposed to meet up Wednesday this week, but I have—I have had a look at the parts of my homework we didn't get to on Friday and it's all just—" He sighs. "It still all just looks like a jumble of letters and numbers to me. I just think I need a lot of help. With math. You know. So I guess I was just wondering if maybe you happen to have a few minutes for me today? I know this is really short notice and you probably already have plans, but I—"

"I have a debate team thing this afternoon," I say, and his face falls.

"No, sure, of course," he says. "It was a long shot to begin with, I—"

"If it's not too late for you, um, we can meet up after that," I quickly tell him. Because I really do need to meet with the debate team; it's our first meeting of the school year. But I'm not going to pass up an opportunity to spend more time with Danny! Plus, I feel really bad that we spent so much time talking about other things on Friday. I don't usually let myself get distracted like that. It was really unprofessional of me. I should have spent more time helping him study.

He bounces a little on the heels of his feet, looking very pleased. "Really? I don't want to keep you from anything. Are you sure?"

I have no idea how cool he thinks I am that I couldn't clear my schedule several hours in advance. But I just shake my head and try to look re-assuring instead of hopelessly ecstatic at the prospect of hanging out with him again so soon. "You are not keeping me from anything. Be-lieve me. It's not a problem!"

"That's so nice of you," he says. "Thank you so much. I really appre-ciate it!"

"The library will be closing, though, once I get out of here," I say. "We should probably meet somewhere else."

"The coffee shop down the block?" he suggests. "You know, where I work. We could meet there. I'll save us a table and get started on some other homework while I wait for you."

I tilt my head at him. "Are you sure you're okay with hanging out in your workplace on a day off?"

He nods. "Sure. It's perfect, actually. I get my employee discount, and also at least there I'm sure that the machines are clean." He laughs. "You like coffee, right?" he asks.

"I'm definitely a coffee guy," I tell him.

"We make this really amazing caramel macchiato," he says. "But I guess you know that since that's what you've been drinking all summer."

"You remember that?" I say, a little confused.

"Yeah, of course. You ordered that all the time." He grins.

"Oh." I let out a nervous chuckle. "I just . . . really like that caramel macchiato, I guess."

"Well, it is delicious."

I lower my eyes, not sure what to say. After all, yes, I like that drink, but it wasn't the reason I kept coming back. I can't exactly tell him that. "You're sure you don't mind waiting?"

He shakes his head. "Not at all! I'm just grateful you are willing to meet up with me again so soon!"

"Of course I am," I say much too quickly, and promptly blush to-mato red.

He keeps looking at me and it's making me a little nervous. So I clear my throat and take a step back. I have to get to class anyway if I don't want to be late.

"Okay, I guess I've kept you long enough. I don't want you to be late for class," he says.

I blush darker and stare at my feet. "I'll see you later," I mumble, and hurry away before my face has a chance of actually bursting into flames.

I also really wish that Meg were here right now. Even if all of this doesn't mean anything and I know I'm way overreacting, I still really do want to talk about it.

At least I manage to get to class two minutes early and I do some-thing I have never in my life actually dared to do before: I get out my phone and send a text to my best friend with the teacher already in the classroom.

I just really need to talk about all of this.

Chapter 23

Meg

WE'RE JUST FINISHING UP ON our late breakfast when my phone vibrates on the table. I pick it up to check my messages. It's Linus.

For a second, I'm confused—Linus never texts in class and class should begin any second now—but then I check what he's written.

Danny found me and asked if we could meet today already! o_O

I can barely contain my triumphant grin; I knew it! He likes him! Danny likes Linus! I was right all along!

I hope you were smart enough to say yes to that! I write back.

He starts typing out a response immediately and I watch the small dots at the top of the screen while I wait. The fact that he is risking this when the teacher could come in any minute tells me everything I need to know about his emotional state concerning Danny. Not that I hadn't already been pretty certain of his feelings for him prior to this.

Of course I said yes! He needs my help. I just have debate this afternoon!

Skip it! I text immediately.

I'm meeting him afterward, Linus replies.

Oh, okay. Even better!

At the coffee shop.

I smile. *How romantic! :)*

Stop it! I'm just excited because I'm silly like that and I needed to tell you.

Have fun! I tell him. *And any details you want to discuss later . . . You know how to contact me! :P*

Need to go! Class! he writes, and I put my phone down.

"Who was that?" Mom asks, looking up from her toast.

I just give her a look in return. "One of the five hundred other friends I have besides Linus."

She sighs exasperatedly. "Well, excuse me for asking!"

"He was texting in class! I'm so proud of him! He's turning into a regular little rebel in his old age."

She snorts. "As if you're so dangerous. Remember how I had to talk you into skipping today?"

"Hey, one of us has to live on the edge," I inform her. "And I'm really glad it doesn't have to be me. And it can't be Sophia anymore since she's no longer one of us, apparently."

She frowns. "Correct me if I'm wrong, but I don't remember Sophia as being particularly dangerous, either."

"Oh no, you're mistaken." I grin. "That one time we went to the movies, she brought in a whole bag of gummy worms and we ate them during the movie instead of buying the expensive stuff there."

"How rebellious," Mom says proudly, and I nod. I remember that afternoon well; most of all how my palms had sweated, heart hammering hard in my chest. I'd missed almost the entire first half of the movie because I'd been so scared someone would catch us and throw us out for smuggling in our own food. Clearly, I am not well suited for a life of crime. But then, Sophia hadn't been doing much better.

It's a nice memory, until I remember everything else, like the fact that there won't ever be any new memories like that with Sophia. She's going to be doing all of this with someone else now. Maybe she's even doing something like this with some other girl right now, I think, and I get sad.

This isn't fair. I don't want to have to remember all this good stuff if all it does is remind me how much I miss her. All I want is for her to be here with me and love me, and that is never going to happen. And maybe, I think, I would have preferred it if none of it had ever happened because you can't miss what you never had.

"Hey," Mom says. "You're thinking of her again, aren't you?"

I sigh. "Sorry. It just—happens."

"Well, that's why we're having this day in the first place," she reminds me. "If you want to forget about shopping and instead just stay in and look at photo albums and listen to sad music, we can do that, too. I'll make cookie dough!"

I straighten my shoulders and shake my head. "No. I don't want that."

The thing is, I am still a little dubious about this whole concept of wallowing in the first place. I don't know if going shopping can really qualify as wallowing, but it's honestly as far as I'm willing to go at this point, and I'm doing it for Mom more than for me, to be perfectly honest. She seems so proud of the idea.

As for the rest, the memories and all that . . . Well, I'm already sad. I don't understand how allowing myself to be super extra sad for a day is going to help matters. I don't believe that there is a certain amount of sadness that I have to go through, and that if I take a day to use up a large portion of it, there will be less of it left for later.

Books and movies and songs promise that eventually, I won't feel it as much. But honestly, I am in no particular rush to get there. The sadness is the last thing I have left of her.

"Okay, fine. We'll go shopping," Mom says. "I actually do need a new jacket."

"I need a new pair of jeans," I decide. "There's this one pair I've been meaning to get rid of for a while."

"Absolutely," she says cheerfully. "Finish your coffee. I'll buy you another one at that coffee place you like later."

Maybe this day won't be so bad after all, I think.

Chapter 24

Linus

I TEXT MY MOM THAT she doesn't need to pick me up after school before I make my way to the debate team gathering. Technically, Meg is on the team, too, but since she's not here today I'll have to fill her in on the details of the meeting later.

Once we're done I make my way on foot to the coffee shop down the block where Danny said he'd be waiting for me. I'll have to figure out how to get home later because I'll miss the bus and I still have homework. But I'll worry about that when the time comes. Right now, I'm still working on keeping my face as neutral as possible in order to not show my excitement too obviously. I don't want to freak him out by seeming hopelessly overeager.

I can already see him through the large front window as I approach. He's secured us a table near the front, which is another nice thing to do—most people I tutored previously would probably have preferred to be hiding in the back because being seen with me does not earn you any status points. I kind of like that Danny doesn't seem concerned about that.

He has a book and a notepad on the tabletop in front of him and it looks like he's working on some other homework assignment.

He looks up as I enter and smiles at me; I don't even have to make a conscious decision to smile back. It just sort of happens to my face.

"Hi," I greet him, walking over to the table.

He closes his book and shoves it aside, gestures toward the empty chair on the other side of the table. "Hey! Sit! You're earlier than I expected. Do you want something to drink? I was gonna get myself another cup anyway just now."

I sit, dropping my bag next to my chair. "Oh, I'm fine, thank you, I'll just—"

"You're in luck," he says. "Joan is working today. She makes the best macchiato."

I glance over to the counter, where a tall girl with blue streaks in her hair is just refilling the water tank on the giant coffeemaker. "Oh. Cool."

"So." He pushes his chair back. "Do you want one of those again? Or something else?"

I am seriously so lost right now. Is he offering to buy me a drink? Because that's not necessary—he's already paying me for the tutoring. "Just a regular coffee," I say, reaching for my bag to get my wallet.

"You sure?"

"Yeah, thanks."

"Okay." Before I can say anything else, he's already jumped up, gesturing for me to stay where I am. "Coming right up! My treat. You know. As a thank you for you making time for me today."

I barely even have the time to nod to acknowledge that I heard him before he's already walked off in the direction of the counter. Since I feel weird just sitting here waiting for a boy to bring me coffee, I start getting my notes from the last session out of my bag and quickly look them over to refamiliarize myself with what we were working on. Also, focusing on my notes is less creepy than watching the adorable back of Danny's head as he leans across the counter to chat with Joan and the older half-bald guy who is working with her.

"Here you go," Danny says a moment later, putting a large mug full of steaming-hot coffee on the table in front of me.

I look up at him. "You didn't have to get me the large one."

He shrugs. "No big deal."

"Let me pay you back," I offer, going for my wallet again, but he reaches out as he's sitting down, putting a hand on my arm.

"It's on me! I told you. Don't worry about it. Besides, I still get a discount here because I work a few afternoons a week."

I open and close my mouth and can't feel much besides his hand on my arm. "Uh, but—" I start, and don't know how to continue.

"Linus," he says.

"Huh?"

"Let me pay for your coffee? Please?"

I hesitate, don't quite understand, and I can't help but glance down at his fingers still touching my sleeve. He lowers his eyes, withdraws his hand far too quickly, and clears his throat.

"Sorry," he says.

"No, no, it's—um." I laugh, a little too shrill probably. I still can't quite wrap my head around the fact that we're here in public together and he remembers me from the summer and he just brought me coffee. "It's fine. Uh. Thank you. I—thank you." And then, to let him know that I get how friendship works and I don't just expect this to be a favor, I add, "But I get to pay for you next time!"

He looks delighted, far more than I would have expected over the promise of a free cup of coffee that is strictly speaking not even free since he already paid today.

"Yes, okay," he says. "You have a deal!"

"Wonderful!" I make sure to smile back at him. Fortunately, smiling at him is really not a difficult thing to do at all. "So, do you want to get started? Sorry you had to wait for me—"

"No, this was good." He bends down to put away his book and get his math supplies from his bag, continuing to speak to me from under the table. "It gave me time to get started on my preliminary notes on *The Misanthrope*."

"Molière!"

"Yes." He sits back up, puts his math book down on the table. "You've read it?"

"I have. I liked it."

"So—you're into books, too? Or just the science stuff?"

I shrug. "I'm into studying, I guess? Learning stuff. You know. I like to read all kinds of things."

"Oh, okay. That's really cool."

I lower my eyes and bite my lip, fingers playing with the pencil resting on my open textbook. He says the kindest things sometimes. "Thank you!"

"Well." He lets out a short laugh. "Shall we get started?"

I look up and nod, relieved. "Yes. Yes, we shall."

Despite the less-than-ideal setting—a library is much better suited for studying than a noisy coffee shop—we do succeed in getting quite a lot of work done over the course of the afternoon.

Danny is a fast learner and not really bad at math at all. Just a little behind because his last school must have used different lesson plans. Which means I can already predict that our sessions will come to an end, which makes me a little sad. On the other hand, helping someone is a good feeling, and helping him is the entire point of this particular exercise and the only reason we are here at all. So I guess we're doing well, all things considered.

I walk out with him once we're done and he keeps talking to me, about school and drama club, and I don't really have anything to add to the conversation. I'm mostly just grateful that I have survived this day so far without embarrassing myself. But I'm more than willing to listen to whatever he has to say. I like his voice a lot.

"Where's your car?" he asks once we're in the parking lot, looking around.

"I don't have one," I tell him. "My dad dropped me off this morning."

He frowns. "How are you going to get home, then?" He looks seriously worried about this.

I wave my hand to indicate it's not a big deal. "I'm going to call my mom and see if she can pick me up. And if she can't, I'll walk; it's only, like, half an hour on foot from here."

He looks guilty. "You missed your lift home because of me, didn't you?"

"It's seriously not a problem. I don't mind walking."

"I can drop you off," he offers.

"You don't have to do that. I'm fine getting home by myself."

"My car is right over there," he insists. "And it's not a big deal. I'd be happy to do it. It's my fault anyway that you're stranded here."

I hesitate. The truth is, I mean it that I don't mind walking, but I do still have homework. And if he does drop me off, I get to spend a few more minutes with him. When it really comes down to it, I'm too weak to resist the prospect of more time with him.

"Fine," I say, and he beams at me.

"Great!"

"Thank you!"

"It's really not a problem. Believe me!"

I follow him to his car, which looks a little dusty, but also like you might not want to wash it in case the dust actually is the only thing still holding it together. I stare a bit, and he follows my eyes.

"Uh, yes." He scratches his head. "I should have mentioned. My car is a piece of crap."

"It's a car," I object. "That's more than I have. And I think it looks, um. Cool."

"That's really nice of you," he says. "But you don't have to say that. It's my aunt Diane's old car and if she hadn't decided to retire it I wouldn't have one, either. It might actually break down any day."

"Meg's car doesn't actually look that much better than yours," I assure him, even though that's not really true. "I've seen worse." That is definitely not true.

He looks pleased and gets in behind the wheel; I slip into the passenger seat. The car is old enough to still have a cassette player. In the open glove compartment, I even spot some cassettes.

"Welcome to the nineties." He laughs, looking a little embarrassed as I pick up one of the tapes to read the writing on the little white sticker on it.

"*Automatic for the People*." I grin as I'm holding up the tape. "R.E.M. You meant that literally about the nineties, didn't you? This is my dad's favorite album."

"Hey, that's a timeless classic!" He sounds scandalized.

"I don't disagree with you," I say, putting the tape back into the glove compartment. *I just think you're getting more and more perfect,* I add in my head. "But do I have to relinquish my cell phone or does it automatically stop working in here?"

He shakes his head. "Oh! That reminds me. I've been meaning to ask you—um."

"What?"

"Just—" He shrugs, hesitates. "I was wondering if I could maybe have your number?"

I . . . pause, think, say, "Oh."

Meg has my number. Sophia has my number. Mom and Dad have my number. And that is the entire list of all the people who have my number. No one else has ever wanted it. This is new. Not unwelcome, but totally and utterly new.

"It's just," he continues, and I realize that I haven't answered him yet. "Since we might have to be able to contact each other, you know. For the—uh, tutoring, just, if one of us is running late or whatever—"

"No, of course," I agree. "Of course. That makes sense. Absolutely. Yes. Of course!"

"Good," he says. "That's—good. Yes. Okay. Good."

I quickly fish my phone out of my bag and hand it to him unlocked, hoping he won't realize how short my contacts list is. "Just type your number in?" I ask.

He hands me his phone in return. "Okay. And you know," he says, "if I give you my number, you know you can totally use it, right? Like, if you ever need a lift home or anything. Please feel free to text me anytime."

I know he's just being nice and probably trying to make friends at a new school. But it still makes me smile as I enter my number into his phone.

Chapter 25

I AM NOT CERTAIN WHY, exactly, but after my day off on Monday the rest of the week goes by relatively quickly. Maybe Mom was right and I did indeed really need a day like that. Who knew? I didn't wallow a whole lot, though. But I did think about Sophia. It made me sad, so I never did it for very long. But yes, I did think about her.

On Tuesday, we have a drama club meeting.

Of course Linus and I are the first ones there; Linus is always so on time it's almost annoying in a very endearing sort of way. I immediately take a seat in the circle of chairs that's already set up in the room. Linus hesitates.

"Shouldn't we . . . wait? For the others?"

I roll my eyes at him. "Come sit down. Don't just stand there."

"What if they have assigned seats?"

"I guess then we can move," I assure him.

He still looks a bit uncomfortable because he doesn't like to do anything wrong, but he sits down next to me anyway.

Slowly, the room starts filling with more and more people, and the fourth or fifth person to enter after us is Danny.

"Hi," I call out immediately, in case he hasn't seen us yet, and his face lights up with a smile as he waves at us.

"Hi!"

He hurries over and right away takes the still-empty chair next to Linus. I'm very pleased with this development.

"Hey," Linus says quietly, and Danny beams at him.

"I'm glad you guys could make it!"

I remember that Danny is new here as well and doesn't really know anyone, and I do my best to keep up random small talk while the room fills with more people. Even Linus participates, and I'm so proud of him because I can tell that he's nervous. This club isn't really inside his usual comfort zone anyway, and now he's also sitting next to the guy he likes. But in typical Linus fashion, he does his best to keep smiling and being polite. If Danny isn't in love with him yet, I don't know what's wrong with him.

We don't do anything much, just sit in a circle and go around introducing ourselves and discussing what we're going to be doing this year.

Apparently our first project, to be put on toward the end of the year in December, is going to be a Sherlock Holmes play that some of the drama club people rewrote last year. Everyone seems really excited about it.

Our faculty adviser, Mr. Walsh, just sticks around long enough for us to elect a drama club president, and I don't really get the dynamics of this club yet, but apparently everyone agrees that it should be this girl named Stella who already had the job last year. I just vote for her, too, to make things simple and because I don't know any of them that well.

Stella then proceeds to explain that we're going to start on the play next week, but that, in the meantime, we should already split into groups for all the backstage tasks, and promptly produces a list of all the extra work we'll need done.

I really don't understand a lot of it, except that it's obviously expected of all of us to help out with something behind the scenes as well. Unless you're playing a lead role—in that case you don't have to because you have more lines to learn or whatever.

I volunteer for props and costumes since I don't expect to get a lead (and I don't want one anyway). Linus volunteers with me, and I'm glad because I don't want to be stuck in that group by myself, even though the girl in charge of it, I think her name was Alyssa or Alicia or Alison or something, seems really nice and smiles at me excitedly when I raise my hand for her group.

This club is going to be more work than I thought it would be. But at least the people seem really nice. And when I look over at Linus and Danny, they're actually talking, so I smile to myself and decide that yes, this is absolutely worth my time.

Friday night, Linus comes over for a *Star Trek* marathon. I'm pretty sure this project will keep us busy until we both go off to college, and I like that thought.

I am aware that once I get him a boyfriend, it will slow our project down considerably. But that's fine. I probably ditched him a lot, too, without noticing when I was dating Sophia.

He's busy clicking through the DVD menu when I walk back through into the living room, carrying the obligatory bowl of popcorn.

"Hey," he says, without looking up. "I just noticed. You put an awful lot of *Deep Space Nine* on your episode list."

I frown. "Not that many!"

"I just thought that Captain Picard was your favorite."

I put the bowl down, drop onto the sofa next to him heavily enough that he bounces a little. "What does that have to do with anything?"

"Nothing, I guess," he says. "I just noticed."

"Your favorite is Janeway and you still put more *Next Generation* than *Voyager* on the list," I point out.

"You counted?"

"Apparently, so did you."

"Okay, okay." He laughs. "For the record, I still think we could have come up with a more sophisticated system for the rewatch than merely sorting them chronologically."

"What's wrong with watching them in the right order?"

"Doesn't it just seem unimaginative?"

"No," I disagree. "It seems sane and like it makes a lot of sense."

"I guess you're right." He sighs.

I pull up my legs and debate whether or not I want to ask this; we are on a kind of tight schedule here. But I'm just way too curious. "How was tutoring today?"

He keeps his face too carefully neutral. "It was okay."

"You guys met up three times this week," I remind him. "And he sat next to you the entire time during that drama club pre-meeting thing on Tuesday."

"Are you trying to demonstrate that you can count?" he asks. "Because we established that literally half a minute ago!"

"Was it his idea or yours to meet up that often?"

He pauses, gives me a long look from the side. ". . . His. He asked to meet up more often. He said he really needed the extra help."

"Ha!" I shout. "I knew it!"

"Knew what? That he needs help with math? That's not a secret, you know."

"Linus, darling," I say. "He is making up excuses to spend time with you!"

"He is not! He needs help with math!"

"Why can't you just trust me on this?"

"Because I have actually spent time with him and you haven't," he points out. "It is all very innocent. Please. Believe me."

At that moment, his phone makes a noise on the coffee table and he picks it up, his face getting these red spots it gets when he's excited or very embarrassed about something.

"Is it Danny?" I ask smugly, picking up the popcorn bowl and hugging it to my chest.

"No," he says.

"Are you lying to me?"

"No."

"Then who is it? Your other secret boyfriend I don't know about?"

"He's not my boyfriend." He sighs, looking oddly guilty. "It's just . . . Mom. I, uh, I guess I forgot to take the trash out—"

"She texts you because of that?"

He shrugs. "Apparently."

"Weird." I sigh. "Mothers, right? Should we just watch the episode? You can't do anything about the trash right now anyway."

He keeps looking at me for a moment, then quickly leans over to give me a hug. Just a brief one, and I don't really know what it's for, but hey, free hugs. Not gonna turn them down. "Of course," he says. "We can do that."

He's still a little twitchy and keeps shifting in his seat and makes a point of seeming really busy with the DVD menu, which makes me think that it probably was Danny who just texted him. And that he's embarrassed to admit it. Maybe he wants to spare my feelings because he has a cute guy texting him while I just got dumped. Maybe he still just doesn't believe that Danny might actually like him. Either way, Linus is such a terrible liar. He gets so nervous.

While he fiddles with the remote, I discreetly watch him out of the corner of my eye and think. I really love hanging out with him, but it's Friday night and he's spending it with me watching TV. While I am one hundred percent certain that he could be just as well spending it with a really cute guy who I am sure really likes him back.

So I know what I have to do. Because at least one of us will be happy. And I have had my turn. Now it's his.

Chapter 26

Linus

SO, AS MUCH AS I'M aware that it means absolutely nothing, I still have a boy's number in my phone now. The number of a boy I really, really like, which is even better. This has never happened before. I'm glad about all of this, but I'm also confused. Especially since Danny actually keeps using my number, which I didn't expect and never dared to hope for. But he does text me, and most of it isn't tutoring-related.

Meg is over on Saturday so we can study together and afterward continue our *Star Trek* marathon, when my phone vibrates on the table.

We're studying in the kitchen because it gives us the fastest access to fresh coffee whenever we require it.

She looks up from her notes, frowns. "Is that your alarm? Has it been an hour already? Does that mean it's coffee break time?"

I can understand how she thinks that, as my parents are in the house and she is sitting right across from me. There really are not that many people who could be texting me on a Saturday afternoon. Or at all, really.

Well, Danny texts me, but it's Saturday. I'm sure he's out with friends or something.

And Sophia texts me. But it's not like I can tell Meg that. I know she didn't buy my excuse about my mom texting me, either, when I was over at her place last night, but I couldn't come up with anything more believable that quickly. I just hope it's someone else this time. I hate that I haven't told her about Sophia yet. We don't talk all the time, but she does text me to check in occasionally and it would just be impolite not to write back.

I pick up my phone to check it and quickly shake my head, can't quite keep in the delighted expression. "It's Danny!"

She perks up at that pretty much immediately. "Oh! What does he want? We can totally reschedule the rewatch and the studying if you have to go and meet him!"

I narrow my eyes at her. "Why would I run off to meet him? He's just texting because apparently he just realized that he must have accidentally packed one of my highlighters after tutoring yesterday."

"He texts you about highlighters?"

I let out a long, patient breath. "He knows how important it is for me to properly color-code my notes?"

She sighs, leans back in her chair, and says sarcastically, "How romantic!"

"He's asking if he should bring it over."

She nods knowingly. "Tell him yes! I can go! Or hide behind the curtains in your living room."

"We have sheer curtains in the living room."

"That is so not the point!"

"No," I confirm. "The point is that I don't need that highlighter today and if I do need one, I can borrow yours. I don't need to make him drive all the way across town to give it back. Because that would be insane."

"I think he knows that, too," she says. "And he probably just wants to see you. It's actually very cute!"

"No, he's just really nice that way," I try to explain, though I can tell that she doesn't believe me. Just then, my phone buzzes again and I look down at it—and feel all the blood draining from my face immediately. It's Sophia. Asking how it's going in drama club. Which I know means she wants to know how Meg is doing.

"Danny again?" she asks, sounding way too pleased.

"I, uh, no, I—" I swallow, mind racing to come up with something believable. This just so doesn't seem like the right time to bring up the fact that I've been talking with Sophia. How would I even tell her? Oh, by the way, ever since the beginning of the school year I've been chatting with your ex-girlfriend behind your back and I haven't told you because I know you're still hurt by her leaving and I didn't want to be a horrible friend. Want another cookie? But oh my god I hate lying to her. I can feel my leg starting to bounce under the table. "Yeah, it's Danny," I say quickly, nodding furiously. "He, uh, yeah, it's just—still about the highlighter. Just—yeah."

"So ask him over," she insists, tilting her head at me. I can tell she's suspecting something, which isn't surprising considering how very, very bad I am at making up lies on the spot.

I know I'm fidgeting like crazy but I can't stop myself; this is all too much. I open and close my mouth a few times, trying to regain some control over the situation. "I'm sure he doesn't have time. And besides, I don't have time, either. You know . . . homework. And stuff. Um."

She huffs out a breath, crossing her arms in front of her chest. "Why are you being so difficult about this?"

I stare at her, and I know I'm blinking a lot, which probably doesn't have the desired effect of making my face look calm and neutral. "Why are you being so difficult about it?"

"Fine!" she exclaims, throwing both hands into the air in frustration. "But I do think you're wrong!"

"I can pretty much guarantee you that I'm very, very right about this," I say, doing my best to look as determined as possible.

She goes back to work while I make my sweaty, shaking hands text the nicest boy in the world to reassure him that my weekend is not ruined by the absence of my pink highlighter.

And then I text Sophia that I can't talk right now, hoping she'll understand.

Crisis averted. For now. I guess. Now I just need to wait for my heart rate to go back to normal. I'm seriously not built for this level of excitement and sneakiness. Good thing I'm not considering a career in politics.

After a nice and (at least mostly) relaxing weekend with a lot of *Star Trek* and hanging out with Meg, I'm actually looking forward to the start of the week.

Meg picks me up that morning so we can drive to school together. She'd been mostly okay this weekend, but I can tell today that she's absentminded and distracted again. I worry about her a bit, but she won't tell me what's going on.

We don't share the first two classes on Monday, but then we have chem together right before lunch and I can tell she's still preoccupied as soon as she walks into the room and sits down next to me.

"Is everything okay?" I ask her, when she simply keeps staring out the window instead of getting her notes and pens in order on the table right before class the way she usually does.

She turns her head, smiles too brightly. "Yeah, just trying to make up my mind whether or not I want to audition for a part in the play," she says.

"Okay . . ." I'm not sure why she's so distracted by this. I think she should go for it and it doesn't really seem like something she would worry about. I'm sure that she's not telling me the truth and I don't quite understand why she's lying to me. But if she doesn't want to talk about it, I'm not gonna pry.

The thing is, I am getting a little antsy, wanting to talk to her. Danny kept texting me all through the weekend and I'm impatient to tell her about it; harmless as it may be, I've never done anything like this before and it makes me very, very happy. And I don't know how much longer I can keep it all inside—I need to talk about it.

I trust that she's going to have time to listen to me over lunch; right now class is starting and I need to pay attention.

I have to stop by my locker after class and Meg trails behind, oddly quiet the entire time. I'll definitely have to find out what's going on with her, if she ever feels like talking about it. But I can tell that she's worried about something. I want to help, but since she won't tell me what's up, I don't know how.

And then when I'm closing my locker and turn around, the first thing I see is Danny walking straight toward me through the crowd of students in the hallway, and I barely register Meg, who's been hiding behind her phone, finally looking up as she notices him, too. I tend to get Danny tunnel vision whenever he's around. It's a serious condition. So far, there's no known cure.

"Linus," he calls out for me, loud enough for people to hear. It's one of my favorite things about him, that he doesn't pretend we don't know each other in public.

"Hi, Danny," I say as Meg pushes herself off the row of lockers she had been leaning against, putting away her phone.

I expect him to tell me he can't make our session this Wednesday or that he has some news about drama club he needs to share, like an emergency meeting or something. I don't know if drama clubs have emergency meetings, but it seems like the kind of club that would do something like that.

He surprises me once again, though, by just stopping next to me, smiling, as if we're old friends and meet up by our lockers right before lunch every day.

"How was your weekend?" he asks brightly.

"Um." I'm not sure how to answer that, since we've been texting all weekend anyway. He pretty much knows everything I've been doing: studying, reading, watching TV, hanging out with Meg. "It was. Uh. Good? I guess?"

"Awesome," he says, and Meg clears her throat next to me.

"Listen," she says. "I have to—um, I got a text. I just need to run out quickly and—I forgot my English assignment on my desk and Mom is dropping it off. I have to meet her in the parking lot."

"Do you want me to come with you?" I offer immediately. We're having lunch together so it makes sense for me to trail behind. The cafeteria is a scary place for one lonely nerd all on his own.

"Why don't you and Danny go ahead?" she suggests, as if it's the most normal thing in the world to suggest such a thing. "I'll be right there. You two can get us a table."

"Oh but—" I can feel myself blushing and I have no idea what she's doing; Danny only stopped to say hi on the way to his own lunch group. "I'm—no, that's all right, I can just—"

"Yeah, okay," Danny interrupts before I can formulate my protest. "We'll save you a seat."

I stare, don't know what to make of this. "Uh, what?"

"Wonderful," Meg says.

"Danny, you don't have to—" I start.

"Let's get going, shall we?" he says cheerfully. "I think there's chocolate mousse for dessert today!"

I'm confused and embarrassed and I know Danny is just being nice; it's like he can't help it, but I'm going to have to have words with Meg once I get her alone. I don't care what kind of stuff she is going through today, she can't put me in this kind of a position with Danny, not when she knows how much I like him!

"Okay," I agree, because there's nothing to be done about it anymore without making everything even worse. Maybe I can just eat super fast and leave so that Danny can rejoin his friends later and won't have to waste his entire lunch period hanging out with me.

Meg smiles and I glare at her, which only makes her smile wider before she pretty much skips away from us.

"So," Danny says, and puts a hand on my shoulder to steer me in the direction of the cafeteria. "Oh, by the way, I have your highlighter in my bag—remind me to give that back to you. Also, I started watching *Firefly* yesterday since you recommended it, and oh my god, the first two episodes were amazing! I can't wait to watch the rest!"

"Um," I say eloquently. Because. Recommended? I did mention that I liked it when we briefly talked about mixed genres in books and television after tutoring on Friday. But I really can't believe he remembered that. "I'm glad you like it so far," I provide lamely.

He beams at me. "You know, I have never watched that much science fiction before, but I guess that's mostly because there's just such a flood of amazing things out there and we all tend to gravitate toward certain genres at some point, don't we? But maybe that's too restrictive in the long run; maybe we all need to start branching out into other genres to keep things fresh—"

I keep walking beside him and do my best to listen and nod, and apparently I am about to have lunch with him and apparently we're going to be talking about television shows.

This is a very unexpected turn of events and I can't help enjoying it a little bit through all my discomfort over knowing that he probably does have better things to do.

I really need to talk to Meg about this. She can't do anything like this ever again. No matter how much I'm enjoying it.

Chapter 27

Meg

I DON'T HATE MONDAYS LIKE so many people seem to. But I know I'm being weird today and Linus can tell. I just don't quite know how to snap out of it. I woke up feeling lonely and even though I know I'm not alone, not really, it's a difficult feeling to shake off.

At least my mood improved considerably when I got my first opportunity at matchmaking right around lunchtime, and the beauty of it is that I hardly had to do anything at all.

It was Danny who found Linus and immediately started talking to him. And even if I am distracted today, I can still see the way they look at each other all the time. Seeing them together at lunchtime was enough for me to have all my suspicions confirmed.

The way Danny keeps smiling at my best friend speaks volumes; he seems so excited and happy and so eager to please, it's the cutest thing I have ever seen. This is going to make everything so much easier.

Because Danny seems more than ready to take things a step further the moment he gets a signal from Linus that his attention is welcome.

Unfortunately, Linus still seems completely oblivious—not that I had expected him to actually realize he's being flirted with, but he almost looks downright uncomfortable.

I don't feel bad for ditching them, though. I'd only be in the way. They might be more relaxed if I leave them alone together and they can be as fluttery and awkward around each other as they like.

I wait around the corner until they've disappeared in the direction of the cafeteria, then I slowly follow them. I have no intention of joining them for lunch, but I am hungry. I'll just have to give them a good head start.

So I swing by the restroom, take the time to check my phone, wait until I can be sure that the line will be short and the two boys will have found a table and hopefully be deep in conversation.

Getting lunch doesn't take long now that lunch period is drawing to an end, and I hurry and keep my head down even though I can't see Danny and Linus anywhere. Which lets me hope that maybe they cannot see me, either.

I finally spot them in the far corner when I've acquired my sandwich and apple and am about to leave the cafeteria to sneakily eat outside. They're sitting at a table by themselves, far away from the Sports Jerseys and Popular Guys, and Linus is talking animatedly, hands waving, and Danny is laughing with such a joyous expression on his face, he just looks absolutely smitten. I cannot believe Linus still thinks he isn't interested in him.

Before they have a chance to see me, I quickly duck away and turn my back to find a quiet spot out in the yard.

"Hey!" a voice to my left calls out, and I turn my head to see a girl walk up to me with a lunch tray, smiling widely. It's Alyssa Valdez, the girl from drama club whose group I volunteered for.

"Hi," I greet her. I'm not quite sure what else to say; people usually don't talk to me in the cafeteria, where everyone sits with their own group of friends.

"I'm Alyssa," she says, and I smile back at her. "Drama club? You're in my group? Costumes and props?"

"I know," I answer. "I remember. Hi. I'm Meg."

"Yes, I know," she says excitedly. "You're Sophia Jones's girlfriend, right?"

My face falls and my mood sinks just a little. "Um," I say. "No. Actually. Not anymore. No."

"Oh." She looks embarrassed. "I'm so sorry. I just—"

"It's okay," I tell her quickly. "She only dumped me a little while ago. Uh. College and stuff, you know? Since she was a year ahead."

"I just came over because we all really miss Sophia and I wanted to tell you to say hi to her from us. But I guess that wouldn't be appropriate now, given the circumstances." She winces. "I'm sorry. I picked exactly the wrong thing to say."

She did, but she had no way of knowing that and she seems nice, so I shrug. "It's okay. Really."

"I'm not usually this insensitive," she promises.

"You didn't know." I twitch a smile at her, and she smiles back.

"Well, anyway," she says. "We have a table in that corner over there. Do you want to—? Where's your friend? He can come, too!"

"Oh," I say, pausing for a second. This is . . . new. "Linus is, um, busy. But—"

"Well, come on, then," she says, and motions with her head for me to follow her. "Sit with us."

"... Okay," I agree, only a little hesitant. I've never had a lunch group before. This is so weird. But from what I've seen of the drama people so far, they're nice enough. I guess I can sit with them instead of hiding away by myself in a quiet corner out in the yard. "By the way," I say, and she looks over at me as we're walking, "I've been meaning to ask—is it difficult for a newbie to get a part in the play? You know. For someone who has never done anything like that before."

She shrugs. "Not if you're good. It doesn't matter how long you've been in the club. Why? Are you thinking of auditioning for a part? Because you should!"

"Maybe." I shrug. This is valuable information. And yes, I think I do want to audition. But I wasn't asking for me. She doesn't need to know that, though. But now I can work on my new plan. This is going to be great.

Chapter 28

Linus

SO, LUNCH WITH DANNY TURNS out to be not as awkward as I imagined it, and he doesn't really seem in any hurry to get up and leave and rejoin his own friends. He's easy to talk to and the more we hang out, the more we manage to avoid those uncomfortable silences that I hate so much.

He's sitting across from me, waving his hands as he talks, and I almost completely forget about my own pasta over listening to him telling me about his old drama club at his last school.

"They called it a pre-performance lock-in," he says. "We usually did it the week before every new play."

"You all slept on the stage?" I ask. It sounds a little crazy, but also kind of fun.

"It was great," he says. "We'd just rehearse a bit through the late afternoon, and then we'd order pizza and watch movies right there in the auditorium."

"Isn't a stage uncomfortable to sleep on?"

He shrugs. "Yeah, a bit. But we didn't sleep that much anyway. And by the time we went to sleep we were so tired it didn't really matter where we lay down."

"That sounds amazing," I tell him.

"It was. Just a fun night with friends, you know?"

"Do you miss them?" I ask.

He nods. "I do. I miss them a lot. But"—he sighs—"Mom got a new job here so we had to move. She's an environmental scientist and she got the chance to be put in charge of a long-term project here, so—" He shrugs.

"For your senior year. That's really bad luck."

"Oh well." He grins at me. "It's okay. I mean, yeah, I miss my friends. But I like this place, too. And new friends are good, too, right?"

I nod quickly. "Absolutely." I like new friends. I like that he maybe kind of sort of is a new friend for me. We're having lunch and we're talking. That's what friends do. I'm really happy about this.

But even if lunch does end up being kind of nice after all, I still really want to know what on earth Meg was thinking by inviting him to lunch with us in the first place. I'm afraid that all of this is still part of her insane idea that there is something going on between the two of us. Maybe I'm being unfair; maybe she thought she was just being nice to him and then something came up and she couldn't join us. She's been distracted all day—it's completely possible that she didn't mean to leave me alone with him.

But it puts me in a difficult position because now I'm worried about her and mad at her at the same time and I can't just walk up to her and demand an explanation.

Because first of all there isn't much opportunity to talk to her between afternoon classes and then there's debate this afternoon, during which she's still distracted and still keeps playing with her phone.

Even our debate teacher seems to notice and calls on Meg to do a mock debate. She only ever calls on students like that when she feels they aren't paying enough attention, and Meg looks mortified at being singled out like that. As a result, she seems to give a hundred and fifty percent—she argues fiercely, way too angrily, way too invested in just a random debate. It makes me think there must be something more behind the way she argues than just humiliation at being singled out in front of the whole class. She wipes the floor with her debate partner. It's this thing she does where she gets so focused instead of letting anyone know how she feels. Our teacher pats her on the back for it, but I'm feeling more than a little unsettled by all of this.

When it comes down to it, I am much more worried than mad. I think something is wrong and I don't want to upset her further. For a moment, I'm afraid she's found out that I've been talking to Sophia. But no. She'd confront me about that. And I doubt she could have found out anyway. I'll just have to figure out what it is that's upsetting her.

Fortunately, she's driving me home today, so I wait until we're walking out to the parking lot before I broach the subject again. If it's something private, she's not going to tell me at school anyway.

"Meg?" I ask, walking next to her down the steps outside the main entrance while she's staring off into the distance.

"Mm?"

"What's going on with you?"

She turns her head to look at me, eyebrows drawn together. "What do you mean?"

I sigh. "Look, you've been absentminded and twitchy all day and then you didn't even show up for lunch, and you haven't even told me yet what that was all about. Which, um. Would be kind of nice to know. I mean. It just made me feel a bit—dumb, being left all friend-less for lunch. Is something wrong?"

"Oh." She laughs. "Don't worry about that. I'm sorry I didn't show. Mom was just running late and there wasn't the time—"

"Are you sure that's all there is?"

"You had Danny, right? I wouldn't have let you sit by yourself. I just needed my assignment. But if you'd been by yourself I would never have—"

"This isn't about me," I interrupt. "Although it was a little weird that you just invited Danny along like that. I mean, he probably didn't really want to—"

"Wait, I thought you guys were friends," she asks, sounding very confused.

"Um." I frown at her. "Why did you think that?"

"Because you kept texting him all weekend!" she exclaims, as if I'm the one not making any sense here.

"Are you mad at me because of that?" I want to know.

"Of course not! I just thought it was no big deal to invite him along if you guys were friends."

"Well, we're not friends," I point out patiently. "I don't really know him all that well yet."

"You hang out with him all the time!"

"It's not all the time and also it's because I'm tutoring him!"

"But you like him!"

"What does that have to do with anything?"

She stops me with a hand to my shoulder. "Linus? Are you mad at me? Because I'm sorry, but I really just had to—I wasn't trying to hurt your feelings or anything. I promise."

I pause, think about it, lift my shoulders. "Okay," I say. "Fine. I'm not mad at you." It's not exactly true, but this is a lie I can live with. Because eventually I won't be mad, and because I don't want to have a confrontation about this, not here, not now.

"I—" She stops, bites her lip. "I—okay. I'm still sorry."

"It's okay," I tell her. "Just—are you sure that you're okay? You seem a little—"

"Oh no, I'm fine." She smiles, so brightly I can easily tell that it's fake, then turns and continues walking in the direction of her car.

I have to jog a little to catch up with her, and more than ever I am convinced that there's something she's not telling me. Or is she still just upset about Sophia?

"You know you can talk to me, right?" I ask her in a final, rather lame attempt at opening up a dialogue between us.

"I know," she says. "There's just nothing to talk about."

I don't believe her, but I don't want to be pushy. So I let it go for now. But I'm going to have to keep an eye on her, because I'm starting to suspect that the breakup is finally catching up with her emotionally, and honestly, it's about time. I have been waiting to provide cookies and a shoulder to cry on for weeks now. If she's finally getting ready to deal with her feelings, then I'm definitely ready to offer support.

I'll just have to make sure to be there for her.

Chapter 29

Meg

I CAN TELL THAT LINUS is mad at me, and I know he has a very good reason. I know it wasn't very nice of me to just invite Danny to lunch with him.

And I feel bad about it, but . . . it turned out all right, didn't it? Because they had fun and they talked and that is progress, and progress is good. It doesn't matter if Linus is mad at me for it. Not really.

Except—I do feel bad for making him uncomfortable. I really, seriously didn't mean to. And I know he gets enough of that from everyone else who ever makes him feel weird and awkward, and I feel terrible for adding to that. But, I keep telling myself, it's all for a good cause. Because, in the long run, he's hopefully going to get something amazing out of it.

When I drive him home, he talks to me and seems cheerful enough, so at least I'm reassured that I haven't screwed up too badly. I just wish I could stop feeling so guilty. But I don't know how to apologize. Because as guilty as I feel, I still think that I'm right. With a little more nudging, I'm sure that he and Danny will end up together. That's good, right? I mean, I don't expect him to be thanking me, exactly, but—I don't know. I'm still right about this.

"Drama club tomorrow," he says, actually sounding a little excited about it even though I know it still makes him feel embarrassed to act and be silly in front of people.

"I'm really looking forward to the play," I say.

"Are you thinking of auditioning for it?" he asks. "Because I really think you should!"

"I want to," I tell him. "But—hey, you know what?" I actually manage to sound as if the thought has only just occurred to me. "You should do it, too!"

"Uh—do what, now?" He blinks at me.

"Audition," I say. "You totally should! I'm sure you'd get a part!"

He laughs. "I most certainly wouldn't. And also, that's a terrible idea. I'm *so* not an actor. I—couldn't. I just—couldn't."

"But why not?" I ask. "Come on. It's fun! And it's just a school play. It's probably just going to be our parents in the audience. No pressure."

"I wouldn't get cast anyway."

"Well, then there's no harm in trying, right?" I grin over at him. "We could audition together."

"Or you could audition by yourself and I can be there in the background to very quietly cheer you on."

"Or you could do it with me," I insist. "Come on, Linus! It's our senior year! Let's take some risks! Try new things! While we still can!"

He shakes his head at me. "I'm all for trying new things. I joined the club, didn't I? And it was my idea to join in the first place, too. But this is just—"

"Too much?"

"A bit, yeah."

I think about it. "You don't have to actually take the part if they offer it, you know?" I try. "You could just try it out and see what happens. And file it away as a new experience."

He shrugs. "I don't know, Meg."

I let it go for now, but I'm sure he'd actually do well if he tried it. I can't make him do this if he doesn't want to, but there's nothing wrong with suggesting it, right? Plus, it would probably make me feel better if I didn't have to do this by myself.

Chapter 30

Linus

MEG SEEMS IN A BETTER mood on Tuesday, so I trust that whatever was wrong yesterday has sorted itself out by now. Since she's back to her usual cheerful self, paying attention in chem class and teasing me about Danny all the time, I don't bring it up again, but I still watch her closely for any signs of sadness.

We have drama club Tuesdays and I do admit that I have been looking forward to it. Kind of a lot, actually. We only had that one meeting before and mostly we just all sat in a circle and confirmed that we were there and some people with more knowledge about these things than either Meg or I possess started bouncing around some ideas and putting people into groups for backstage stuff.

Meg and I are on our way to the auditorium when Danny suddenly jogs up to us, smiling.

"There you are! Hi!"

"Hey," I greet him back, and Meg smiles at him.

"I'm glad you decided to come back this week," he tells us, and I laugh.

"I told you. I had a lot of fun last week!"

He shrugs. "But you're in, like, fifty different clubs. So I really appreciate that you're taking the time to hang out with us. Otherwise I'd have to think about joining astronomy club or whatever." He winks.

It makes my heart stumble in my chest for just a moment, but then I remember that he's the new kid at our school and is probably eager to make friends any way that he can. That's why he's being so nice.

I shake my head at him. "I'm in three clubs. And it's fun! I mean, if you do want to join astronomy, you're welcome to tag along next time. But I know that it's not everybody's cup of tea, so—"

"I don't know if I'm actually smart enough to hang out with you guys," Danny says. "But I think it's really cool that you're interested in all these things."

"You're as smart as the rest of us," I assure him.

"Says the guy who's spending pretty much all of his free time tutoring me in math."

"Being good at math is not the same as being smart. And just because numbers aren't your thing, it doesn't mean that you're not smart or anything."

"You really are too nice to me." Danny smiles at me and I can't look away.

"Linus is always really nice," Meg chimes in. "But he's also right, you know? I bet you could teach him a lot about literature and art. He's creative, but he doesn't have an artistic bone in his body."

I give her a grateful look. "Exactly!"

"So, what you're saying is that we're all really smart?" Danny asks, grinning. "Because I can totally live with that."

"We could take over the world anytime we want," I confirm.

He bumps our shoulders together and nods enthusiastically. "Let's draw up a plan for world domination after tutoring tomorrow. It shouldn't take more than a few weeks, right?"

My insides keep fluttering and I'm feeling a little light-headed, but it's a good feeling. He's being so nice and I have a hard time keeping the insane grin that wants to spread across my face down to a smile. This feels so much like friendship. "A few days at most," I answer, rolling my eyes at him. "Please. Like it's going to be difficult!"

I am enjoying this. Talking with him. Joining drama club was definitely a good idea. I've never had anyone to talk to like this except for Meg and Sophia. But somehow, it feels different with him. And I don't think it's just because I like him. He's just—amazing. He's amazing and the fact that he actually does seem to be enjoying my company most of the time in some way makes me like him even more. I'm not used to this, but I really like it.

Chapter 31

Meg

"DO YOU THINK PATRICK STEWART did drama club when he was at school?" Linus asks as we set down our bags by the pile of everyone else's bags in the corner of the auditorium.

I raise both eyebrows at him. "What? You don't have that part of his biography memorized?"

He laughs and slaps at my arm. "Shut up! I was just wondering. You know? How early do most stage actors actually start acting on-stage?"

I shake my head at him. "You'll turn everything into a statistic if it stands still long enough, won't you?"

"Probably." He shrugs and grins at me. "But seriously. Now I really do kind of want to know how many *Star Trek* actors have drama club experience."

"Oh, you should change that up a bit and write fan fiction about it," I suggest. "Not with the actors, of course, but the characters? I'd totally read it. You know, an alternate-universe thing where Captain Picard and some of the others all go to school together as kids. And they all have to put on a play together? Make it a Shakespeare play—that could lead to all kinds of hilarious drama and stuff."

"You know I can't write," he says sadly. "But hey, if you find a fic like that, definitely send me a link, okay?"

"Maybe we can get Danny to write it." I wink at Linus. "Of course, you'll have to spend several afternoons introducing him to the characters first. . . ."

"Cut it out." He waves a hand to shush me, lowering his eyes and biting his lip to keep the smile small. "Also, the rewatch is our project."

I pat his shoulder and sigh loudly. "You know I'd gladly stop monopolizing you and give you a few afternoons off, right?" I say, but then I do shut up about it because I know he's worried about Danny overhearing us, and I don't actually want to make him uncomfortable. Besides, everyone else is gathering in a circle, so I guess we're about to start.

We're doing some kind of improv exercises in drama club today and I'm kind of amazed at how much fun it actually is. I can see why Sophia used to love it so much.

I like the idea of pretending to be someone else, but it's not just that. These people are crazy. The warm-up exercises alone are insane and I'm honestly not sure why I haven't tried this before; it is hilarious. We have to make all kinds of weird noises and jump around and shake out various body parts and do things with our faces like mimic various emotions someone shouts at us. It's so much fun.

But as much as I love this, I can see that Linus is having a much harder time with all of it. He tries, but his face is already as red as a fire truck and he's still standing a little awkwardly back in our circle of theater kids. I want to help him, but I have no idea how, so I offer him a little smile before we launch into the next exercise.

He gives me a tight-lipped, wobbly smile back, and very obviously resists the urge to run from the room as every single person there gets down on all fours to howl like werewolves.

Through my own howling, I can see Danny catching Linus's eye across the circle and, while Linus goes even redder, Danny starts scratching at the floorboards before rolling over onto his back to flail his arms and legs like a puppy, howling twice as loud as the rest of us. And I can't believe my eyes, but it seems to be working: I can see Linus relax just a little, his smile suddenly real, and some of the nervousness fading from his face.

Danny keeps this up through the rest of the warm-up, exaggerating his movements and just being extra silly, and Linus watches him in a way I bet he thinks is stealthy and smiles to himself. I'm sure Danny is doing it to help him, and I was so right about them. They are obviously good for each other.

Linus still spends the afternoon mostly trying to stay out of everyone's way and be involved as little as possible, but he doesn't look quite so panicked anymore. I could hug Danny for this.

I make more attempts at participating because I know I'm probably being extremely awkward and clumsy, but I don't even care right now. Most of them don't look all that elegant, either, doing any of this. And no one laughs at me, for which I'm very grateful. They're all really nice here. Which seems to be just the way theater people are, I guess. The only theater person I was ever close to is Sophia, but I always did like her theater friends. Most of them graduated with her, at least most of the people we used to hang out with after school, but I always did feel accepted by this crowd.

Everyone is really helpful and patient with me, and with Linus, too. They let him stay in the back when he doesn't want to try something and instead show him how it's done by example until he feels confident enough to attempt it himself.

And me—well, apart from finding out that I'm really into all of this, I'm having so much fun watching them having fun. Seeing people enjoying themselves is always, always worth it. There are too many people in the world who focus on the negative. I like being around people who have no problem making fools of themselves just because it's entertaining for themselves and others. It makes me regret never doing this with Sophia.

Danny stays glued to Linus's side the entire time, offering help and advice and partnering up with him and just watching him occasionally; he has that look on his face when he's sure that Linus isn't paying attention to him. I can see that he likes him. The more I observe them together, the more I'm convinced that I'm right about this.

Alyssa finds me when we're taking a little break, excitedly bouncing over to where I'm having a sip of water.

"Do you like our little club so far?"

I smile and nod quickly. "Yes! This is so much fun," I tell her. "I mean, it is going to take some getting used to, but I definitely want to get used to it, I think. I should have tried this sooner."

"Yes, it's probably a little weird if you've never done anything like it before." She laughs. "And hey, you're trying it now! Never too late to try something new, right? And from what I can tell, you're doing more than okay."

"Oh." Well, that is nice to hear, that I'm not making a complete fool of myself. "Thank you!"

"I think you're going to like it here," she says.

I laugh. "I think I already do."

"Oh, by the way, if you ever need any help with anything, come find me." She pats my arm. "I mean, if you want to. But I'm always happy to help."

"Thanks," I say. "That's really nice of you."

She grins. "Well, you're one of us now."

"Thanks!" I lean back against the wall behind me and she turns to stand next to me as if we're old friends already. Her eyes land on the group across the room where Linus is leaning against the wall, with Danny bending his head toward him to whisper something in his ear that makes both of them break into a fit of laughter.

"Well, those two seem to be really getting along, don't they?" she comments.

I manage to not punch the air in triumph, but I immediately like her a little more than I already did a moment ago. If she can see it, too, then that means I am not delusional; there is something there between those guys.

And now it seems I have a new friend who agrees with me. This is great.

Chapter 32

Linus

SOMETIMES I CANNOT BELIEVE HOW slowly time passes when you're embarrassed. And I'm feeling so embarrassed this afternoon. Mortified, even. Drama club is fun, but it's also, well, embarrassing. I'm not really good at any of this and I don't really like people looking at me and in here I can't shake the feeling that everyone is staring at me. And everyone who even just glances at me will be able to tell how absolutely awkward I am at all of this.

It's not really all bad, though. No one is laughing at me and I don't think they're actually judging me, and also . . . there's Danny.

Danny is being very helpful, making me laugh and offering advice, and I'm so, so eternally grateful for that, because I don't really know what I should be doing a lot of the time.

"Don't worry about that," he tells me, when I voice my concerns to him. "Today is all about having fun and getting used to one another.

Just do what feels right and have fun with it—no one expects you to spontaneously start reciting Shakespeare or whatever."

That is good news because I don't really have any Shakespeare lines memorized. So I try my best just having fun with it and not second-guessing myself, and I think this could really be something if I just give it a chance.

By the time the club ends I'm really tired, but I'm still just a tiny little bit sad that it's over. I'm very happy that I can stop making weird noises and jumping up and down all the time, but as uncomfortable as that part of it was, I really liked this feeling of kind of maybe bonding with Danny a little more. He's just so nice. He didn't have to help me out like that, and now that I feel safe from spontaneous embarrassment again I really do feel very happy about the way this afternoon went.

Meg is packing up her things in the opposite corner of the room and she's kind of beaming—I could tell how much fun she was having with these exercises and I like seeing her in such a good mood. She deserves it after everything she's been through.

"Hey," I say, walking over to her, bouncing on my feet a little. I can't help it, I'm still kind of buzzing from all the talking and hanging out I got to do with Danny, even if it didn't mean a thing. "This was nice, wasn't it?"

She nods. "Yes! I liked it. I think I could get used to it."

I'm glad that she didn't hate it. I would stay in the club even if she decided to leave, because I've made a commitment and also Danny is here, but it's going to be more fun if we can do it together.

Danny walks over to us as the club slowly disperses, bag already slung over his shoulder. "So, what's the verdict?" he wants to know. "You both coming back later this week?"

I nod quickly. "Definitely! Yes! I wouldn't miss it for the world!"

"Absolutely," Meg confirms. "This is a nice counterbalance to all the dry academic stuff, and probably just the boost my college application still needs. I'm in!"

"I'm glad to hear it," Danny says. "Anyway, I guess I should get going." He smiles at me. "You don't have a car, right? Need a ride home? I just got mine back from the garage yesterday!" He looks very happy about it.

"I—uh—" I have no clue what to say. Meg is going to drop me off at home as always and I don't want to bail on her. But . . . it's Danny!

Meg checks her watch and frowns—we still have homework and she is probably impatient to get going, and I'm just about to politely decline Danny's offer when she sucks in a breath and looks up, waving her wrist with the watch on it at me.

"Oh, shoot," she says, eyebrows drawn together. "I totally forgot that I have this eye doctor appointment this afternoon. I really have to get going, I—"

"Wait, what?" I try to remember her saying anything about this before, but I'm coming up blank. "What eye doctor appointment?"

"It's, uh—" She waves her hand again, sighs. "Yeah, it's totally last minute, sorry."

"You didn't say anything about that before," I remind her.

"It—got rescheduled," she says, and picks up her bag from the floor, wincing apologetically. "I'm really sorry, Linus. I can—I mean, I guess I could drop you off at home first, it's not a big deal, but—"

"I . . . guess I can go with Danny?" I say, heart hammering in my chest, not daring to actually look at him in case he just offered to be polite. But if he meant it . . . this is a good development, right? A bit sudden, and I wasn't prepared for it, and I'm not sure how someone as organized as Meg can forget about an appointment, but—well. "Or I'll walk. I can walk. I don't mind walking."

"I just really—they called yesterday and apparently someone had canceled, so they could fit me in earlier, and I just totally forgot—" Meg looks really sorry. Too sorry. I'm almost one hundred percent sure that she's running out on me on purpose and while this means more time with Danny, which is what I wanted, I'm not sure how I feel about her making this decision for me.

"Are you okay?" Danny asks her, sounding concerned. "Like, is it anything urgent?"

"Oh!" She shakes her head. "No! I'm fine. It's a routine checkup. And I may need new glasses. So I can—you know"—she gestures wildly—"drive Linus home safely in the future and all that. I don't know yet. I'll talk to you guys later, okay? Bye!"

And with that, she hurries from the room and I'm left standing there, not quite sure what the hell just happened.

"Uh, I guess I should get going, then," I say, after I've just stood there staring for a minute. "Since I still have homework and stuff."

"Don't be ridiculous," Danny says, putting a hand on my shoulder. "I'll drive you."

"You don't have to do that!"

"You don't have to keep pointing that out! I'm offering, okay? And since your usual lift home is indisposed—"

"I really don't mind walking," I let him know. Because, well, I don't. "But—uh, I mean. I'd be home quicker if I could go with you, just, if you're sure it's not too much of a detour—" I know I'm stammering, but I'm afraid he might have figured out as well that Meg was making up that appointment. Meg just sounded as if she was making it up. She has always been a worse liar than she cares to admit to herself. But then, Danny doesn't really know her that well. I'm probably worrying about nothing. And, well, he did offer to drive me home. It's all okay, I tell myself. I just wish I was better at this whole social-interaction thing. I want him to drive me home; I just don't want to be a burden.

"It's okay," he says. "I'd really be happy to take you home!"

"I can call my mom. Maybe she's home by now. Or my dad."

"If you'd prefer that, okay. But it's really no trouble at all!"

I take a breath, put on a smile, and tell myself to stop being weird already. "Okay. Yeah. If you're sure, that would be so nice of you. Thank you! I just feel like you keep getting stuck with me," I admit. "I'm really sorry. I swear that I am usually way better organized than this!"

"What are you talking about?"

"Just—" I shrug, shoving my hands into my pockets. "Lunch yesterday, and now this. I feel bad for taking up so much of your time constantly!"

"You're joking, right?" he asks. "You spend several afternoons a week tutoring me when I know you probably have a million better things to do."

"But you pay me for that!"

He lowers his eyes a little, nods. "Right. But it's still just—really nice of you."

"I like tutoring," I admit.

"Well." He takes a deep breath, lifts his head again to meet my eyes. "And I'd like to be allowed to take you home right now. Is that okay?"

I deflate a little, and I don't really know why I should keep saying no to this. I mean, I want to have him take me home. It means I'll get to keep talking to him, and I really can't imagine in what universe I would ever actually say no to that. Unless there's a universe in which I am straight and blind and someone who doesn't like nice people.

"Yes. Okay. That's more than okay. Thank you!"

He smiles and I go to retrieve my bag while he waits for me by the door, starts walking next to me down the by-now-deserted hallway.

"You really do enjoy the tutoring, don't you?" he wants to know.

"I really do. Why?"

"Just." He shrugs. "You're good at it. You're patient. Like, I'm never afraid to ask you stuff because I trust you won't tell me it's a stupid question or anything."

"I would never do that," I promise. "Why would I do that? If it were a stupid question, you wouldn't be asking it. No good teacher should ever make you feel like you're not allowed to ask if you don't understand something!"

"I feel like that's a really unusual attitude, though," he says. "You're kind of a natural at teaching. I'm really glad that Meg recommended you to me."

"Oh. Yeah. Thanks," I say quickly, trying not to let him see as my face falls a little. This was Meg's idea? Well, now at least I know why he approached me. It's not like I ever actually thought it was because he liked me, but this is . . . Has she been lying to me? She never mentioned this. "I . . . try."

"You do more than that," he insists. "I've had a lot of different math teachers over the years, and, I mean, I learned math, I got good grades. But I never really got why math was exciting or fascinating. You know? Until you started explaining it to me. I can listen to you when you talk about it. And the way you talk about it helps. You talk about it as if you actually love it."

"Well, yes, but that's because I do actually love it."

"I know. And that's awesome. And it shows when you're trying to teach it. It makes me almost feel excited about it, too. Or at least—at least like I want to try to understand it better, because if you can be so passionate about it, it cannot be completely stupid."

"But today, you made me feel the same way about acting," I tell him.

He laughs. "No, that's different. You were already excited. I just— helped. A bit."

"That's what I'm doing, too. I don't see the difference."

"Have you thought about becoming a teacher?" he asks. "I mean, obviously you can do whatever you want. And I have no doubt you could build space probes or cure cancer or become president—"

"Oh no! I do enjoy a good debate, but I couldn't even imagine going into politics!"

"But, well, you know." Our shoulders touch as we walk next to each other, and I can't tell if it's an accident or if he bumped our shoulders intentionally. "I think you have a real gift for teaching. And it seems as if you're enjoying it!"

"I have thought about it," I admit. "A lot. But I don't know yet what I want to do. I know most people probably have it figured out by now, but I just—I can't decide."

"You still have time."

"Not that much time!"

"Enough time." He smiles at me. "I can help you. If you like. You can use me as a sounding board. Or we'll act out different futures for you. Whatever you need."

"You're nice. But I'll be okay. Thank you!"

"Well, if you need me, I'm here," he says.

I don't know what to say to that and I can feel myself blush dark red, my face burning with it, so I quickly change the subject as we exit the school building and walk across the almost-empty parking lot in the direction of his car. So even if he's just hanging out with me for my math skills, he still always manages to make me feel kind of really good about myself. And I guess that's worth something.

"What about you?" I want to know. "Do you know what you want to do yet?"

"Not really. I mean, yeah, in theory I'd like to be a writer. But it's not like you can just make up your mind to be that and make it work. So, in the meantime—well, I do know that I want to go to college. And major in English because I love it. And I'll figure out the rest."

"I'm sure you will," I say, and add because he has offered it first, "If you ever want to talk it out with someone, I'm here for you, too. You know that, right?"

"Thank you." He sounds surprised but pleased all the same. "And, you know, I actually think that a lot of people our age don't really have any of this stuff figured out yet. I think it's a little difficult even to imagine what you want to be out in the real world when all you have ever known is school, you know? How are we supposed to know what it's going to be like, actually doing other stuff? It's always going to remain a bit of a surprise. So I guess taking the time to properly make up our minds is a good thing."

"Oh, I absolutely agree," I assure him. "It's like—all I know for sure is that I want to do something that makes me feel like I am doing something. I mean, I want to feel like I'm contributing, you know?"

He nods. "Yes, I get that. And I like that you think of it that way. I guess that also means becoming an investment banker is not on your list of possible career choices?"

I shake my head firmly. "God, no! Absolutely not!"

He grins, gets out his keys as we finally reach his car. "You want to use your awesome math powers for good!"

That makes me laugh. "I guess you could say that."

"I couldn't see you as an investment banker anyway. You are far too nice for that."

"Uh," I say eloquently. I'm never really sure what to do with compliments like this one. Probably because I don't get them a whole lot. "It's like—um. There's this episode on *Star Trek: The Next Generation*," I tell him. "Sixth season, I think. It's this thing Picard says that's always sort of stuck with me, it's something along the lines of 'the most important thing in a person's life is to feel useful.' I've always really liked that. I think we all want a purpose in life, you know?"

He unlocks his car, smiles at me over the roof of it. "Your Captain Picard is right," he tells me. "I think I like that quote!"

"It's also why I like tutoring, I guess." I open the passenger-side door and slide into my seat as he gets in behind the steering wheel.

"It makes you feel useful?"

"It makes me feel like I'm doing something to help someone."

"You are," he says, and starts the car. "Doing something to help someone, I mean. And I can absolutely assure you that you're really good at it."

Hanging out with Danny is definitely going to be very good for my ego. Regardless of why he is actually hanging out with me in the first place.

Chapter 33

Meg

ONCE AGAIN, THE FIRST THING I do as soon as I get home is to take my afternoon coffee upstairs (in a new mug Mom brought home for me from the museum yesterday; it says I DIG ARCHAEOLOGY on it) and boot up my computer.

The idea to fake an eye doctor appointment when Danny offered to take Linus home was a good one. And while I didn't stick around to see if it worked, I'm confident that Danny did indeed drive Linus home. If everything went according to plan, they should be pulling up in front of his house together any second now. And hopefully they spent the entire drive talking and getting to know each other even better.

But from what I can tell after seeing them together earlier, they already do get along pretty great.

The thing is, I can't really keep just ditching them all the time. I know it looks weird, and also I don't want to be a bad friend to Linus.

I can't really keep putting him in these awkward situations that probably make him feel all kinds of nervous.

It would be so great if those two just had another reason to spend more time together. And I still believe that Linus taking on a more active role in the upcoming play would be a great way to accomplish that. But the problem with that idea is that I really don't know the first thing about auditions and what's important to know if you want a part in a play. I'm not exactly the best person to help him with this and to give him advice.

And I do know someone who might be able to provide some helpful tips, but . . . I can't exactly ask her anymore, can I?

I mean, that option has been there all along, even if I have hesitated considering it for obvious reasons. I don't really know if I want this, but on the other hand, it's for the greater good. It's for Linus and Danny!

Maybe my own feelings in this don't matter. I can make them happy. Isn't that enough to make it all worth it?

All I need to do is keep a level head and get it done. It's not a big deal. And she may not want to talk to me anymore anyway. Who knows?

I take a deep breath and turn toward my laptop.

The fastest way to get the required information would doubtlessly be a text message or a phone call. But somehow, I can't really do that yet. I don't want to talk to her. I just need her help.

For the greater good.

So I open my e-mail in-box and pull up my contacts folder—I don't remember her e-mail address, since we never really e-mailed much before. We mostly texted. And instant messaged. And spent every possible waking minute together.

But there's a first time for everything, I guess.

So I gather all my courage and start typing: *Dear Sophia...*

It feels weirdly formal. Like I'm writing to a stranger instead of to the one person who knows me better than anyone. And I don't like this. All it does it make me remember that she's so far away, doing new things, meeting new people, while I'm still here, the same old Meg stuck in an all-new life. One without her. It hurts. But I don't have a choice. I have to keep writing. For Linus.

Once I have written it all out—four paragraphs, and I have already left out some of the less important details—there is nothing to do but focus on my homework until she finds the time to write back to me. If she even wants to write back to me. I don't know that she does. She called and texted a lot, the first few weeks. And then, when I never responded, she stopped.

But I do have enough to do to keep me busy for the rest of the day, at least until Mom gets home later tonight. So I don't have to dwell on this; I can simply dive right into my homework instead.

I gather all of my courage and press SEND.

Chapter 34

Linus

OVER THE COURSE OF A week, I keep tutoring Danny, I keep participating in drama club and debate and astronomy, and really, everything is pretty much business as usual except for the fact that something is definitely going on with my best friend and I cannot figure out what it is.

She's distracted one minute and attentive the next. She still hasn't apologized for ditching me after rehearsal right after she promised she wouldn't abandon me again, and I don't quite know how to bring it up without sounding too whiny. Plus, she let me believe that it was Danny's idea to approach me about tutoring, while really she was the one who told him he should do it. I mean, it's not like she outright lied to me, but she didn't tell me the whole truth, either. And that's just not like her at all. Also, it makes me feel stupid for thinking Danny might have asked me because he wanted to. Because maybe he liked me. Clearly, it was Meg's doing all along.

During drama club, she keeps to herself most of the time and then throws herself right into the middle of the action. It's almost like she's avoiding me. I don't really mind her leaving me on my own in there; Danny is very nice and always willing to partner up with me and even gently encourages me after rehearsal, when Meg keeps bringing up the topic of auditioning for parts for the Sherlock Holmes play.

"I just think it could be fun," she says, shrugging.

"I'm not an actor," I point out once again. "I wouldn't get a part anyway."

"Do you want a part?" Danny asks. "Because if you do, it can't hurt to try, right?"

For a moment, I'm not sure if I like him taking Meg's side in this, but he's not pushing me to do anything. He's just being helpful. So I smile and think about it and the thing is, I don't even know if I want a part or not anymore. It really might be fun. Trying new things is good, right?

But no, really, I can't figure out why Meg is acting the way she's acting most of the time. She keeps up her weird habit of disappearing during lunch period. She's done that every day this week. At least Danny always hangs around to keep me company, which is nice. I'm not a big fan of eating on my own.

I mean, maybe she just wants to give me some space with Danny. But I worry about her. I can just see her sitting alone in some secluded corner of the school yard, eating her lunch by herself, face sadly buried in some old sci-fi novel. Like she did that one time last year when she was fighting with Sophia. I don't like that thought.

Things have started feeling so tenuous between us that I'm almost a bit nervous to bring up our plans after drama club.

"So, *Star Trek* marathon at my place today?" I ask as we're packing up our things for the day. "After I'm done tutoring?"

She looks up, a little startled, and I can practically hear her thinking. "Uh," she says. "I'm—sorry. I have—I can't today, I have . . . Grandma."

I blink at her. "You have what now?"

She shrugs and doesn't meet my eyes. "Yeah, my grandmother is coming over today. Spontaneous visit. Sorry. But I really cannot just skip out on her; I never get to see her. . . .'"

I shake my head and I'm honestly so confused. Meg's grandmother is eighty-six years old and in a wheelchair and lives five hours away by car. How can she be making a spontaneous one-day trip to visit her grand-daughter? "Okay," I say, because I have no idea how else to react to such an obvious excuse. No, it's more than that. It's such an obvious lie.

"I'm sorry," Meg says again. "Rain check?"

"Sure."

"Awesome. Thanks, Linus!"

I watch her walk away and I just wish I knew what this was all about. I get it if she wants to be alone. What I don't get is why she can't tell me that instead of making something up. She knows that I, of all people, would understand. And yet she prefers to lie to me.

She keeps making up excuses and avoids any real conversation, when I know there are things on her mind. She never even told me that she was the one to tell Danny about me. That still stings.

She also keeps bailing on me when she has promised to drive me home after school. And I don't exactly mind that, either, because she doesn't have to drop me off. It's nice of her when she does, but really, it's up to me to find a way to get home. I just don't fully understand why she keeps telling me that she'll do it and then she ditches me, but I'm worried that she thinks she might be doing me a favor, stranding me with Danny.

I'm not sure if this can all still be attributed to Sophia and the breakup. All I know is that I don't know how to help. I'm supposed to be her best friend. But all I feel is powerless. It's like she doesn't even want my help, and that hurts a bit. Best friends are supposed to be there for each other when something bad happens, and yet she acts as if everything's completely fine in her life. I want her to feel like she can trust me, like I can handle being there for her. But maybe I was wrong about how close our friendship is? I get why she stopped answering my texts and dropped off the face of the earth at the end of the summer, right after Sophia dumped her. But I feel like I'm still cut out of her life even now and I'm not sure why that is.

Of course, I don't want to upset her even more by telling her that she is sometimes kind of annoying me a little with the way she keeps disappearing on me and giving me meaningful looks when she sees me talking to Danny. But I know that eventually I am going to have to bring it up.

Her behavior is harmless now but I don't know what's next and I don't know why she keeps doing this. Whatever her reasons, her actions seem unhealthy. But what am I supposed to do? I can't help her if she won't let me.

For now I let her go and instead follow Danny out to the parking lot so we can go get some tutoring done.

"You're quiet," Danny says, smiling at me once we're seated at the coffee shop table where we are going to be working on his math skills today.

"I'm sorry," I say. "I'm worried about Meg."

He frowns. "She does seem distracted. But I don't know her that well."

"Yeah." I sigh. "I'm afraid the Meg you did get to know so far this semester isn't really the Meg she usually is. She seems—I don't know. Sad?"

"You know her better," he says. "But if you're that worried, do you think we should do something to cheer her up? Like, do you think there is anything that we can do for her to make her feel better?"

I think about it. "Maybe," I say. "I don't know. I did already try to cheer her up, but I don't think I've been very successful yet. It could be that she still just misses Sophia."

"That's always a possibility," he confirms. "They were together a long time, right?"

I sigh. "Yeah. I've been talking to Sophia a bit, and she seems really sad, too. She used to write to me pretty frequently, actually."

"Why did they break up?" Danny asks.

"Oh, it was just because Sophia was leaving for college," I say. "Or at least that's the way Sophia tells it. Meg still won't talk about it, so I don't know her side of the story. Sophia seemed to really regret breaking up with Meg at first. She wrote to me all the time. But lately she's gone quiet."

"Could she maybe be dating someone new and she doesn't want Meg to find out?" he suggests.

I do my best to imagine that scenario, but somehow, I just can't. I don't really think that there is a way that Sophia could be with anyone else. But maybe that's just because my brain rejects the idea after having seen them together. I can still only see them as a unit in my head. Maybe also because Meg has shown no sign at all of being ready or even wanting to move on.

"I don't think so," I say. "A while ago Sophia said she was single. I don't think that has changed." I hesitate before admitting: "I really thought they were going to be together forever. Meg used to talk about what their wedding would be like. And now—this."

Danny nods. "Well, they were young to be talking about their wedding. Not that I think there's anything wrong with it. When you're sure, you're sure. But maybe Sophia got freaked out? I mean, obviously I don't know her, so I may be wrong. But maybe she just panicked."

I think about it, but what it comes down to is that all of this is still nothing more than guessing. I shrug. "I really just don't know."

"Well." He scratches his head. "Maybe they both just need time to get over it. Maybe Meg just needs to find something to take her mind off things. I'm sure you're helping her by just being around and stuff."

"I really want to help her," I say. "Just not like—trying to set her up with someone new or anything like that. I don't think she's ready for that yet."

"I wasn't even thinking about anything like that," he assures me. "Just—if there's anything I can do to help, let me know? We can round up the rest of the drama people and all do something together. Maybe that would be a good distraction."

"That is really nice of you," I tell him.

He beams at me. "I mean, we're all friends, right? Friends have one another's backs."

I lower my eyes and bite my lip and whenever he says things like this I can almost imagine that Meg is right and there actually is something between us. But I don't want to get my hopes up in case I'm mistaken.

"At least we have an astronomy club field trip coming up," I say. "That will hopefully cheer her up a little."

Danny tilts his head at me. "Field trip? That sounds important. And kind of cool. What do you do?"

"Stargazing." I laugh. "Literally. We just sit and watch the night sky. That's all; that's the entire trip."

"I always assumed astronomy club would hang out at observatories, filling out star charts or whatever," Danny says, grinning.

"Oh, we do that, too," I assure him. "We're visiting an observatory later this semester. This time it's just all of us out on the field behind the old cement plant. Ms. Heller, our faculty adviser, is bringing a telescope. We all take turns looking through it."

"That actually sounds really cool," he says.

I hesitate, but there's no harm in suggesting this. It's just a field trip. "You can come along, if you want," I tell him. "There's only five of us so far. And it's really fun. It's this Friday, sunset until nine p.m."

He seems to think about it. "Are you sure that's okay? I'm not even part of the club. . . ."

"So?" I shake my head. "It's just for fun. And it's not even a weekly club thing. We just go on excursions together. We literally just sit around on a field. But the telescope is really cool. Ms. Heller usually doesn't mind people tagging along if they're interested in what we do."

"I've never looked through a telescope before," Danny says. "I've always wanted to."

"Yeah. Everyone should do that at least once in their lives."

"If you're sure it's okay, I'd love to come along." Danny smiles at me. "I should probably ask this teacher of yours first, though."

"I'll see her tomorrow anyway," I say. "She's my physics teacher. Do you want me to talk to her?"

"That would be amazing." He looks really excited about this. "Is there anything I need to bring?"

"Flashlight and a warm jacket." I am really excited about this, too, if I'm being honest. "Meg has a picnic blanket to sit on. I usually bring a thermos with some cocoa, but mostly because that's what they do in the movies."

"Of course."

He smiles so widely and I lower my eyes and blush and prepare to go back to explaining calculus to him. Because as much as I might want to believe that this is a date, calculus is what we're really here for.

Chapter 35

Meg

I AM DISTRACTED AND CAN'T quite focus, my eyes wandering back to my laptop screen with the e-mail in-box open in the browser every few minutes. There is still no reply from Sophia. It's been a week now and I don't even know if this is still her current e-mail address and how often she checks it. Maybe she exclusively uses her university e-mail now. Who knows?

I should probably let it go, but my brain keeps coming up with all sorts of reasons for why she's not writing back to me. I'm a little angry with myself for not being able to concentrate on something as important as homework, but there's not much I can do about it.

Well, I guess I could close my laptop and make a conscious decision to not check my e-mail again until I have at least completed my mini-essay on nineteenth-century urbanization. But somehow, I don't really have that level of self-discipline today.

I'm a little nervous and jittery and maybe I should have gone without the coffee this afternoon. On the other hand, no, the coffee is necessary. I always have a coffee when I get home. I need it. So I'm weirdly wired and restless; that was to be expected, wasn't it? I haven't talked to Sophia in so long and it's making me nervous, waiting for a reply from her.

If she did get my e-mail, I'm almost sure she's going to write back. I did get messages from her the first few weeks of school, after all. I just never responded to any of them. She did text, she did even try to call a few times. But I ignored her because I didn't want to hear any of it.

What if it's too late now?

This is insane. It's not even like I want to get back together. I just asked her advice about a friend. A mutual friend. I know she cares about Linus.

I kind of want to talk to someone, but Linus is not an option for this and I'm not sure I want to tell Mom. Because I'd have to tell her about stranding Linus at school after drama club, too, and I don't know if she would approve. Technically, it wasn't very nice of me to bail on Linus so that Danny had to take him home, and I do know that. I just think that in this case, it was an okay thing to do. I didn't really abandon him, after all. I just made it so that he had to get a lift home from the boy who offered to give him a lift home, who obviously wants to spend time with him, if those looks they share are any indication.

I'm through with history and have just moved on to English when my e-mail in-box shows one unread e-mail and I almost knock over my mostly empty coffee mug in my haste to get at the mouse.

It's from Sophia, she has replied! Finally!

Quickly, I open the e-mail, then just sit there for a second with my eyes squeezed shut, not sure what to do or whether I actually want to know what she has to say.

Forcing myself not to hold my breath, I make myself open my eyes.

Dear Meg, it says, and I read slowly, not skipping ahead. It's several paragraphs and I'm relieved to find that it's not personal in the way I had feared it would be. I should have given her more credit than that. Sophia would never use the opportunity to help out a mutual friend to pursue a personal agenda, like trying to convince me not to hate her.

I'm so sorry for the late reply! I didn't get this until now, I promise. I only use this e-mail for newsletters and stuff now; that's why I rarely check it anymore. I didn't mean to ignore you. If you want, you can from now on reach me at . . .

I slump back in my chair and let out a breath, relieved. She wasn't avoiding me, then. We can still have a conversation. That's good. I lean forward again, reading on.

This is very exciting news, she continues. *I am happy that you're enjoying drama club, and I absolutely think that both you and Linus could get a part if you auditioned. There's no guarantees, of course. But here's my advice:*

And what follows is a lot of advice about how to choose the part to audition for and what to avoid and just a lot of general stuff that does indeed sound very, very helpful for someone who doesn't actually know the first thing about acting.

She ends the e-mail with the words: *If there is anything else I can help you with, like, if you need someone to brainstorm ideas with, you know I am always here for you! I'll do anything to help Linus out, and Danny, too, he sounds really nice! I hope things work out for the two of them!*

I think about it. The truth is, as nervous as I had been ever since I wrote to her, and as weird as it feels to just casually talk to her like this—it also doesn't feel as weird as I feared it would. It's just e-mailing. I can almost pretend I'm talking to someone else. And I think I actually could use someone to help me with this.

Before I can talk myself out of it, I open a new e-mail, copy her new e-mail address into the address field, and start typing.

And this is why I contacted her; I know Linus and I know what I want to achieve, but Sophia knows people and knows how to make friends and what is necessary to create opportunities for conversation and bonding. This is exactly the part I knew I needed help with and I'm so glad she has agreed to provide just that.

I make sure to thank her for the suggestions, telling her if she has any ideas that would mean I could stop abandoning them for lunch, I'd be glad to hear them.

She offered to brainstorm and, honestly, I can use the help. Obviously what I've been doing so far with setting them up to have lunch together and making them carpool occasionally and encouraging them to run lines together for drama club is working in a way, but I'm not really any closer to getting Linus to audition for a part.

I promise to send her regular updates on drama club since I know she must miss all of her friends there, and then I go back to my homework.

I have a new e-mail from her when I get back to my desk after dinner, and I open it immediately. Hearing from her is exciting. I can't help it. It just feels like . . . a connection. And maybe this is a really bad idea, connecting with her again, because she's still so far away and still not my girlfriend again, but it makes me happy. I've missed her.

And it's not like I'm getting my hopes up or anything. Definitely not. We're just talking about Linus, not us. It still feels nice, being able to do that again. Maybe that's enough.

In her e-mail Sophia suggests trying to manipulate drama club to make them put on something romantic for a school play, and maybe getting the two of them to rehearse romantic lines together. But I'm not sure I know how to do that. Sophia might have been able to influence what play they put on when she was part of the group, but I'm pretty sure that I can't do that. I've been sitting with Alyssa for lunch sometimes, but that still doesn't mean I'm a real part of the group yet who can just make suggestions like this.

Also, even drama club, which is a pretty liberal group of people, wouldn't dare cast two guys as the romantic leads for fear of ugly repercussions. And we could maybe push Danny into playing the lead, and then I'm quite sure I could get Linus to help him learn his lines by reading the female parts for him. But then what? Also, that might backfire. He could choose to rehearse with the actual female lead instead. And that's not even considering the fact that I probably wouldn't be able to influence who gets what part anyway. Maybe Sophia could accomplish all of this, but she can't exactly abandon college and come back for that, which I do understand, of course. Even if it would be very helpful if she could. On the other hand, I'm glad I don't have to spend any actual time with her. E-mailing is more than enough for now. And then, if we can accomplish this together, we can see what comes next.

But that means that now we don't have a plan for what to do next, and something obviously does need to be done.

I write back to her and explain why her idea wouldn't work this way. It's a great idea. But it just . . . wouldn't work.

Maybe we should just focus on getting Linus to audition for something for now. We can worry about the rest once that is accomplished.

She must be online, probably doing homework, too, or something, because it's just a few minutes before she writes back.

You don't actually have to put on a play, she writes. *We can make this really easy. Just bring up the idea of gender-bending some romantic scenes just for fun, and I can guarantee you most people in that club will totally go for it! Suggest making up only same-sex couples and that you all have to take turns, and then Linus will have to do the scene with Danny, right? From what he tells me, he doesn't actually talk to anyone else in the club and he's not going to want to do something like that with a stranger.*

This is exactly the kind of elegant, smart solution Sophia always seems to have up her sleeve. I think about it, and I like the idea; I think it could actually really work—until I realize what she just told me.

From what he tells me . . .

I freeze, eyes fixed on that little sentence fragment, and suddenly I feel cold.

From what he tells her? When has Linus been telling her anything? Are they talking to each other? Behind my back? Have they been talking this whole time?

I swallow heavily and lean back in my chair and I don't know what to think. Because Linus has never said anything. This whole time, ever since I told him about Sophia dumping me, he hasn't said anything about talking to her.

And yes, I know they're friends, but he's my best friend and why has he never said anything? Why did he hide this from me? What have they been talking about? Have they been talking about me?

I open up a chat window instead of e-mailing back, and type: *You've been talking to Linus? How long has that been going on?*

I'm sorry, she answers. *I thought you knew.*

He never said anything, I tell her.

She writes back: *I've just been checking in occasionally. That's all. There's not really anything to tell. I haven't written to him in a while anyway.*

I bite my lip and take a deep breath, and then another one, and another one. There's really no point in me getting angry, I tell myself. They're friends, I knew that. They're allowed to be friends. This is nothing to be angry about. And it's not exactly as if I have been completely honest with him lately, either.

I still am angry. It feels . . . it feels not good. I don't like this. I don't like that he never told me about this. More than that, I think—I think I can reasonably assume that he went out of his way to hide it from me. Like all of those times we hung out and someone texted him and he said it was his mom or Danny. Was it Sophia some of those times? Would he lie about something like that?

And yet, I try to convince myself, even if he did, it doesn't change anything. It doesn't change what I'm trying to do here. I need to stay focused. I can't let my emotions get the better of me. Maybe he made a mistake. So what? It happens, even between friends. Even between best friends.

Whatever, I write.

Are you mad? she asks.

No, I lie. *It's okay.*

And then I simply close the chat window and sign off. I don't want to talk about it.

It will be okay. It will all be okay. It has to be. I just need to walk away from the computer and get another cup of coffee and it will all be okay. Eventually.

It has to be.

Chapter 36

Linus

WEDNESDAY MORNING I GET TO drive my dad's car because he has the day off, so I pick Meg up for once and drive the two of us to school. She's already waiting outside when I pull up in front of her house and comes running up to the car as soon as she sees me.

"Linus! Hey!"

"Good morning," I say, waiting until she's fastened her seat belt before I turn the car around to get us to school.

"Beautiful morning, isn't it?" she asks, and while I'm still nodding she's already reaching for the car stereo, turning up the volume. "I love this song," she shouts over the music, dancing a little in her seat.

I nod along to the beat and can't really answer because of the noise. This is a little weird. Meg is never exactly in a bad mood early in the morning, but she just seems—a little over-the-top today. Suspiciously cheerful.

We arrive in the school parking lot, where I can at least finally turn off the music, and Meg is out of the car before I've even turned off the engine.

She hurries around the car while I get out and manage to slam the door behind me as she is already threading her arm through mine and starting to pull me along with her, a spring in her step I haven't seen very often lately. I barely manage to beep the lock closed before she has pulled me out of range.

"Are you prepared for the stargazing field trip this Friday?" she asks, voice just a little too loud. "I can't really decide what jacket I should wear because the weather has been so weird lately; it's still so warm in the afternoon and then it already gets so cold when the sun goes down. . . . You're going, right? Because, you know, Friday night, you don't have other plans? We'll have to reschedule the *Star Trek* marathon again. . . ."

"Yeah, I'm going," I assure her, but she's already talking again.

So I keep quiet and just nod at the appropriate places. There's not much else that I can do.

After being so weird that morning Meg keeps avoiding me for most of the rest of Wednesday, but by Thursday she is almost back to normal, if still a little distracted. I just wish I knew how to help, but she still doesn't even want to talk.

Friday we'd usually go right to one of our houses after school to order pizza and watch TV, but this week there's the astronomy club field trip, so we can't do that, obviously. Instead Meg drops me off at home with the promise to pick me up again later so we can drive out to the field together after picking up Danny, who's coming with us.

I half expect Meg to back out of driving all of us and coming up with some excuse the way she's done for a while now; she seems really intent on leaving me alone with Danny a lot of the time. But she just smiles, says, "I'll see you later," and drives off.

I spend the rest of my afternoon getting a head start on some homework so I'll have more of the weekend for myself, and then have a quick dinner with my parents before Meg picks me back up. Together we leave for Danny's house.

Astronomy club is a small group, but it's always fun—and I'll never turn down an opportunity to look through a telescope. Even if it's just a small and not very good one. It's still a telescope.

Most of us have brought picnic blankets and within a few minutes we're all scattered across the field lying on our backs and staring up into the night sky while Meg helps Ms. Heller set up the telescope.

"This is really pretty," Danny says from the other side of the blanket, and I turn my head to look over at him where he's stretched out with his hands folded behind his head, looking up.

"We're lucky that it's such a clear night," I say. "You can really see everything."

"Yeah. There's Cassiopeia." He points up, traces a W-shaped line into the air with his index finger.

"You know constellations?"

He shrugs. "My grandpa's really into that. He taught me. Oh, look, Pegasus!"

I smile to myself and look where he's pointing. "You want to have a look at them through the telescope?"

He laughs quietly and turns his head at the same time I do, smiles at me. "In a minute. I'm comfortable. Don't want to get up yet."

"Yeah." I smile back, pat the blanket softly. "This is a nice picnic blanket. Nice and soft."

"And the ground's not too cold yet." His smile turns into a grin. "When I was little I used to sit out in the backyard with Grandpa for hours, even in the middle of winter. And he had these little folding chairs, you know, for camping and stuff? I used to fall over in mine when I leaned too far back to get a good look at the sky. But I really liked just sitting there."

"That sounds amazing."

"It was."

"Do you still do that?"

"Fall over?"

I blush and shake my head. "Watch the sky with your grandpa."

"Oh." Danny shrugs a little. "Not really, no. He's—really old now. He doesn't go out much anymore, not since Grandma died anyway."

"I'm sorry."

"It's okay." He rolls his head to look back up at the stars. "It's just— this used to be our thing when I was growing up, you know? And some- times I just like looking up and thinking of that."

"Yeah," I say, and look up, too, very aware of him right there next to me, the warmth he gives off in the cool night air. "I get it."

"Meg's taking a while with that telescope," Danny comments.

I nod. "As soon as we feel like getting up, we should go get our turn."

"In a little while," he answers.

And I'm in no hurry. This is nice. Comfortable, just like he said. I'm perfectly content just lying out here on the ground for a few minutes.

Chapter 37

Meg

AUDITIONS FOR THE SCHOOL PLAY are this week and I haven't convinced Linus yet to try it. I don't know if I actually can. But I have thought about Sophia's idea of suggesting that exercise for rehearsal, and that at least is something I'm pretty sure I could actually accomplish.

I haven't seen much of Linus this weekend and I haven't e-mailed a lot with Sophia—I guess I just needed a while to wrap my head around the idea that those two were talking behind my back the whole time. I'm sort of ignoring that for now. I mean, I can see why Linus didn't tell me. He probably knew I wouldn't like it. And I obviously can't tell him who to talk to and who to avoid. I'm not that kind of friend. I don't want to be controlling. He's allowed to talk to Sophia if he wants. I don't like it, but I have bigger things to worry about for now. They're not going to make me give up on my project with all of this. I'm so close to getting Linus and Danny together, I can feel it.

My chance finally arrives that Tuesday in drama club. We're having a bit of a rehearsal before the first round of auditions tomorrow, and while Linus is still saying hi to Danny, I find Alyssa and some of the others and take a seat close to them.

"Hi," Katie greets me. "Ready for auditions?"

I nod. "Absolutely."

"Nervous?"

"A bit." I shrug. This is the moment. "But I've been reading up a bit on different techniques and I've come across something really interesting in the process. And I was wondering if we could maybe try it?"

"What is it?" Alyssa asks.

"You know when you take a scene, some scene from a play, and you swap everyone's genders? Could we try something like that?"

"Oh, we've done that a bunch of times," Stella speaks up, and Katie next to her nods emphatically. "Always a lot of fun. Sometimes we do scenes from movies or books, or combine two scenes to make things even more interesting."

"I was thinking we could pick romantic scenes and just swap one half," I say. "You know. Make them a little . . . gayer."

Alyssa's eyes light up and she's smiling at me really widely. "I like that."

"Yeah?"

"If everyone else is in, I'd really love to do it!"

"Awesome," I say, and can't keep the grin off my face. Mission accomplished. Well. Half of it. Now I need to wait and see if Linus and Danny agree to do a scene together.

It turns out that everyone really likes the idea and pretty quickly the room is splitting up into pairs, because apparently we're doing this right now and everyone has to take a turn. I can see Linus sitting there slightly wide-eyed and a little red in the face, but then I can also see Danny turning to him and talking really fast and Linus nodding vigorously and saying something back. I assume my plan is working.

I partner up with Alyssa because she asks and I feel relieved that I can do this with her—it might have been my idea and I might like all this drama club stuff, but I'm not really all that comfortable yet acting out romantic scenes with random people. This is one aspect I haven't considered in my planning. I'll have to pretend to be in love with someone who isn't Sophia.

But Alyssa is nice. I can do this. And it's for the greater good. It's for Linus and Danny, who are still talking, probably trying to decide on a scene, one that they both know.

There isn't a whole lot of romance in our Sherlock play that we're putting on this December, so everyone's choosing their own scene for this.

Alyssa and I, after much thinking, go for the ending of *Shrek*, the wedding scene, which we look up on my phone and watch the scene several times over. Everyone else is doing the same with their own scenes. We get Malik to play our Lord Farquaad for us because it's his favorite movie and he knows most of the dialogue by heart anyway.

Danny and Linus have decided to act out the ending of *When Harry Met Sally*, combined with some *Pride and Prejudice*, as I understand it. Linus will make a very interesting Sally or Elizabeth, I'm sure. Right now he's quiet, watching the others perform, and I know that after this I won't get him to audition for a part right away. But maybe if all of this has time to settle a bit until tomorrow, he'll feel ready by then.

For now, I can file this away as a success and enjoy the rest of my afternoon.

Chapter 38

Linus

I WAS ABSOLUTELY NOT PREPARED for having to actually act in front of everyone today. Just . . . absolutely not. I have mostly avoided acting in drama club so far. But this time there is no backing out of it: All of us are doing this, and I am a part of this club. There is no point to me being here if I don't participate, I tell myself. Repeatedly. I also tell myself repeatedly that no one will expect me to be perfect. It doesn't do a lot to calm my nerves.

"You okay?" Danny whispers in my ear, and I realize that my leg is bouncing and I'm biting my nails. Which is something I never do.

"Fine, thanks," I tell him, lowering my hands and pressing them down over my bouncy leg to still the motion. No need to draw attention to myself before we've even started, right?

I'm so eternally grateful that he asked me to act out the scene with him because I would never have been able to make myself ask someone. I'm even more eternally grateful that he suggested a combination of two scenes that basically gives me an excuse to just stand there while he talks at me. I do have some lines, but he has way more. I'm glad we're combining the scenes, because that way if I forget some of the original lines or don't react like in the movies, it's less noticeable. I'm just really no Meg Ryan. I'm also no Keira Knightley and no Jennifer Ehle and oh no, why am I doing this, what was I thinking? I cannot measure up to any of them. I just had to take a mix of parts previously played by some of the most gorgeous people to ever walk the face of the planet. *Of course*. And I'm pretty sure I won't be able to cry. Well, maybe I will start crying out of sheer nervousness. But that's not really the sort of emotion the scene calls for, is it?

We've watched each scene several times on my phone and I've made notes of my important lines even if Danny assures me I won't have to get the wording exactly right.

"It's just an exercise," he says. "It's about the emotion."

Which actually doesn't help me at all because learning whatever scene we come up with by heart I could have done in a matter of minutes, but getting the emotion right in front of a room full of people . . . Well. My palms are sweaty for a reason. "Cool," I say, trying to sound confident.

"Just remember," he tells me, smiling encouragingly, "let me do all the pushing. All you need to do is react to me. Okay? You're the smart one, the strong one, and I'm the one who's just figuring out what he's feeling. So I'll babble on pretending to be eloquent, and you can just let me do all the work, all right? I'm telling you that I want to be with you. You're pretty sure you like me back, but I've been kind of a tool, so you're not gonna make it that easy for me. You want to make sure that I'm done being an idiot first. Sound good?"

"Sounds awesome," I assure him, and my voice only wavers a little. I'll take that as a victory.

It's our turn sooner than I would have liked and I stumble after Danny into the center of the room. Everyone's sitting around us in a semicircle, staring expectantly.

"Like the Globe Theatre," I say, realizing we're pretty much surrounded by our audience.

Danny grins at me. "What?"

"Uh, you know." I shrug, blushing as I wave a hand around the room. "The stage. At the Globe. Shakespeare's theater. The stage was surrounded by the audience on three sides. That was actually quite common for the time."

Danny shakes his head and laughs, crinkling his nose at me. "Of course you know that."

I make myself laugh, too, trying my best to forget there are other people in the room with us. Which . . . sort of doesn't work at all. I'm still nervous.

"Ready?" Danny asks.

"No," I admit. "But let's do it anyway."

"You'll be fine," he assures me, taking my hand and squeezing it before turning toward Stella and Alyssa, who seem to be in charge today. "Uh, hi, okay. We're doing this thing inspired by *When Harry Met Sally*? And *Pride and Prejudice*, and . . . you know, you get the picture. The whole big emotional confession. I'm Harry. He's Sally. Or . . . I'm Mr. Darcy and he's Miss Bennet. Basically, I've been behaving like a bit of a jerk, because I'm emotionally confused, and now I have to try to win him back. Totally out of the blue, like your typical romantic hero." I can hear the grin in his voice. His shoulder brushes mine, and he's still holding my hand, which just makes me very, very aware of how gross and clammy my palm is. Not that I'm complaining about the hand-holding. Danny's hand is warm and smooth and I could absolutely get used to this feeling if I ever got the chance.

"Cool," Stella says, nodding encouragingly. "Awesome choice! Very cool combination. Let's see it, then."

Danny turns to me, letting go of my hand at last. My fingers curl into a fist almost automatically, feeling even colder now that his hand's gone. "Ready?" he asks.

I exhale slowly, nod once. "Ready."

He takes another step back and I can see his face changing, from his nice smile to something a little stressed, a little desperate, a little determined. I'm pretty sure I'm still mostly looking as if I just woke up in a strange room filled with feral dogs. I don't know if I can do this.

"I've been thinking," Danny says, already in character, a bit breathless, as if he's just been running, "and I'm pretty sure I need to tell you something. You see, the thing is: I love you. Is that okay?"

Oh. So obviously we're starting, then. Okay. I mean, I knew we were, but this still feels sudden and I can't figure out how to get myself to feel like I'm Sally. Elizabeth. One of them. Or both. Acting is hard. I open and close my mouth, trying very hard to remember my line. Any line. I know we're acting. I know this is a part he's playing. But I can't help it: Hearing those words, even if they're not real, is doing something to me. And I don't know how anyone can expect me to suddenly learn how to improvise when the boy I'm in love with is standing across from me playing not one fantastically romantic part but *several at once*.

"Um," I say, face burning. "What?"

"I love you," he repeats, like he's stating a fact. "I think I have for some time."

"I—uh." I shake my head, doing my best to clear my thoughts. The words are gone, but after a bit of head-shaking I remember the gist of it. "Okay. And what do you want me to say to that? I—don't—I mean . . . That's—You can't just . . . say stuff like that." I know this is totally lame, but it's the best I can do. Luckily, Danny has it under control.

He shrugs. "I'm sorry. I know it's kind of a lot. But it's the truth, you know? And I needed to tell you. This is the kind of thing I figured you should know. About me. Since we're best friends and all."

I wave my hands, which is less of an acting choice and more a way to stall for time while I figure out my next words. "Yeah, but . . . I have no idea what I'm supposed to do now," I say, which is true for me as well as for my character. Maybe I can make this work, I think. Sally was pretty much thrown off guard by Harry, too, wasn't she? And Lizzie Bennet didn't even accept Mr. Darcy's love just like that. So maybe my stuttering can yet sound like cool aloofness. I mean, probably not, probably it just sounds like stuttering. But at least I'm trying, right? I clear my throat because my voice is all scratchy and quiet and that just won't do. "Maybe it's best if I just . . . leave," I say in a louder voice, sounding angrier than I meant to. I take a step back, not quite sure what direction I'm supposed to pretend to walk off in since there are people on three sides and a solid wall on the fourth.

But Danny grabs my sleeve before I can take more than two shaky steps anyway. "Wait!" he calls out. "You can't just . . . I mean, please don't just go. Don't you have anything at all to say to me? If you need space or time or whatever, I get that, but please don't tell me that my words meant nothing at all to you!"

And oh my god, I need to react to that. *What would Elizabeth Bennet do? What would Sally do?* I have absolutely no clue. Linus Hanson's impulse is to either faint or run screaming from the room, but that simply won't do. I blink at him. "It's—not that simple?" I try, and okay, I'm fairly certain that I sound absolutely nothing like Sally or Elizabeth. Sally and Lizzie were strong and confident characters. I feel like the perfect opposite of that. Also, there was way more text in their scenes. I take a breath and do my best to reassemble either scene as well as I can. "I mean—you can't just—show up here and expect that to fix everything. You haven't really been behaving like a best friend lately. You can't just tell me you have feelings and expect that to make everything okay. It doesn't work that way." Well. That was completely over the top, I'm sure of it, but Danny breaks character for just a fraction of a second to nod and flash a smile at me before his face is back to serious and desperate. So apparently it doesn't have to be perfect.

"Then what do you want me to do?" Danny asks. "I'll do anything."

"I don't want anything from you." This line I'm pretty sure is the lamest cliché ever, but at least it sounds fairly dramatic. Maybe I am slowly getting the hang of this after all! "This is just all a bit sudden."

"It's not so sudden for me," Danny says. "I've realized some things lately."

I swallow. "What kinds of things?"

Danny takes a step closer, his fingers brushing my sleeve again for just a second. "Things like. . . . The fact that I've never met anyone like you and that you're the first person I want to talk to every day. Things like the fact that I love the way you stare at me when I'm being an idiot." And, okay, that makes me realize that I am kind of staring at him, so I make myself blink, can't quite keep in the embarrassed grin. And Danny just keeps on improvising. "I love that after we've spent a day together, my clothes smell like coffee."

"You work in a coffee shop," I can't stop myself from pointing out, which earns me a few laughs around the room. I bite my lip.

"Yeah, well." Danny lifts his shoulders. "It's not just all that, though. I just really like you, you know? You're my best friend. And you're also kind of more than that. You're completely awesome and you're so kind and funny and just the best person I know. I can't stop thinking about you. Like, ever. And I know I've been a jerk. I'm sorry. I really am. I didn't know what to do with all these feelings, with all these thoughts I'm having, which is not an excuse, I know. But the thing is, I've realized that I don't *want* to stop thinking about you. Because when I think about you I'm—happy. And I thought . . . I just had to let you know. If it doesn't change anything between us, then that's the way it is, but I *had* to let you know. Because this isn't just going to go away for me. This is the real thing. And you deserve to know. And you don't have to say anything back, and I'll stop behaving like an entitled idiot now and leave you alone, but I needed to tell you. That you're the coolest, nicest, most amazing person I have ever met in my life and that I'm sort of head over heels in love with you."

I sigh, close my eyes, and shake my head to gather my thoughts. I need a moment after listening to that speech. "Oh," I say finally. "That's—that's just . . . Um." I look at him, and my voice is sounding all scratchy again. "Are you sure?" I wince.

"Of course I'm sure," he tells me. "I ran all the way here just to tell you this, didn't I?"

I have to grin, I can't help it, even though my heart is pounding. Acting is nerve-racking work. "You did."

He tilts his head at me, which has no right to look as adorable as it does. "Do you hate me now?"

I shake my head emphatically. "Of course I don't. I—well. Maybe a little. But it'll pass."

"So . . . where does that leave us?" he asks.

I heave a sigh that sounds actually really put-upon and dramatic, and for a moment I'm very proud of myself. "You're an idiot," I say. "But it's not like I didn't know that already."

"So we're okay?"

"Yeah," I say. "We're okay. We're very okay."

He laughs and he sounds relieved. I offer a small grin, which feels like an appropriate way to end the scene. We don't kiss. That would be taking it too far. But he does hug me and I just squeeze my eyes shut again for a moment, don't really know what to do with my own arms, and finally just settle for patting him awkwardly on the back.

He lets go of me with a small smile to the sound of our friends clapping all around us, and I'm surprised to discover that I'm still in one piece and no one's throwing rotten fruit at me. If that's a thing that actually happens to actors these days. Which it's probably not.

He's still smiling at me and I'm sort of smiling back and can't figure out how to look away when Stella's voice jostles me out of my semi-frozen state and back into reality.

"You guys!" she calls out to us, still clapping enthusiastically. "Good work! I think even Meg Ryan and Billy Crystal would have approved!"

I laugh along with Danny and catch Meg's eyes across the room. She's bouncing in her chair a little, giving me two thumbs-up, and okay, I am a little bit proud that I made it through this. It was just about one of the most mortifying things I've ever had to do in my entire life. But you know what? It was fun. Sort of. At least . . . I can definitely see the appeal of doing this more often. Or maybe that's just the leftover floaty feeling from having Danny say all those things to me, even if none of it was real. But I don't care. I'm going to count this as a success. I did something new, and it was pretty awesome.

I am happy to be allowed to sit back down now, but it's weird—it's giving me a real sense of accomplishment, having been able to pull this off. I'm starting to think that maybe a tiny little role in the play wouldn't be the worst thing in the world, and I know that Meg really wants me to audition with her. It seems important to her. And if she keeps insisting, I guess I could at least try it.

No one's laughing at me, so they're probably not going to laugh at my audition. And also, I'm not exactly sure how this club works yet, but I'm a little bit afraid that it might be rude to simply show up for all the rehearsals and then refuse to participate in the actual play. I don't want to be rude.

The rest of rehearsal goes by pretty quickly. Everyone else is so great at this. It's fun, watching them. Meg does a really good job, too, and I can tell she's having a lot of fun with it. She also looks really cute together with Alyssa. They seem to work well together. It's good to see her happy. So I make up my mind to say yes to auditioning together if she asks again. Maybe she's right. Maybe we do need to take more risks and try new things. Because this is our last year of high school and it seems like the perfect time to live a little before things get serious out in the real world.

"That was fun today, wasn't it?" Meg asks, digging through her bag for the car keys as we're walking out to the parking lot that afternoon.

"It was," I confirm. "I really liked you as Shrek."

"You made a great Sally." She grins at me. "It looked like you were kind of enjoying it."

I shrug. She's not completely wrong. Even if it was embarrassing. "I think I'm slowly getting the hang of this."

"So, does that mean we'll audition for parts tomorrow?" she asks, voice hopeful.

I sigh and roll my eyes at her. "Fine. Yes. We'll audition."

"Oh, thank you!" She bounces a little on her feet before throwing her arms around me in a hug. "You won't regret it, I promise!"

"I just hope you're right," I say, hugging back quickly before we resume walking. "So, how does this work?"

She finally pulls her keys from the bag, waves them triumphantly. "Ha! Found them. Um. I don't know. Alyssa gave me a bit of advice earlier. And I was hoping you could ask Danny for help?"

"We're not meeting up today, actually."

"Oh. Uh. Okay. In that case—want to come over so we can rehearse something?"

"Sure." I like this plan. I like not having to prepare for this by myself. "We can do that."

Chapter 39

Meg

THE PLAY THAT THE DRAMA club is putting on is not based on an actual Arthur Conan Doyle Sherlock Holmes story, because apparently that would be unoriginal or something. Some of the more experienced drama club members have written their own story and also updated it into the twenty-first century. It's all a bit insane but I love it.

Linus and I audition together with a scene from the Benedict Cumberbatch BBC version because it's our favorite, and everyone laughs and seems to enjoy it. We had a lot of fun rehearsing it the night before, and I really like performing in front of other people for our audition. Even Linus seems to have fun playing Inspector Lestrade while I play Sherlock Holmes. I'm excited for the play. Of course I don't want to be Sherlock, though. I don't want a lead. But something small with a few good lines would be wonderful.

For a moment, I imagine Sophia in the audience. I don't know if she's going to come to the performance, but she'll most likely be home for the holidays, so there's a very good chance that she'll be there to see her old friends. I think I'd like her to be there, and I'd like to impress her with my acting abilities, even if I'm new to all this. It would give us something else to talk about.

"That was really good," Danny tells us once we're done. He's already waiting backstage in the auditorium; he's going to audition, too, today. For a bigger part, probably, since he's a lot more experienced than Linus and I are.

"Thanks," I say. Linus just blushes.

"Are you sticking around later until they put up the cast list?" Danny wants to know.

I exchange a look with Linus. I had no idea they were going to put the list up today, but I really want to be here for it, actually.

Linus shrugs, nods. "Sure."

"Absolutely," I agree.

"Cool, I'll see you then." Danny turns for the stage when they call his name, looking incredibly calm for someone who's about to audition for a play. I guess he's done this more often than we have.

"Good luck," Linus says quietly, but Danny hears him anyway and offers a grateful smile.

"Break a leg," I throw in. I remember this from the time I accompanied Sophia to these things.

In the usual rehearsal room we find almost the entire club assembled, waiting for the list to go up. We sit with them and talk, and I really do like these people. I can't believe I didn't try this earlier.

"I'm just saying, it would have been a great musical," Stella says loudly, waving her plastic cup at Malik enthusiastically enough to spray

Katie and Linus with large drops of iced tea. "You can't deny that it would have been a great musical!"

"Yeah, okay, but . . ." Malik shakes his head at her, rolling his eyes. "Everything makes a good musical in your opinion."

"Well, everything does," Stella insists.

Katie frowns at her. "A Sherlock Holmes musical? For real?"

"Why not?" Stella huffs out a breath. "We could have done it."

"Not all of us can sing, though," Katie reminds her.

Stella shrugs. "I think everyone can learn to sing with the right training."

"I couldn't," I jump in, and they all look at me. "I mean, I'm good enough for the shower, but I wouldn't want to put any of you through that."

"I can confirm that," Linus says, grinning a little crookedly. "I've heard her sing. I mean, not that I'm any better."

I shake my head at him. "You're actually not that bad, you know?"

Malik tilts his head at us. "I feel like the only way to settle this is dragging you along to karaoke one of these days."

Linus looks like he's considering it, but I don't know if I'm ready. I don't think I am. Karaoke was Sophia's and my thing. I almost forgot it was a drama club thing, too.

It's about an hour after our audition when Mr. Walsh walks in with a piece of paper and pins it to the bulletin board next to the door. I surge forward with the rest of our new friends to get a look at it.

I see Linus's name almost immediately—he's Mrs. Hudson, the landlady! Well, Mr. Hudson, the landlord, in this case. He's also really very, very red in the face and I know he's probably freaking out internally because he didn't even want a speaking part. But I know he can do this.

I keep scanning the list, then scan it again, and then a third time, my stomach sinking as realization slowly sets in.

My name isn't on it. I didn't get a part.

Joining drama club and auditioning for the play was my idea, and I didn't even get cast.

Chapter 40

Linus

I DON'T KNOW WHAT TO say. I have no idea what happened. But people are patting me on the back and congratulating me and Meg is kind of staring at that list hanging up there on the bulletin board and . . . that's my name right there on that list. Next to an actual speaking part.

I can't believe this.

I mean, sure, I knew that in theory this could happen. If you audition for a part in a play, then there is a slight chance that you might actually get one. But the thing is, I told them I was looking to maybe be an extra or something. Just something in the background. Not a speaking part. Not Sherlock's landlord.

This is insane. I'm not really sure how I feel about this. But . . . it is exciting, I have to admit that much. And that they thought I was good enough, that they trust me to do this, and do it well . . . I can't lie, that makes me feel really, really good.

"Linus!" Danny calls over the crowd of people, and I look up at him.

He gives me two thumbs-up and grins excitedly and I flicker a smile back at him.

This just needs to sink in a little before I can actually believe it.

I scan the list again. Danny is playing John Watson. It seems fitting. He's going to be so great.

Meg's name isn't on the list.

I look it over again, and again, but no, she's not on there. I swallow, turn my head to look for her. She really wanted a part. I know that, even though she pretended it was no big deal when we were practicing last night. But she was good! I'm not an expert at these things, but I think she was really good. And I know she was really excited about it.

She deserves some good news. Maybe we can switch. She can have my part. It's not that important to me, and it seems really important to her. I have no idea why I got it in the first place. But it doesn't seem very fair to me.

Meg's standing a little way off, arms wrapped around herself, and she's smiling but I can see the sadness behind it.

"Hey," I say, walking over to her.

"Congrats," she says. "I told you you could do it."

I shrug. "I'm not sure I want it, though. You know I didn't aim for this."

"Oh, shut up. You're gonna be great. This is a good thing."

"Yeah, but—I don't know, do you want to . . . We could switch? If you want?"

She laughs. "That's very sweet of you but they obviously didn't think I could do it. I don't think you can just exchange your part for another one if you don't like their decision."

"Meg—"

"Besides, you're really going to be great in it. You have to do it."

"I don't know if that's such a good idea."

Suddenly, she looks almost angry. "Of course it's a good idea."

"But you want it more than I do. You should have it, I—"

"I'm fine, Linus," she interrupts. "It's all good. Seriously. It's not a big deal. Don't worry about me."

"Of course I worry about you. I really wanted you to get it. I don't want to do this without you."

"That's not up to me anymore, though."

"Maybe we can—"

"Linus," she says, finally uncrossing her arms to put a hand on my shoulder. "It's okay. And you don't have to do this by yourself. You have Danny, right? I'm sure that he's going to be happy to help you out. And if he's ever too busy, you can come over to my house to rehearse your lines or whatever. It's okay. Really."

I give her a quick hug and don't really know how I feel about all of this. Mostly I just feel really bad that I got something that she wanted. I already feel so guilty for spending so much time with Danny instead of being there for her like a good friend. I know she's still going through a lot and maybe I haven't been the most supportive friend over the past few weeks.

"Let's go home?" I suggest. "You could come over and we can watch the rest of the extras on the *Firefly* box set. I have chocolate chip cookies."

She laughs and squeezes me a little before letting go. "Thanks. But I should get started on my homework. And I know all you really want to do right now is go and congratulate Danny."

"No, that can wait," I insist. "Really, we can just go."

"Don't be silly," Meg says, and smiles at me. Her smile doesn't look honest. "I'm okay, I promise. I just want some alone time with my homework."

I don't want to leave her alone. What I want to do is go home with her and make coffee and watch our *Firefly* DVD extras, or whatever movie she is rewatching this week: *The Mummy*, or *The Princess Bride*, or *Return of the Jedi*. But I know she gets this way sometimes, and she needs to be alone to process things. I don't understand it, but I know I have to respect it. Maybe if I want to help her, I have to give her some space right now.

"Okay," I say. "Promise you'll text, though, if you change your mind about wanting company."

Her smile looks a little more genuine when she rolls her eyes at me. "I promise."

I smile back, and then I go to find Danny.

Chapter 41

Meg

I KEEP IN THE BACKGROUND a bit while Linus goes over to join the small group surrounding Danny. I smile when anyone makes eye contact with me and give out congratulations to all those who got cast. But other than that, I mostly keep to myself. I want to leave, and I'm going to slip out the first chance I get, but the moment doesn't seem right and as disappointed as I am, I don't want to seem rude.

I watch Stella, the five-foot-nothing green-haired firecracker who got the lead, high-fiving Katie and then hugging Alyssa. There's no use denying it; this kind of hurts. I wasn't that bad, was I?

Sure, I'm the new kid in the group, but so is Linus. And so is Danny, for that matter, and he got a lead. Sort of. Watson counts as a lead, right? But, okay, I guess he does have more experience than Linus or I do.

"Hey," Alyssa says, suddenly showing up next to me. I know she's on the casting committee. She's been in this club for years. But if she's on the committee, that means she probably didn't like me, either.

"Hey," I say, not sure how friendly I want to be right now.

"I'm sorry it didn't work out for you," she says. "There's just not that many roles, and we're a pretty big club, so—"

"No, I know," I say. "I get it. No big deal. I guess I wasn't that good."

"No, you were," she hurries to assure me. "You were really good. And—I just wanted to say, you should definitely audition again for the next play once we start rehearsals in January because you're pretty much guaranteed a part since you didn't get one this time around. It's just—"

"It's really okay," I interrupt, because I'm not sure I want to talk about this.

"We just liked your idea of gender-bending so much," she goes on to explain. "That's why we cast some of the roles the way we did. That's why Stella is playing Sherlock and Katie is Inspector Lestrade. If it hadn't been for that, we would have probably given you Linus's part. It was a tie between the two of you, but we had so many girls in male roles, we found we should cast one boy in a role that's traditionally played by a girl."

"But you thought he was good, right?" I ask, raising both eyebrows at her.

She nods. "He's gonna be great. Of course. And . . . we wanted to do something different. You know? We were going for the unexpected."

I sigh. "So I wasn't just way too bad?"

"Of course not." She shakes her head. "Meg, you were really, really good. And I hope you're still going to stick around without a part? Because there's so much behind the scenes. I'm actually not performing, either. And I could really use your help."

"With what?"

"They made me stage manager for the production," she says proudly. "I can't do that by myself. So, if you want—I could really use you on my team. Wow, that sounds so official, sorry." She laughs. "What I meant was: Would you like to help me behind the scenes? I could really use some help."

The more I think about it, the more I have to admit that it does sound really cool. It's not what I wanted, but I can't bail on the club and on Linus. At least they can't think I'm completely horrible if they'll still let me participate like this. And I guess I need to be involved somehow if I want to stick around without seeming weird.

So I swallow my pride and nod. "Okay," I agree.

It could be worse, I guess. I'm still sad, but at least it wasn't personal. Maybe being a simple stagehand could be fun, too.

I'm still wondering if I'm always going to be rejected for everything that I want. First my girlfriend dumps me and now this. But whatever, right? It really could be worse. That's not much of a consolation, but at least Project Danny is still in full swing and going better than ever because now I can really push them to run lines together. Maybe I should just focus on that for now.

Chapter 42

Linus

I DO HAVE TO ADMIT that I am a little bit nervous meeting Danny at the coffee shop on Saturday. At the same time I'm kind of grateful that we're not meeting at either one of our houses. We haven't met up just the two of us since we had to do that romantic scene in drama club together on Tuesday and after that, I'm afraid that meeting up in private might just feel a bit too intimate. Fortunately, he has two younger siblings, twins, who apparently make too much noise to get much studying done, and he hasn't really asked why I don't want to meet at my house.

The truth is, I love my parents, but if I ever brought a boy home even under completely innocent circumstances, I'd never hear the end of it. It's not that I'm afraid they'd embarrass me . . . well, yes, okay. I am a little worried that they might embarrass me.

So I arrive at the coffee shop almost exactly on time—Mom let me use her car today since she doesn't have anywhere to be anyway. Once again, Danny is already there before me.

I can see him through the coffee shop window, sitting at the table that we could probably be calling "our usual table" by now if there was a need for us to have things like a usual table at our favorite coffee shop. Even calling it "our" favorite coffee shop feels different to me today and while it's a good feeling to some extent, it also makes me feel a little uncomfortable because I'm still pretty sure that it's a completely one-sided feeling. Or at least I haven't had any concrete evidence disproving this hypothesis so far.

The thing is, he makes it really almost impossibly hard to not be feeling these things. I'd have a hard time not feeling them if it was just him sitting there looking so cute with his black spiky hair and that adorable face. But as if that isn't enough, I can see the two coffee cups in front of him, and no matter how many times I tell him that I can get my own coffee, he always gets here before me and buys me one. So, he gets his employee discount, but he should at least let me pay him back for some of those coffees. I know he works here to save up for a better car. He shouldn't be spending all of his money on coffees for me.

And then there's the fact that he's just so nice all of the time and he even didn't have a problem doing that romantic scene with me in front of people, and all of this is just too much for my poor little heart to handle.

Which is probably the reason I'm still just a little bit upset with Meg. She knows how I feel about him and she must know that I don't stand an actual chance with him, and I know she was the one who suggested the gender-bending exercise. I don't know why she keeps insisting on pointing out this one thing I know I can never have.

But even if I'm a little upset with her, not even that can spoil my mood today. Danny has been so nice about helping me, has even offered to run lines with me, and now we are meeting for coffee (and math) and all of that is still good even if it's not precisely what I wish it could be. But I'm content taking it for what it is. Maybe he's never going to be my boyfriend, but he can still be my friend, and that's a really nice thought.

I walk into the coffee shop and he smiles when he sees me and no, I really don't know how I could possibly be in a bad mood today.

"Linus," he says. "I got you a coffee!"

"You seriously don't have to keep doing that," I tell him, sliding into my seat and dropping my bag next to my chair.

"It's no big deal," he assures me. "So. You're an actor now!"

I laugh. "Hardly. But getting cast was certainly a nice surprise."

"You've earned it. And—I like that we can practice together now."

"Oh, I, uh." I laugh. "Yeah, um, same here. Definitely!"

"You wanna start next week? I was thinking we could just extend our tutoring sessions. Just get all the math out of the way and then go right to the fun stuff."

I nod emphatically. "Of course! We can do that! Absolutely!"

"Good. I'd really like that." He beams at me.

"But you know you don't have to, though, right?" I hurry to assure him, because I don't want him to think I expect his help in exchange for the tutoring or anything.

"I know," he says. "But it's going to be fun!"

"Just—I don't want to monopolize your time like that. I'm grateful for any help, though! And I'm sure you have a lot of helpful advice. I honestly don't know much about acting at all, but that means I should probably read up on it. I mean—do you know any good books on acting?"

He lowers his head, fingers playing with a napkin. "Linus—if, um. You'd tell me if you ever, you know. Wouldn't want to hang out or anything, right?"

"Uh." I pause, gaping at him, a little taken aback at this weird change of topic. "What?"

"I just—" He sighs, shrugs. "I'm a little worried that—that maybe you're getting a little sick of me always being around."

"What—no. No! What?"

"I mean, you're always pretty fast at pointing out that we're just studying together or that you don't really need me to drive you home or that you're only working with me in drama club because I give good acting advice or whatever. And, um. If I'm . . . annoying you, ever, could you—you can just tell me, you know? I won't be offended. I promise. I don't ever want to crowd you or anything, and I don't want to be that annoying sort of friend who constantly overstays his welcome."

I'm feeling a little panicky, a bit like I just sidestepped into an alternate dimension. "I—um. That's not—why did you—"

"I just really like hanging out with you, you know?" he cuts off my stuttering. "But I know we've been hanging out a lot and, I don't know, I never meant to—I get that you have other things in your life—"

"You like hanging out with me?" It's certainly not what I meant to say, but it's what comes out when I open my mouth again.

He grins, rolls his eyes at me. "Of course I do! We're friends, right?"

"We—are?"

"I—thought we were. I hoped we were. I mean—"

"But, but—"

"Oh god, I'm sorry. You only ever agreed to tutor me. I totally misinterpreted everything, didn't I?" he asks, horrified.

"No!" I am completely in over my head with this and I don't have the slightest idea what to do, but I absolutely cannot let him think that I don't want to be friends with him. "Of course we are friends. Of course we are! If you—if you want to?"

"Linus," he says. "Of course I want to. We have fun, right? You're smart, and you're funny. And—and—" He breaks off, blushing dark red and lowering his head. "I'd be honored to call you my friend."

I have never had a friend before who I am also in love with. But I guess high school is a good time for new experiences, isn't it? "If by smart you mean good at math and by funny you mean clumsy, then I guess you have a point," I joke.

He laughs. "So, to seal our new friendship, can I buy you a cookie? Or maybe a new cup of coffee before we get started on the tutoring?"

"No," I say firmly. "It's my turn to buy you a coffee."

"But you're already giving up your afternoon to teach me all about how numbers aren't actually evil!"

"Don't mention it," I say, and grin. "That's what friends are for, isn't it?"

His answering smile is all I need to fully restore my good mood from earlier.

Chapter 43

Meg

THE WEEKEND IS INCREDIBLY BORING. I am bored and lonely and Linus has even canceled our *Star Trek* rewatching plans because apparently Danny needs more tutoring and then they have to work on memorizing their lines for the play or whatever. The play that I am not a part of.

I have to study, too, so it's not like I don't have anything to do. But the thing is, I can't really focus on anything all Saturday, and Sunday isn't much better.

Mom has brought work home and doesn't have time to listen to my whining. And I don't really want to write to Sophia because . . . well, I'm mad at her. Again. All her advice about drama club and yet here I am, by myself, not included in all of their fun. I got what I wanted, I try to tell myself. I got Linus to hang out with Danny even more. But in the process I also apparently managed to end up completely alone and abandoned and friendless. Which is just perfect.

I sigh and roll my eyes at myself so hard I almost give myself a headache. I'm seriously starting to annoy even myself.

There's a slight chance that I have simply forgotten how to be by myself. It's a possibility. I have been in a steady relationship since I was fifteen, and we spent almost every waking moment together. And when we weren't together, I was hanging out with Linus. I don't think I have actually had to spend an entire weekend by myself in . . . two and a half years?

Can you forget how to be alone? That seems stupid, because you cannot actually keep yourself company, can you? So can you really have to learn to live with yourself? Isn't that just something that you do anyway?

But honestly, I have no wish at all to answer any of those questions. Because they don't matter. I'm just being dramatic and feeling down because I still hate being single and because my best friend has someone new to hang out with now. And Linus has always been there for me before. So I am simply very unused to this kind of situation.

It's just . . . maybe it's time to face reality? The reality is that I'm alone. Sophia and I can talk, but she's never coming back. And I can keep trying to set up Linus, but if it works he won't have time for me anymore and if it doesn't he might end up being mad at me for pushing him into this. It seems like either way I can only lose.

There's a knock on my door and I sit up quickly on my bed. "Yes?"

Mom sticks her head around the door frame. "Meggie?"

"What's up?" I don't even find it within myself to protest the stupid nickname I hate so much.

"I've decided that I can read the rest of that paper on Monday and wanted to know if you were maybe up for pizza and *The Matrix*?"

I frown at her. "You said you needed to read that as soon as possible because Professor Clarke coauthored it and he was your new boss and he expected all of you to—"

"Yeah, well," she interrupts me, mouth set in a grim line as she takes another step into my room, "Professor Clarke can take a long walk off a short pier, for all I care. I have already given up several hours of my precious weekend trying to read his pretentious and tedious and quite possibly terribly, terribly wrong excuse for a paper and I'd really like to watch TV with my daughter now."

"Are you sure?"

"About pizza and *The Matrix*? Do you even need to ask?"

I smile and just like that I'm already feeling better. Maybe I really just cannot be left on my own for too long. "I'll be right down," I promise.

"I'll order the pizza," she says. "Extra olives for you?"

"What kind of a question is that? Start ordering, woman!"

She rolls her eyes at me. "Jeez, your manners are impeccable. Were you raised by wolves?"

I throw my pillow at her and she quickly ducks back out the door, laughing all the way down the stairs.

I find Linus by his locker Monday morning and Danny is standing right there next to him, watching him in this way he does when Linus has his attention elsewhere. Despite my growing feeling of loneliness, I'm really glad that they're spending so much time together. And, come on. I am a little bit responsible for that, am I not? You can't deny that I helped.

"Hey," I greet him, walking up to him.

"Hi," he says, looking up at me.

"How was your weekend?"

He smiles a little shyly, exchanges a look with Danny, closes his locker door. "It was fine. Thank you. How was yours?"

I shrug, and think, *Lonely. Boring. Never to be repeated, if possible.* What I say is, "It was okay. Mom and I watched movies. There was pizza."

"Pizza is good."

"Yeah. I really like pizza."

Danny stays quiet throughout the entire exchange, and sometimes I do wonder what these two talk about when they're on their own.

"Are you prepared for debate this afternoon?" Linus asks.

"Oh! Absolutely! So prepared! You?"

"Have I ever been unprepared for a debate?"

I laugh. Linus has no business being a good debater, with his endless patience and kindness, at least not if you ask most people. He always leads the winning team, though. Patience and kindness win more debates than rudeness and raising your voice a lot of the time.

"Do you need a ride home after school?" I ask.

He bites his lip and shifts a careful step closer to Danny. "Uh, we're—studying, this afternoon. At the coffee shop. So no. Thank you!"

This is what I wanted. This is why I've been doing this. To make the two of them want to spend time together. I've accomplished my goal! Then why does it sting like this when he suddenly doesn't need me anymore?

"Cool. Have fun with that! Wait," I say to Danny, attempting to lighten the mood. "Is it mean to say 'Have fun with math' to someone who doesn't like math?"

Danny shakes his head. "I don't think so. I know how you mean it. And it's like, it's not not fun, if you know what I mean? I, uh, I still prefer words over numbers, but Linus is an excellent teacher. You are!"

he adds when Linus opens his mouth to protest. "You're making it interesting."

"He is good at that," I agree. "He is good at many things."

And, really, just the way they look at each other, this shy, awkward little glance—what even is that? They spent the entire weekend together. They spend so many afternoons together. How are they not boyfriends yet? I don't understand it.

Just then Danny turns his head, eyes sort of lighting up as he sees someone down the hallway. "Oh," he says, "there's Stella. I just have to—I'll catch you later, okay?" He directs that last part at Linus, who nods and doesn't seem worried at all, but I watch closely as Danny walks away in the direction of Stella, who's just a few lockers down trying to wrestle several heavy-looking books into her book bag.

Linus, who had been busy opening his own locker, turns his head to look where I'm looking. "Huh," he says, frowning. "I didn't even know they were friends. It's nice that they're friends, isn't it? Like, outside of the drama group? Since he's new here and all?"

I think I can detect just a touch of jealousy in his voice, and I do share his worry, if I'm being honest, but I don't want to say anything in case I'm wrong. "What do you mean? That's just Stella. You know her. She's our Sherlock."

"No, yeah. I know. I didn't mean—forget it."

"They're probably talking about the play." I can't look away from those two. The way Danny is leaning against the lockers next to her, and he's smiling so widely, and—is she putting her hand on his arm? What is going on there?

He sighs. "He was just saying something earlier about having plans to see a movie with someone. It's probably about that. Or about the play."

I bite my lip and really hope that he can't tell how much I'm freaking out on the inside. I'm really afraid all of a sudden. What if Danny isn't gay at all? Or bi? "Yes. Probably."

Linus stares at his shoes. "Do you think they are—um. A thing?"

I shrug. "Why would you think that? They're just talking." Friends talk. Linus and I talk. This doesn't have to mean a thing.

"Oh!" He looks over at them, too. "I have no idea. He never said anything."

I let him take my arm and pull me away from the lockers and down the hall so that we won't be late for class. But I can't stop thinking. My brain literally won't shut up about this. Danny and Stella. *Danny and Stella?*

We have only walked a few steps when I spot Alyssa a few lockers down, and I stop in my tracks. "Hey, um, meet you in class?" I say to Linus. "I just need to ask Alyssa something."

"Oh," Linus says. "Sure." He lets go of my arm and waves at me before hurrying down the hallway by himself.

I quickly make my way over to Alyssa, who smiles at me when she sees me.

"Hey," she says.

"Hi," I say, smiling back at her. "Hey. Good to see you. I—uh, can I ask you a quick question?"

"Yeah, sure." She grabs a book from her locker and works on shoving it into her backpack while I lean my hip against the locker next to hers, trying to figure out how to ask this.

"It's—um. Promise you won't tell anyone?"

She gives up on wrestling with her book and looks up at me. "Of course."

"Is—I was wondering—do you know if Danny is gay?"

"Oh, uh." Alyssa frowns. "I—no idea. I didn't think so?"

"Oh." I can feel my heart sinking. This is not good. "But I thought—

in drama club, when he and Linus performed that gender-bent scene together—it just seemed—"

"Danny is a really good actor," Alyssa says, but she must see something in my eyes, because she bites her lip and seems to think for a minute. "But, you know," she continues, "I don't really know him that well, so don't take my word for it. It's totally possible that he's gay. It just literally never crossed my mind. Like, this is honestly the first time I've ever thought about his sexual orientation. So, I guess it's possible?"

I look over at Danny and Stella, who are still talking. Danny looks really, really happy to see Stella. And they just—the way they're leaning their heads together as they're talking . . . they just look awfully friendly. "What about Danny and Stella?" I can't stop myself from asking.

Alyssa follows my line of sight. "Maybe?" she says. "I don't know."

"Does he have any close friends here who might know?" I ask. "Anyone he might have told about it if he likes anyone?"

"You should ask Linus," Alyssa points out. "I thought he was Danny's closest friend, honestly. Or—oh. Wait. Are you asking for him?"

I feel almost sick. What if I have made a terrible, terrible mistake? Have we ever had any sort of confirmation that Danny was into boys? Because I have always just assumed that he was gay or bi, but what if . . . oh my god, what if he does like Stella and isn't into guys at all?

Have I seriously orchestrated this whole thing without ever even getting all of the facts? I can't believe I could have been so stupid.

I can feel my face getting red and I feel so bad for talking about Danny behind his back. I know how much I would hate it if I ever overheard some guys speculating about whether I was gay or not behind my back. I feel like a terrible person.

"Sorry," I say. "This is really none of our business, is it? I shouldn't have asked."

Alyssa smiles. "Well, it's not like I could really help you out anyway."

"I have to get to class," I say, hoping my voice doesn't sound as shaky as I feel.

"Oh, okay." She nods. "Of course. I—I'll see you in drama club?"

"Of course," I promise, and throw one last look back at Danny and Stella. They seem really happy together. Maybe Danny did just want to be friends with Linus?

I've not been feeling very good all weekend, but suddenly I feel way, way worse. Because if my suspicions are confirmed, I have not only hurt myself but my best friend as well.

Oh no. What have I done?

Chapter 44

Linus

SOMETHING IS DIFFERENT SINCE THAT day in the coffee shop when Danny told me that he actually liked hanging out with me and I don't have to assume he is just being nice all the time.

I guess it makes sense that he wants to be friends, especially since he's new here, but I have to be honest, I really had no idea. It's just that the possibility had never even crossed my mind. I'm not usually the kind of person that good-looking new guys single out to be their new friends. And it's baffling, to say the least—Danny already has friends from drama club. Friends he is not seeing as much because he spends so much time with me. It's a simple mathematical fact. A day only has so many hours. And we're usually meeting twice a week now, and one extra afternoon over the weekend. I tutor him, and then he helps me run lines for the play. Which was his idea, because I would never have dared to ask. That's a lot of time to spend together, isn't it?

My own social life has never been exactly flourishing, but even I notice how much less time I suddenly have for spontaneous Thursday afternoon coffee with Meg or even our carefully scheduled *Star Trek* rewatch. We are already way behind schedule with that. And once again I'm spending my afternoon at Danny's coffee shop tutoring and running lines.

"Do you think you can try that scene without the script just once?" Danny asks, and I look up at him and can feel myself going pale.

"Without the script?"

"Come on." He laughs. "I bet you have that entire thing memorized by now. Just try it. Just once."

"I—no, I—" I swallow heavily and don't quite know what to say. I do have the scene memorized, and all my other scenes as well. Memorizing things isn't the problem here. It's more that I kind of like being able to hide behind my script. And yes, I know I have to get over that. Just . . . not now. Not yet.

"If you get stuck, I'll help you," Danny assures me.

I shake my head and lower my eyes. "I don't—just one more time with the script? Please? Just to make sure?"

Danny tilts his head at me. "You said the same thing last time."

"I know. It's only—"

"You're doing great, you know?" he interrupts, and smiles at me encouragingly. "And I'm not just saying that. I like what you're doing with the character."

"Thanks," I say lamely. I'm not sure I believe him. I'm not sure that Mr. Hudson is supposed to be so shy and awkward. "This is just . . . new."

"Of course," he says. "It can be weird at first."

"I'm still afraid I'll forget my lines in rehearsal next week and make a fool of myself in front of everyone," I confess.

Danny laughs. "I don't think you'll forget your lines. And if you did, no one in the club would care. It happens. You won't be the only one who forgets something. You're allowed to mess up at first. No one expects you to start out perfectly."

"I guess it's mostly that I don't know all of them that well yet," I admit. "I'm still stuck on trying to make a good first impression."

"Hmm." He picks up his coffee mug, wraps both hands around it as if soaking up the warmth of the drink. "You know, we could do something about that quite easily, don't you?"

Danny is not popular—he's not one of those guys who always have to be surrounded by a million people hanging on their every word—but he seems to be slowly building a nice, solid circle of friends and I feel honored to be included, like I have accidentally fallen into a different dimension where being me is way cooler than it actually is. Because he still hangs out with me so many hours in a week.

But he also keeps bringing this up, keeps trying to get me to meet the rest of the drama people. Or, well. I have already met them, since we're all in the same club, obviously. But he wants me to keep meeting them, even outside of drama club. I know they're all friends and do stuff together outside of school; Danny has mentioned it a few times. But even though I have apparently suddenly transformed into someone who is acceptable company for an entire group of people, I'm not quite sure that I am ready for that yet.

In fact, I am quite sure that I'm not! I may be a little cooler than I thought I was, but I'm still not a social butterfly. I fear I may be perpetually stuck in the caterpillar stage. Because it's been weeks now of hanging out with Danny, and I still prefer the company of one or two people I like over the company of large groups of people.

"I know," I say hesitantly. "I just—I'm not really a party person, I guess."

"Well, I'm not saying we have to go to a party," Danny says over the rim of his coffee cup, and I sigh in relief.

"Oh, thank god!"

"I'm not even much of a partygoer myself. But how about a movie? We were all going to go tomorrow night. You could come with us!"

"What movie were you thinking of seeing?"

"Does it matter? We haven't really decided yet."

"How does that not matter? Don't you go to see a specific movie? Otherwise what's the point?"

"The point is to do something with your friends that you can talk about later!"

"Okay, but—how can the movie not matter to you? Especially if you plan to talk about it later?"

"It's not so much like it doesn't matter at all. It's just not the entire point of going."

"Then why don't you just go bowling or to a pizza place?" I have no idea if kids these days go bowling or to pizza places to hang out with their friends. But I've seen it on TV a lot and it seems like a nice, fun way to spend an evening. A lot saner than sitting through a movie you decided on last minute. You can't even talk to your friends during a movie. And if you do, Meg will murder you and I will go looking for the remote to rewind what we have missed due to all the talking.

"Maybe we could go bowling," he concedes. "Would you like that? I'm sure the others would be on board. I haven't been bowling in ages. The more I think about it, the more I like this idea."

I have to think about it, because while it does sound awfully tempting, it also sounds a little scary. I'm in drama club with those people, but I don't actually know them all that well yet. I like them well enough, though, and if they don't laugh about me for my nonexistent acting skills, they might be okay with my complete lack of proficiency at bowling. I still don't know if I can manage small talk with an entire group of people in a loud public place like a bowling alley.

"No, a movie sounds good," I tell him. "I'm sorry, I didn't mean to be difficult, I was only—"

"Linus!" He reaches across the table to cover my hand with his own and for a second I wonder if I have spontaneously developed asthma because breathing becomes a bit of a struggle just then. "You're not being difficult. If we all go out, it should be fun for all of us, right?"

"I like movies. It does sound like fun. We can do that," I mumble. If it's this important to him, I think I can even live with their chaotically random system of picking a movie and tag along and I have absolutely no doubt that I'll manage to have fun. This is just all so new. I am not used to having friends with whom I have to agree on those things. Meg and I pretty much always liked the same things anyway and Sophia was always cool with everything as long as Meg promised to make out with her afterward.

"I'll text the others and ask around, okay?" he suggests.

"Okay. Cool." I suck in a breath; time to dive in headfirst. New things. I have read somewhere that trying them is good for you. "But if everyone would rather go see a movie, that also sounds really good."

"Awesome. I promise that you won't regret it. I'll even pick you up and drive you home after!" Danny beams at me before picking up his phone to start texting.

Well. Look at me being a teenager with friends and plans for Friday night. This is all kinds of exciting.

Chapter 45

Meg

"WHY WOULDN'T IT BE A date?" I ask, sitting cross-legged at the foot of his bed while he ruffles through the shirts in his closet.

I've decided I'm going to keep acting confident in front of Linus, even if I'm still a little nervous that I've misinterpreted Danny's interest in Linus. Ever since I saw him talking to Stella I've paid close attention to Danny's interactions with both boys and girls, and the only thing I've found out for sure is that he's friendly. Very friendly, in fact. To pretty much everyone. Everyone likes Danny and Danny is nice to everyone in return. I overheard one girl in my math class whispering to her friend about how she thought he was cute and wondering if he had a girl-friend, but I know that doesn't mean anything. It just means that she thought he was straight, and that happens to queer people all the time. To straight people, too, I guess.

But this invitation is a good development. Danny asked him to hang out. It has to mean something, right? Maybe I'm wrong after all about Danny being straight. At the very least it's a reason to be hopeful.

"Because we are not dating, we are friends, and also all of his friends will be there and—oh my god, Meg, you can't stop with all of that even now? Seriously?"

"You're canceling our scheduled TV night to hang out with a boy! I just want the juicy gossip I am entitled to by being your best friend!"

"No. You just want to find new ways to push us together! You really have to stop doing that!"

"Fine." I groan. "I solemnly swear to not bring it up again. I didn't even mean it like that."

He lets his hands drop from his shirts, shakes his head. "It's useless. Why do I only own nerd T-shirts or dress shirts with sweater vests?"

"What qualifies as a nerd shirt in your vocabulary?"

He holds up a shirt that says NERD in big bold letters across the chest. I wince a little. "Yeah, don't wear that."

"But I don't have anything!"

"Why do you care what you're wearing if this so clearly isn't a date?" I ask. I just really, really need to know what's going on between them. In case Danny really isn't interested.

He glares at me over his shoulder. "I just do, okay?"

"Okay. Fine. I'm sorry. Do you want my help?"

"No. Thank you, though."

"Do you want me to go down to your kitchen and make us a cup of coffee?"

"That—would actually be wonderful, yes."

I get up, look at him standing there in front of the open wardrobe all fluttery and excited about his night, despite the fact that he is not even expecting anything from it other than to go bowling with a bunch of theater geeks. "Danny would be lucky to have you, you know?"

"Meg, please, don't start again!"

"Sorry, no. Sorry."

"Are you sure you don't want to come with us?"

I shake my head. Alyssa and Danny had both texted me and invited me along since technically I'm a part of their group, too. But—I can't help it, everything about them reminds me of Sophia and I can handle that during rehearsal but I can't hang out with them on a Friday night. "Mom bought the *Eureka* box set. We were gonna start on that tonight. She even made cookie dough; I can't bail on her."

"Your mom is awesome."

"Yeah. She is."

"I'll miss you, though!" He pouts at me. "And I'm sorry about the rewatch project. I'll make it up to you."

I laugh and hug him tightly because honestly, my best friend is the cutest best friend ever. "You can make it up to me by having an amazing night with your new friends! And then tell me all about it!"

"They're *our* new friends, you know? They won't stop being your friends just because you're not coming along tonight."

"I know. I'll go make coffee, all right?"

"Yeah, okay. And, Meg?"

"What?" I ask, stopping to look back halfway out the door.

"If I haven't found anything to wear by the time you're back, you may help me."

I bounce a little on my feet and grin at him. "I'll be quick! You won't regret it."

He heaves a sigh. "You always say that. And then you try and make me wear my Yoda T-shirt."

I wave at him and hurry down the stairs.

And I have just realized: He is right! They are my friends, too! So if he's not willing to tell me about Danny, I am sure I can get the full story of tonight from someone else at drama club next week.

I'll try not to do anything. Unless—well, unless stepping in appears to be absolutely necessary.

Chapter 46

Linus

THE GROUP ACTUALLY LIKED MY idea of going bowling, which I almost regret even suggesting in the first place because a movie is so much more comfortable, but I'm not letting myself dwell on my fears. I'm doing this.

Danny picks me up like he'd promised and we listen to his nineties cassette tapes in the car on our way over to the bowling alley.

"I should put some newer music on tapes so I can listen to that in the car," he says.

"You could also get a new car stereo," I suggest carefully, but he shakes his head.

"Where would be the fun in that?"

I nod along to Savage Garden, and I kind of have to agree. This is awesome. I feel a little like I'm in a nineties high school movie.

We're six people: Alyssa, Stella, Malik, Katie, Danny, and me, of course, and I know all of them from drama club. We all know one another and have seen one another making fools of ourselves during drama club, which I guess means we have already bonded. That makes this evening a lot less intimidating in my mind.

We meet up outside in the parking lot so we can all walk in together and, first of all, go and rent our shoes.

While we're waiting for the guy behind the counter to find all six sizes we ordered, Alyssa taps my shoulder. "This was a really good idea," she tells me. "I love bowling."

"I don't even know a lot about bowling," I admit. "I just thought it sounded like fun."

"Meg didn't want to come along?"

I shake my head. "I tried to persuade her, but no. She already had plans for tonight."

"That's too bad," Alyssa says. "Maybe next time."

"Yeah."

"Well, at least you're here." She smiles, and I smile back because Alyssa is nice and I like her.

"Does anyone want pizza?" Malik asks. "I kind of want pizza."

"Yes!" Stella nods enthusiastically. "Absolutely!"

"Pizza is always good," I agree.

Since everyone seems to share that opinion, once we've put our shoes on, Stella and Malik go to get pizza and sodas for everyone while the rest of us go ahead to claim our lane and enter our team names into the computer. Then, as soon as Stella and Malik are back and have set down their trays with our drinks and the giant pizza they got for all of us, we start playing.

So far, being out with people is not as awkward as I thought it would be at all.

I was right about one thing, though. I completely and utterly suck at bowling! Which was to be expected since I have been, like, three times in my life so far. That hardly makes me an expert. But it's not about winning, and the playing in itself is actually a lot of fun.

To my utter delight, Danny sucks as well, so I'm not the only one here who's looking a little silly.

My first try, I don't even knock over one single pin. Neither does Danny. On my second try, I get two—Danny once again gets none. His ball ends up in the gutter. He turns around to the rest of us, grinning widely, bouncing up and down on the heels of his feet.

"How bad was that?" he calls. "I missed two in a row! If I keep this up, is there an award for worst player?"

Everyone laughs and I say, "I guess you'll have to fight me for that title."

Danny comes over, one hand lifted up in the air, and it only takes me a second before I realize I'm supposed to high-five him. "It is on!" he promises.

I'm still going to try to hit the pins, though, and I know Danny will, too—this is the purpose of the game after all and also everything else would be unfair to Alyssa, who is on our team and actually kind of amazing at bowling. She even got a strike. Thanks to her, mostly, we're not doing too badly.

On my next try I knock over one pin, which is at least more than Danny had done. Katie raises both eyebrows at me. "I assume you were trying to make it go to the right like that?"

I grin at her. "Of course! That was my intention."

"Good job, in that case," she says, giving me a thumbs-up and grinning back. "I'm starting to suspect that you're some sort of secret agent and you're really playing for our team. You and Danny both," she adds, smirking up at him.

Danny laughs. "Shut up, you're blowing our cover!"

"Ohhh," she whispers loudly, exaggeratedly waving us away from her. "Sorry! Go back to secretly losing. I didn't say anything!"

"Katie, would you kindly stop intimidating my teammates? That would be awesome, thanks," Alyssa jumps in, handing Katie another slice of pizza. "Here, stuff that in your face and stop it with the slanderous accusations!"

"It's not accusations, darling; the evidence is right there in the computer," Katie says, but she takes the pizza. "Your team is going down." She does an evil laugh that is honestly impressive before reaching for her soda, focusing back on Stella, who is just now rolling her next ball. "Watch how it's really done," Katie says, taking a huge bite of pizza and nodding toward her teammate, then flinching at the flash of light and the clicking sound of a cell phone camera. "Hey!" she manages around a mouthful of pizza, lips greasy and a string of cheese clinging to her chin. She glares at Malik, who is examining his phone screen with a grin.

"Yup, I'm uploading that right away and you're getting tagged," he announces.

Katie groans and swallows her bite. "Oh my god. You suck so much. This will have dire consequences, my friend! When you least expect it!"

Malik rolls his eyes at her and proceeds to upload his photo.

"Oh, team selfie?" Danny suggests, throwing a questioning look at me and Alyssa.

I shrug. "Sure."

"Malik, you can take one of us while you're being lame and waving your phone around anyway," Alyssa decides, pushing Danny and me together and putting an arm around my shoulders. I'm tightly sandwiched in between her and Danny all of a sudden, Danny's arm landing across my shoulders from the other side, and it's really not very difficult to grin into the camera from this position.

Just as Malik is snapping the picture, Stella, who must have sneaked up behind us, shouts "Boo" and gives us a little shove, so as the camera flashes we're all screaming and making weird faces and the picture comes out looking rather funny, all of us with wide eyes and our mouths open and hands flailing.

"Can you send me that?" I ask Malik, looking over his shoulder at the screen. I really want a memento of this night and that picture is kind of hilarious.

"Sure," he agrees, and as I give him my number, everyone else realizes they don't have my number yet, either, and suddenly they're all getting out their own phones so we can exchange contact info. And just like that, for the first time in my life, the contacts list in my phone looks as if I actually have a group of friends.

We go back to playing after that, and Katie goes back to teasing us for playing so badly, but in a friendly way. Nobody really cares that our bowling balls keep rolling off the lane into the gutter. Everyone laughs with us, and Danny and I keep high-fiving each other after our worst shots. Rolls? Well, whatever you call them.

The best thing about the night, except for getting to hang out with Danny, is how no one seems bothered by the fact that I'm here. They act like I'm their friend, they don't make me feel weird about being the new guy in the group, and they don't have a million inside jokes that make me feel left out—something I had definitely been a little afraid of. Though, to be fair, Danny is new, too. But he has been out with them before. I'm newer. And I was afraid of just not being able to settle into the group dynamic.

But no, they are just genuinely nice people and I really like hanging out with them. A lot. More than I expected.

And this doesn't mean that I am magically transformed and that I'm going to buy T-shirts without prints on them tomorrow and start hanging out with the cool kids during lunch break. This doesn't mean that I want to spend all of my evenings like this. But for tonight, it is fun. And I can definitely imagine doing it again.

Malik, Stella, and Katie on the other team beat us in the end, which surprises pretty much no one and doesn't even really seem to matter. Katie gloats, but only until Alyssa and Stella physically pick her up and threaten to use her as a bowling ball until all three of them collapse into a laughing heap.

Bowling is definitely a sport I could get behind.

Danny drives me home once we're done having fun and it's dark out with millions of stars overhead, the air cool and crisp in November. I'm looking forward to winter. I really want to build a snow Vulcan.

"Did you have a good time?" Danny interrupts my thoughts.

I turn my head against the backrest of the passenger seat, smile at him. "Yes. I did. You couldn't tell?"

"No, I could. I guess I just wanted to make sure."

"It was amazing. Thank you for making me come along."

"It wouldn't have been the same without you," he says quietly, and I have to look away and clear my throat.

"You probably wouldn't have lost quite so badly without me, though."

"Hey, did you see me play? And it's not about winning anyway."

"I agree. There's just something so satisfying about—what exactly? It's not even knocking over pins. I didn't do that a whole lot, so that can't be it. Why is it even so much fun?"

"I—honestly have no idea. But it's kind of addictive, isn't it?"

"A little, yes," I agree. "We should do it again sometime!" The words are out before I can stop them, but Danny looks delighted.

"We should! Whenever you want! Just let me know."

"And whenever everyone else has time, right?"

He pauses. "Or we could also, um. Go by ourselves? One day? Just us?"

"That way each of us would get more turns!"

"Precisely. Yes."

"We could do that."

It's dark in the car so I'm pretty sure he can't see me blush. I hope he can't see me blush.

"I'm looking forward to it," he says quietly.

Chapter 47

Meg

I KNOW FOR MOST PEOPLE Thanksgiving break means family reunions and stuff. But that's not how Mom and I handle things. Mostly because Mom's parents live on the other side of the country and the flight is very expensive, so we're saving the reunions for Christmas. And Mom's sister has a huge family of her own, also on the other side of the country. And from what I understand, Dad's family lives only a few hours away, but neither of us really wants him or any of his family (or any of his current girlfriends—who knows how many he has right now) at our holiday celebration.

So in the week leading up to it, we start preparing for a holiday of our own the way we do every year: lots of food, board games, and a movie marathon for Friday because we'll be too tired and too lazy to move. We've done it this way for the past few years and I am looking forward to it a lot. It's the best holiday ever, almost better than Christmas.

The only thing that dampens my excitement is remembering how it was last year. How Sophia had come over for the movie marathon on Friday. It had been so nice, having her here and imagining what it would be like a few years ahead, when we'd be making our own holiday traditions, celebrating in the spacious yet cozy apartment we were always talking about renting together.

But it's fine, really. I'm fine. I'm just wondering how long it will take until all those memories will stop haunting me. I just . . . miss her. That's all. I'm also aware that she's most likely back in town for the holiday, and I don't know what I'm more afraid of: that she's going to ask me to meet up or that she's not going to ask. I don't think I'm ready to see her. But if she asks, I don't think I could say no. And if she doesn't ask—what would that even mean? That she doesn't miss me at all? On the other hand, I'm not asking her, either, am I?

Anyway. I know that Linus is doing the traditional Thanksgiving experience with his family; he doesn't have any brothers and sisters, but he has something like fifty thousand cousins and two full sets of grandparents and I don't even want to imagine what his tiny house looks like with all of them crammed in there.

I am usually really looking forward to my four days of not moving from the house, except that this year that's kind of all that I've been doing for weeks. Even if I really like being by myself a lot of the time, all of this sitting and not having anyone to talk to is making me more than a little antsy at this point. At least once the holiday is over we're almost into December, which means just a couple weeks until the play, and that means things will be busy. Even if I'm not onstage, Alyssa has me doing all kinds of things behind the scenes. It's actually exciting.

So, my Thanksgiving is just as calm and uneventful as I am used to. And, like every year, we have prepared way too much food for the two of us and will probably be living off the leftovers for several days until we have to throw them out. This is also nothing unusual.

We only leave the house for a short walk on Friday just to stretch our legs a bit and get some fresh air, and then it's right back to watching movies for the rest of the day. I do my best not to miss Sophia, to not even think of her. My Thanksgiving tradition with my mom is older than my relationship with Sophia was. I just have to go back to the way things were before.

Just like every year, I fall asleep on the couch before midnight and Mom has to wake me to send me up to bed once the movie is over.

And this is exactly why it is (usually) the perfect kind of holiday: no responsibilities and nothing to do; the most exhausting thing we had to do was to wash the dishes.

I sleep in on Saturday because I can—once I am properly rested I will have to get started on my studying, but for now I am happy extending my holiday a little bit and getting the rest I want for some reason after doing nothing but resting for two days straight.

After a late brunch and some TV while Mom finally sits down in the big armchair and resumes reading her new boss's paper, murmuring insults aimed at him under her breath the entire time, I finally pull myself out of my weird funk to get started on everything I have to do this long weekend.

Starting the Monday after Thanksgiving we have extra rehearsals for drama club every afternoon because the first performance is just about two weeks later, and the days fly by.

We're doing six performances altogether, mostly because our auditorium is small and doesn't seat a big audience.

This means we've had to cancel all our other clubs for the duration of this school play craziness, but only for a couple of weeks before the

Christmas holidays, so that's okay. And also I assume that for Linus it's absolutely worth it.

I tell myself that whether Danny is straight or not, Linus is obviously at least getting a friend out of it. And there's still a chance that Danny is, after all, interested in him. The bowling invitation has given me a bit of hope back in that regard. Mostly because I still don't really want to think about what I did in case Danny has no romantic interest whatsoever in my best friend. That would just be—not good. Seriously, seriously not good.

I've never seen Linus fall for anyone before—I'm not counting his online flirtation with the guy from Portugal, because I think that was more wishful thinking than actual attraction—so this is all new. But seeing him with Danny now makes me realize that he really is in love, whether he wants to admit it to himself or not. And after the way I've encouraged him to give this a try, I don't know if he could forgive me if it turned out it was all just false hope. I don't know if I could ever forgive myself.

So I spend my afternoons backstage with the other club members who didn't get cast and help out making everything run smoothly. I tell myself I am working backstage, not hiding from anything.

Organizing is my thing, so I do manage to have a good time. Whenever I succeed in focusing on what we're doing here instead of dwelling on all the happy memories this setting evokes. Memories of me hanging out here with Sophia back when she was part of the club. I used to accompany her to her auditions and sometimes I picked her up from rehearsal.

I still miss her so much. I don't know how to stop. It's even worse after the holiday and all those happy memories I just can't seem to shake off no matter how hard I try.

But anyway. Alyssa takes care of all the actual cues and rehearsal reports and whatnot, but I'm mostly in charge of props and costumes and making sure everything is where we need it and I'm good at that. Organizing things calms me.

And yet I can't help it, I'm still . . . jealous. I spend a lot of time just watching the rehearsals go on up there on the stage and it looks so amazing. It looks like so much fun. Fun that I'm left out of. Because they didn't want me. That seems to be a pattern developing in my life.

Girlfriend, best friend, drama club—they're all perfectly fine without me. I'm not necessary. I'm not needed. And, okay, I pushed Linus into spending time with Danny, but once it turns out that Danny doesn't in fact want him, Linus is never going to talk to me ever again and I'm going to be completely alone at last.

Luckily, there isn't too much time to dwell on anything because on top of rehearsals we still have exams and homework and holiday preparations. I'm grateful for all of that, and still I feel a certain sense of relief when I finally wake up and it's Friday the eleventh, the day of our first performance.

I'm one of the first people to arrive that afternoon. I may not be needed onstage, but I still have props to sort so they're ready to be used. I take my job seriously even if it's not the one I wanted.

Before my weird mood can take over once again I just decide to dive right into work instead and drop my bag and jacket in the rehearsal room before making my way to the auditorium to start setting things up backstage.

I'm about to wipe down the blackboard we need for Sherlock to explain his theories to Watson when I finally hear footsteps approaching.

It's Linus, way too early as well, but that was to be expected. He likes being on time almost more than I do.

"Hi," I greet him. It's weird, seeing him like this. If things were normal, I'd have been the one to drive him here. We would have been running lines for weeks. But he has Danny for that now. He doesn't need me.

He looks pale and a little sick, needs a moment before he answers. "Hi. You're, uh. Early."

"So are you."

He holds both hands to his stomach. "I feel sick."

"Nervous?"

"A bit." He shakes his head. "But, I don't know, maybe I'm coming down with something? My dad's coworker has the flu, maybe he brought it home and I—"

"You don't have the flu," I interrupt, rolling my eyes at him. I should have known he'd try something like this.

"You can't know that."

"Yes, I can," I assure him. "You're fine. It's just nerves."

"How would you know?" He sounds a little angry. "You can't know how I'm feeling."

"No, but I know you," I point out. "And I figured you'd be getting cold feet just about now." I want to take it back the second the words leave my mouth—that was uncalled for and I know it.

He goes even paler, silent for a long moment. "What's that supposed to mean?"

I lift my shoulders, hold up my hands in a placating gesture. "Nothing, oh my god. I just meant—"

"You think I want to miss the performance." It doesn't sound like a question.

"I didn't say that."

"You kind of did."

"Did not. But, come on, you can't tell me that you're not nervous. And, I mean, that's okay, it's fine to be nervous."

"Well, thank you very much for your approval."

"Just don't bail on the show."

He gasps. "You really think I'd do that?"

"Isn't that kind of what you're considering?"

"I'm here, aren't I?"

"But if you were sick, you could go back home." I have no idea why I'm saying this. I have no idea what's happening. But on the other hand, I kind of do. It feels a bit like that summer day when Sophia broke up with me. "You should be glad you get to do this; not all of us were so lucky."

He looks actually hurt now. "I offered you the part. I didn't even want it."

"Oh, how generous!" I throw my hands up in the air. "Because that's everyone's dream, getting a part out of pity! I can't believe I didn't jump at the offer! But also, you don't make the casting decisions, do you? They chose you. They didn't choose me. It was their choice."

"Why are you acting like this?" he asks. "I didn't do anything wrong. You pushed me to do this. You spent weeks trying to convince me this was a good idea. And then when I actually go and do it, you're mad at me? I don't get it."

"I was only trying to help," I defend myself.

"I thought you of all people would have my back," he says. "Aren't we supposed to be friends? If you're so unhappy about me doing this, why didn't you talk to me? Why didn't you say something sooner? Like, maybe not right before I have to go onstage, which you of all people should know is really hard for me?"

I let out a bitter laugh. "I should have said something sooner? Are you serious right now? Like you told me that you were talking to my ex-girlfriend behind my back?" I ask, and his mouth drops open.

"Meg—"

"Because how did you think that would make me feel if I found out about it?"

"I didn't mean to—" He looks panicked. "I never wanted—"

"Didn't think I'd find out?" I can't keep the bitterness from my voice and I'm not even trying to.

"It's not like that," he says. "She contacted me. And—she's my friend, too. I just wanted—"

"She dumped me," I say, and I kind of feel like crying, but not here, not now. I have been so good about not crying so far. "She dumped me and you know how much that hurt me, and yet you went behind my back and . . . Did you guys talk about me?"

He hesitates. ". . . Yes."

I let my shoulders slump, and I'm just done with this conversation. "Awesome. Just perfect."

"She just wanted to know how you were. We didn't—I didn't mean to keep it from you, I'm sorry, I—"

"It doesn't matter now," I say. "But, yeah. So much for having each other's backs."

"I'm really sorry," he says. "Please believe me."

"I'm sorry, too," I say. "But I really need to not be here right now." I turn around and abandon my props. I'm allowed bathroom breaks, after all. And I just hope there will be more people here once I return so I won't have to talk to him again.

I really feel like crying now because I guess on top of everything else that went wrong this year I have also just effectively ended our friendship and I really just don't know what the hell is wrong with me.

Can't I just have one thing in my life that's not completely messed up? Is that really too much to ask?

In the bathroom, I spend a long moment just staring at my own face

~ 251 ~

in the mirror, willing myself not to cry. It'll show if I do. I get all gross and splotchy. Everyone will know.

I manage to fight back the tears, but it's hard. Because after Sophia, I could easily blame her for the breakup. This time, it's a little harder to see who's really to blame.

Chapter 48

Linus

THE GOOD THING ABOUT THIS is that suddenly I'm not nervous about the performance anymore. Well, I am, but it seems kind of insignificant all of a sudden. I have a far bigger problem now.

I don't know how Meg found out about me talking to Sophia, but it doesn't really matter. I assume Sophia told her. That seems to make the most sense. But the only thing I care about is that she wasn't happy with it.

Which—I knew she wouldn't be happy with it. This is exactly the reason I never found a way to tell her. I didn't want to upset her. And now I've managed to make her really angry with me and the worst thing is that she looked so hurt. I never meant for any of this to happen and I have no idea how everything could get so out of control.

Because here I am backstage in the auditorium, dressed up in a tweed suit and an apron because the costume department thought that was funny, and in a little while I have to go out there and perform in front of an audience.

It just all suddenly hits me all at once and I'm not sure I remember how to breathe. Because. Oh my goodness! I have joined the drama club and even landed a speaking part. Yikes. Am I completely out of my mind? Oh, man. This is not good. And I have spent weeks talking to my best friend's ex-girlfriend behind her back when I knew how sad she still was about the breakup, and instead of telling her or making every effort to make her feel better I chose to spend more time with a boy I just met this summer, and I didn't even really try very hard to make her come along when we all went out. I am not a very good friend.

But then, Meg hasn't been a very good friend, either, has she? She has been talking to Sophia, too? Why didn't I know about this? And then all of her comments about Danny and me, and the way she practically forced me into this audition and . . . They were setting me up this whole time, weren't they? Pushing me into spending time with Danny.

I definitely do not appreciate being manipulated like this and humiliated and—do they think I can't find a boyfriend by myself? Do they think they have to fix my life for me?

Yes, I'm sorry, I'm so sorry, but I am also really upset. I feel betrayed. And I have never liked it when people patronized me, and this feels a lot like it: Let's find the fat little nerd boy a boyfriend because he's just too awkward and shy to manage by himself.

I know Meg. We have been friends for years and I know that it wasn't her intention to belittle or hurt me.

The fact remains, though, that she did.

"Hey." Suddenly, Alyssa is standing next to me. "Have you seen Meg?"

I nod. "Yeah, I, uh. She went, um. Just in that direction. Bathroom, I guess."

"Oh, okay, thanks," Alyssa says, then narrows her eyes at me. "Everything okay with you? You look a little—"

"No, yes, fine, I'm fine," I assure her, putting on the best smile I can muster right now. "Just—nerves. You know."

"Why do you think I prefer hanging out backstage?" she asks, and winks at me before clapping a hand to my shoulder. "Welcome to the wonderful world of theater."

"If it helps, I think a little shyness can only add to your interpretation of the character," Danny speaks up behind me, and I look up at him and the smile just happens to my face, even if I'm not in the best mood right now.

"Thank you."

"Always," he says, and, well, now I'm definitely not pale anymore at least.

Chapter 49

Meg

"OH, THERE YOU ARE," ALYSSA greets me as I arrive back at my blackboard that still needs to be wiped down. "Do you have the folder with the lighting cues? Because I can't find it."

"Oh." I shake my head. "You gave that to Malik the other day."

"Right." She slaps a hand to her forehead. "Of course I did. Sorry."

"No worries. This is why you have me as an assistant."

"Deputy stage manager," she corrects me, grinning, then squints her eyes at me. "Hey, are you okay?"

"Yeah," I lie quickly. "Why?"

"Nothing," she says. "Just—it's nothing."

I manage to find a laugh for her before I turn away, but that just makes me suddenly look right at Linus, who looks right back at me, and we both sort of freeze before looking away.

This is the worst. It's just the absolute worst. I was so worried about messing everything up with Linus getting hurt over Danny, but now I've hurt him myself.

I did all this to help him. I just wanted to help. And I've made everything fifty thousand times worse in the process.

Things backstage are busier than I ever imagined they could be, but I still get to observe most of what's going on out there on the stage. That's sort of my job, watching the play and handing people things when they need them. It sounds more boring than it is, I swear. It's actually really cool.

Linus does really well in the first scene. Really, really well. At least that calms my nerves a bit—I had started to worry about him. If he'd screwed up now it would probably have been my fault for fighting with him right before his first-ever performance.

But he pulls it off like he does it all the time. He speaks loudly enough, even though his volume had been an issue in rehearsal a few times, and he doesn't miss a single cue, and, well, I'm not a professional critic or anything but I find his performance perfectly convincing. I'm still mad at him, but I can see through my anger that he obviously practiced hard and that he deserves the role. So I guess if even I like his performance, then everyone else must, too.

Chapter 50

Linus

THE PLAY IS NERVE-RACKING, BUT not necessarily in a bad way. I have three scenes in which I have to talk and a few more where I'm only in the background, dusting and carrying a tray or just standing around while Sherlock and Watson are talking.

I know my lines and I know how to deliver them, thanks to Danny's endless patience with me. I'm still nervous. But at least this nervousness distracts me from being upset over the fight I had with my best friend. There honestly isn't much room in my head for anything that was said between us. I have to focus on my lines and blocking.

I'm right there in the second scene in Sherlock's study, because it's Mr. Hudson's job to show in the visitor who will turn out to be Sherlock's client for the story.

Just as rehearsed, I rap my knuckles against the ladder we've put up as a door frame and clear my throat loudly. "There's a visitor at the door for you, Sherlock," I say. "Do you want me to show him in?"

Stella, who is our Sherlock Holmes, waves her hand impatiently and heaves a sigh. "If this is about another house cat who ran away, I'm jumping out the window," she declares dramatically, green hair flying as she drops onto the ratty old sofa.

Danny, who is sitting in an armchair pretending to read the paper as John Watson, lifts his head and looks over at me.

I wait patiently while Stella keeps ranting on about how they haven't had any interesting cases in months. I'm still impressed that she can remember all of her lines. She has a lot of them. I'm good at memorizing things, but if I'd had to memorize all of her lines, I would be freaking out by now with the fear of forgetting something.

My eyes keep flickering over to where Danny is sitting and he looks back at me, winks at me from behind his weeks-old newspaper. I can barely hold back the smile, but I do feel better all of a sudden.

"Show him in," Stella finally says, and I nod in her direction.

"Just a moment." I breathe a sigh of relief as I exit the stage. That was my dialogue for my first scene. I've made it through my entire first scene without a hitch! I didn't fall down and I didn't forget my words and they didn't have to stop the play because I messed up (which had been a recurring nightmare for the past few nights).

Backstage, Alyssa slaps a hand to my shoulder and grins widely. "See?" she says. "Not that bad."

I laugh a little breathlessly. "It's not over yet!"

For a moment I think about finding Meg and talking to her about our fight earlier. But we're in the middle of a performance and now is just not the time. Also, I'm a little afraid of losing my cool after all and becoming so nervous that I'll start forgetting my lines for the next scenes. So I stay where I am and wait until it's time to go back out. I'll have to find her as soon as the play is over.

My next scene is once again in Sherlock's study, where I am dusting off the coffee table while Stella and Danny are arguing about their case, and I have a bit more dialogue because Mr. Hudson keeps commenting on their theories and inadvertently gives them the vital clue that leads them toward the solution.

Once again I make it through the entire scene without falling flat on my face or saying the wrong thing.

I'm still nervous, but I'm starting to think that this acting thing is kind of fun. I can at least see the appeal of it now. It's an incredible feeling, going off the stage knowing that I did well. Once I make up with Meg, I have to remember to tell her this.

Chapter 51

Meg

THE PLAY IS SILLY. I knew that from the beginning, but seeing it now only confirms it.

But silly as it is, I still kind of love it. It just makes me wish even more that I could be an active part of the whole thing instead of having to stay backstage helping out everyone else.

So Alyssa keeps telling me that I'll probably get a part in our spring play. I guess I should be looking forward to that. But first of all, I don't know for sure that it's going to happen and also, it doesn't really do a whole lot to make me feel better about missing out on this play.

Stella is amazing as Sherlock, the perfect mix between bored and just plain rude, and then adorably excited every time their case takes a sinister turn and things get more complicated. And Danny is such a mild-mannered Watson, patient and quiet and the perfect counterpart to Stella's exuberant energy. They work really well off each other. Really well.

I mention as much to Alyssa during a rare time things are quiet for her backstage, and she nods, grinning widely.

"We made good casting choices there."

"You did," I confirm, because, well, they did. "It helps that they're friends, right?" I can't help it. I'm still a little worried. They just . . . they work so well together.

"Oh, of course it does," she says. "But they also rehearsed a lot. They were really committed. And it shows. It also helps that they're incredibly talented."

None of that really tells me anything and it just makes my stomach sink even further. I can't shake the feeling that I've screwed up absolutely everything. But there's nothing to be done about it now, is there? It's too late.

I don't stick around once the show is over. I help clean up and put things away, but then I see to it that I get home before someone can insist I go out for pizza with them. I'm not in the mood today, and also I don't want to spoil the night for Linus. I've done enough of that already.

Alyssa looks a bit disappointed that I'm not coming along, but she understands when I say that I have a really important essay to work on. There hasn't been much time for schoolwork with all the rehearsals lately.

So I hurry out as soon as I can, find my car, and start making my lonely way home. Tonight, I really feel like I deserve every bit of loneliness this has brought me.

Chapter 52

Linus

DANNY IS WAITING FOR ME in his car when I walk out of the auditorium and I hurry across the parking lot, slip into the passenger seat, and firmly close the door behind me. Then I lean back, take a deep breath, and close my eyes.

"Did you find her?" he asks.

I breathe in, breathe out, and slowly shake my head, my eyes stinging just a bit. "No. She was already gone. Alyssa says she went home. I think she hates me now."

"I doubt that."

"She wasn't happy with me. You should have heard her. I've never seen her that upset before. And she was right. I should have told her. I can't believe that I didn't. She's my best friend. I don't think she trusts me anymore."

"That is entirely possible. But she doesn't hate you. It's impossible to hate you."

"That's very sweet of you, thank you."

"Just telling it like it is," he says, and starts the car.

We have some hanging out to do with some of his—our—friends. I don't really feel up to it, but I can't say no to this. Danny seemed really excited about it and I guess it is a nice thought. It's not their fault that I had a fight with Meg.

I need to apologize to her. I think she also needs to apologize to me, but . . . well, we just need to talk about this. If she still wants to talk to me. But we're not going to accomplish anything tonight. Maybe I'm still too angry.

Anyway, I promised that I'd go out with the drama club people after the performance and I don't like breaking my promises and I don't feel like explaining why I can't.

But tomorrow, I'm going to have to really find a way to fix all of this.

Once we're seated around the table at the pizza place I get out my phone, and then I just sit there and stare at it. I could text her. But what would I even say? I feel bad for looking at my phone while in company, but I just can't stop thinking about this. I've never fought with anyone like that before. I don't like it.

"You're really worried about this, aren't you?" Danny asks quietly.

"Well, yes. She is my best friend." I shove my phone back into my pocket and take a sip of my water. "If she hates me forever now, that would just really, really suck."

"I still don't think that she hates you. I think you both just need a little time. You're not going to solve this tonight. But I don't think it's possible to hate you."

"Why are you always being so nice to me?" I want to know, lowering my voice so that our friends can't hear us, even if they do seem to be deep in conversation themselves. And dammit, I am blushing again.

He props his head up on his arm, looks at me with an expression I can't quite decipher. "Have you really not figured that out yet?"

I don't think I have. But the way my stomach does this weird little swooping thing tells me what I want the reason to be.

Chapter 53

Meg

MOM HAD TO GO TO the museum because she needed to use the computer there, so my house is empty pretty much all Saturday. I'm grateful for that, because I have some serious thinking to do and I would like to not be interrupted while I'm doing that. There are performances today and tomorrow night, so the weekend isn't completely mine, but I'm good at keeping to myself when I want to. And I'll do my best to get most of my thinking done before I have to meet up with the others backstage.

I have the coffee ready and have even opened a fresh box of cookies, and with that and my laptop I sit down at the kitchen table and then don't quite know what to do.

This is all my fault and I'm well aware of it. If I hadn't had the genius idea of interfering and meddling in my best friend's love life, none of this would have happened. But if I broke our friendship, that means that I have to find a way to repair it. And I'm just not sure how to do that, because I've never had a fight like this before. I've never had any-one be mad at me like this. I've never given anyone a reason to.

Maybe, I think, the best place to start is to make a list. Lists help. And while I'm at it, I can try to figure out whether I need to apologize to Sophia as well because I dragged her into all of this and I've pretty much been ignoring her texts and e-mails ever since I found out she'd been talking to Linus.

I still just don't get why they had to do that. But they are the only friends I have. If I don't forgive them for this, then I'll really be alone. And as much as I value my quiet time, I'm really just not good at being alone.

Monday morning I feel tired—I've spent my entire weekend thinking but I haven't really been able to come up with a solution to anything. Maybe I'm still too angry. I don't actually feel that much like apologiz-ing. At least I managed to come up with a good excuse why I couldn't go for pizza with everyone after the play on Sunday night. It's Decem-ber. Everyone tends to just believe you when you tell them you're com-ing down with something. And I didn't want to spoil Linus's fun. So I went home instead.

I should have found a way to make up with him by now, but I don't know how. Every time I tried to text Linus, I couldn't do it at the last second. I have no idea how many text message drafts I deleted over the course of the last few days. But there were a few. And after the perfor-mances I managed to avoid him so things wouldn't be awkward. The silence between us is seriously getting to me.

I see Linus by his locker, and he's alone, and I do think about walk-ing up there to talk to him the way I do every morning. But I can't.

So I look away and walk off toward my own locker, but I can see him watching me as I look back before turning the corner.

We have another three performances this week, Wednesday night, and then Friday afternoon and the last one on Saturday. It's going to be a busy week.

"Good morning," Alyssa says, and I look up, surprised to find her walking next to me.

"Morning."

"We missed you last night," she says.

"Yeah, sorry, I just—"

"Homework, yeah," she says. "I get it."

"I know it's super lame, but—"

"Hey, no." She grins. "You have to defend your valedictorian spot. That's not lame. But . . . you're coming to the party after our last performance on Saturday, right?"

I nod. "Of course." I can't miss everything. And I'm still hoping for a part in the next play. I should probably stay on their good side. Also, making a few more friends can't hurt. Maybe I've been wrong to stay in the background so much to give Linus some room to hang out with them. I'm just not good at this.

"Good," she says. "See you later?"

"Yeah, sure."

She smiles again and I stop by my locker, watch her walk away. I don't know if we're friends. But at least she keeps talking to me, and she's nice. And . . . kind of cute, with her crazy long hair and that constant amused sparkle in her eyes and the way her smile always starts off a little crooked, the left corner of her mouth always twitching up first. Even if all of that's completely irrelevant because I don't need another disaster like Sophia and the way that ended. But . . . I'm almost looking forward to meeting her backstage tomorrow and working with her. That's something, I guess.

Monday crawls by slowly and Tuesday is a blur of activity with an extra rehearsal to keep things fresh in our minds and trying to squeeze in some studying in the library between classes and drama club. Wednesday is much of the same, only that we have a performance that night instead of rehearsal. On Thursday I'm so exhausted I just get through my classes and then go straight home to take a nap before getting started on my assignments. Even with the play going on, we still have exams and the holidays coming up and I'm starting to feel a little stressed out. Maybe it's good I didn't get a part. I can't imagine how Linus gets it all done.

But now all that's left is just Friday afternoon and then Saturday afternoon and then it's finally, finally over and the world will go back to normal.

I haven't had a chance to talk to Linus all week and I really miss him so much, but maybe I'll figure out a way once all of this drama club stuff is over. I hope so. I just want my friend back. Nothing's the same without him.

Chapter 54

Linus

THE WEATHER IS GETTING COLDER all the time now and it's snowed a few times already. Not so much that I can build a snowman or a snow alien. But enough to look pretty when you open the blinds in the morning and look outside.

I love winter. I am already looking forward to winter break, to snuggling up under a mountain of blankets with a cup of hot chocolate and a pile of books or a nice game or a movie. Even being inside is more fun when the weather outside changes.

It's Thursday and I'm meeting Danny in the library again—we haven't gotten much tutoring done since that Saturday after Thanksgiving, what with the play and everything. I feel a little guilty for that because I know how important it is to him to catch up in math. But we don't have a performance today and no other clubs or appointments or anything, so we can get in one more afternoon of tutoring before the holidays.

I'm first in the library today since I have hurried here, and I start spreading books and notes strategically across the tabletop. I am prepared! Danny has been so nice, constantly telling me that I am a good teacher, the least I can do is try to live up to it. I haven't really felt nervous about spending time with him for a while now, but today I am feeling a little fluttery again. I can't stop thinking about what he said at the pizza place, about me figuring out why he's being so nice to me. I just wish I knew for sure what he'd meant by that. Wanting to spend time together is something that friends do, but—it's also something that more-than-friends do, and I just wish I could make sense of all of this without feeling silly for daring to have hope.

He enters the library just minutes later, and I offer him a wide smile as he quickly crosses the distance between the shelves and slides into the chair next to mine.

"You're here before me," he says.

"I have a reputation to uphold! I am always ridiculously early everywhere; it was seriously starting to hurt my pride that you kept showing up earlier than me!"

"I wasn't aware that we were in competition over who was the most punctual." He sounds amused.

"Everything can be a competition if you have the right attitude," I inform him.

"True."

"Are you ready to do some calculus?"

"Actually—" He squirms a little in his seat, lashes fluttering as he looks past my head at some spot on the wall. "There's, um. I wanted. I was wondering—"

"If today's not good for you, we can meet up anytime over the weekend," I offer. "It's not a problem! Well, I mean, Saturday afternoon we have the play, but I'm free in the morning and on Sunday and—"

"No," he says. "I mean, yes, I would like to meet up over the weekend, but—uh."

"You're just full of ambition, aren't you?" I laugh proudly. "If you don't end the school year in the top five percent of the class—"

"I wasn't actually thinking—I mean, I don't want to study over the weekend."

I frown at him. "Okay. Then what—"

"I was hoping we could see a movie on Friday. After the play, since it's a matinee. And maybe do dinner after?"

I nod enthusiastically. "Oh, of course! Absolutely! Who else is coming along?"

"No one, I hope," he says.

"What do you mean?"

He sighs, turns a little in his chair so that he's facing me, takes another deep breath. "Linus, would you like to go to dinner with me tomorrow?"

"I—don't understand. Like, just us? As in—" It hits me out of nowhere what he's asking me and I can feel my eyes widen, breath hitching in my throat. "You—oh. You mean—"

"I am trying to ask you out on a date, you doofus!" He lets out an embarrassed little groan, hides his face behind his hands. "And it's not going well, apparently. I'm so sorry. If you don't want to, we'll never have to speak of it again—"

"Of course I want to," I manage, a little breathlessly. "On what planet would I not want to?"

"I, uh—really? You want to?"

"Do you want to?"

"I asked you!"

"Yeah, but—" I wave my hand at him. He's just sitting there all cute and kind and dreamy and I still cannot really understand what's happening right now; things like this don't happen to me. "Are you really sure? I mean—you don't have to, if you're just being nice, you don't have to, I—"

"Linus!" He leans forward in his chair and I snap my mouth shut, stare back at him, and I don't even dare to blink because I don't want to miss a moment of this.

"Yes?"

"I do want to. I have wanted to for quite a while."

"You—wait, what? Why?"

"I like you," he says. "Why is that so hard for you to believe?"

"Because you're kind of perfect," I say before I can stop myself.

"No, I'm not."

"Uh," I say, suddenly feeling shy. "I just meant—"

"I like you," he repeats. "And if you want to, I'd really love to spend more time with you, and not just to study or to carpool home after school."

"Technically that was never carpooling, that was just you providing a very entertaining taxi service free of charge," I mumble.

He laughs. "Has anyone ever told you how entirely adorable you are?"

I blush darker. "No, I can't say that they have."

"Well, then." He catches my eyes again, smiles carefully. "I think it's about time that someone started doing that regularly."

I am not sure how we're supposed to go back to math after this, but I figure it's his own fault if I'm distracted today—he can't spring something like this on me and expect me to keep it together afterward. He could have waited until after tutoring if he expected to learn something today.

Not that I am in any way opposed to this turn of events. Not. At. All!

The rest of Thursday flies by and I'm really surprised that we actually manage to get any studying done. I'm feeling . . . flustered is the word, I guess. And a bit like I'm sleepwalking. I can't quite believe what's happening yet.

He drives me home after tutoring and this time when he smiles at me as we say good-bye it means something different and I'm so . . . I don't have a word for it, but my palms are all tingly and I can't stop grinning.

Chapter 55

FRIDAY MORNING I HONESTLY CONSIDER faking a stomach flu and staying home.

I smack my palm down onto the alarm clock harder than necessary to silence it and pull my blankets up to my nose, curling in on myself.

I've just had it with this week. I'm feeling exhausted. And it's not the extra stress from having to sit backstage while everyone else is performing. It's . . . everything. I'm feeling overwhelmed and lonely and the thought of having to go out there into the world and interact with people is almost too much.

But on the other hand, it's just today and tomorrow. And then this play will be over and it won't be long until winter break, and bailing on them today would probably only make me feel worse than just battling on and somehow making it through this day.

And, I tell myself, as I miserably stare at the display of my alarm clock, if it turns out that I really can't do it, I can still fake sickness later and go home. But I know myself and I know I'll feel horrible if I don't go at all. I might not have the part I wanted in all of this, but they're still counting on me. And the thought of actually doing what I accused Linus of secretly contemplating—faking sickness and staying home—makes me feel awful.

I do feel nauseous, but I guess that's just the crippling guilt I'm feeling for the whole Linus situation. But I deserve that. I messed up. Badly. I guess it's only right that I'm feeling like a despicable human being for that.

No, I decide, throwing off the covers and sitting up on the edge of my mattress. Feeling sorry for myself isn't going to fix this. Even if all I want to do is hide, I don't think I've earned the right to do that.

And now I'm feeling sorry for myself again. Ugh. What is wrong with me?

I take a shower and get dressed and do my best to brush the knots out of my hair, which is somehow looking particularly orange today, and even that annoys me. But there's nothing I can do about it right now, other than put on a hat so my head doesn't look quite as . . . glowy. It really doesn't mirror my mood today.

Mom is down in the kitchen microwaving a stack of pancakes left over from yesterday by the time I finally make it downstairs.

"Morning," she says.

"Morning," I grumble back at her, walking over to the fridge to get the syrup. Day-old pancakes are really only edible drenched in syrup.

"You look cheerful," she comments, but I can tell from the way she looks at me that she's worried.

I don't want her to worry. I just don't know how to snap out of this. "I'm okay."

"You guys have another performance today, right?"

"Yeah, this afternoon," I tell her. "I'll once again be standing back-stage holding a clipboard."

"Well, I'm still looking forward to seeing it tomorrow," she says.

"You don't have to. Seriously. I won't be upset."

"I would be." She looks at me. "You know what you're doing is important, don't you? I know it's not what you wanted, but—"

"I know." I sigh. "I do know, I promise. It's just—maybe joining Sophia's favorite club right after she dumped me was a stupid idea after all."

"Oh, honey." She gives me a quick side-hug as I walk past her toward the coffeemaker, before the microwave pings and she goes to retrieve our pancakes.

Maybe it really was a stupid idea. Maybe I'm not mad about not getting a part at all, maybe I'm just upset because everything reminds me of Sophia, everywhere I go. Or maybe I'm upset about everything at once. I really don't know. But I guess eventually I'll have to figure it out so I can really work on fixing it.

Chapter 56

Linus

FRIDAY I BARELY REGISTER WHAT classes I'm sitting in; I have a bio exam but I'm so well prepared I'm sure I did well anyway.

The performance is pretty much right after class at three that afternoon, which means the theater kids even get to skip last period to prepare.

I know that I'm a rather perky and scatterbrained Mr. Hudson-the-landlord today, but I can't help it. I still feel like I'm in a dream. Because once this performance is over I have a date. My first-ever date. With a boy I really, really, really like. I have no idea what to expect, but I'm looking forward to it so much.

I just wish I could tell Meg; I almost feel like I'm going to burst if I don't talk to someone. But instead I just keep it to myself and pour all of this excess energy into my performance and, judging from the way people slap me on the back as I go offstage, I guess I did well.

I don't think that being on a date is going to be so very different at all from the two of us hanging out with the rest of the drama people, and yet I can't help being a nervous wreck.

We both rushed home real quick to get changed after the play. I told Danny that my dad could give me a lift to the movie theater; it wouldn't have been a problem. It's a Friday afternoon and my parents are home early for once; they actually have a date night of their own later.

I could probably even have borrowed a car, but Danny insists on picking me up, says it's more romantic this way. (Romantic! No one has ever wanted to do anything romantic with me before!) And to be honest, I'm glad that I don't have to drive in the snow that started falling heavily the day before.

I am standing in front of my open closet trying to find something to wear, but I have no idea what to pick. I mean, he knows what I look like. Would it be weird to dress up? Am I making too big a deal out of this? It would probably be silly to dress up too much. And besides, we have been alone together countless times before, in the library or at the coffee shop for our tutoring sessions. So this is not all that new, not all that different—except for the million ways it is completely and utterly new and different and a little scary and exciting and overwhelming.

I wish Meg was here. She'd help me pick out a shirt and she'd find something to say to make me calm down a bit. I miss her. It seems wrong that she's not here to calm me down; it's kind of how we work.

My parents are here, but they are no help at all. On the contrary, they're sort of making everything a million times worse. Dad is downstairs searching the kitchen drawers for batteries for his camera (luckily he hasn't figured out yet how to take photos with his phone), and Mom keeps popping into my room to entertain me with all sorts of advice and offering to fix my hair. Which just makes me panic that my hair looks weird and might need fixing. That particular worry hadn't even occurred to me before.

"He respects you, right?" she asks for the millionth time. "That's important. Don't let him pressure you into anything you might not be ready for. You don't have to do anything just because everyone else is doing it—remember that!"

"Oh my god, Mom." I sigh. "He's not like that, okay? He's—"

"This is just a really big step and I want you to be prepared," she says, and I'm about to just climb into the closet and lock myself in there and breathe into a paper bag when Dad shows up in the door.

"Linus is a good judge of character," he tells my mom. "Don't worry about him." I have no idea where he got that idea, but I'll take it. "Linus," he continues in my direction. "I found batteries, but I'm not sure about the light in the entryway and it's too dark to take the pictures outside, so if I set things up in the living room, do you think you guys have enough time for him to come in for a few minutes?"

My stomach drops. "Set—up . . . what—Dad, what are you setting up?"

My dad reaches around the door frame and waves a tripod at me. "I think the wall next to the fireplace would be a good backdrop. I'm just going to take down the pictures because those picture frames reflect the light from the ceiling lamp and—"

I hold up a hand to silence him. "Please," I manage. "Please don't take down any pictures. This isn't prom night or anything. Just—I think I'm just meeting him outside anyway."

Dad frowns and exchanges a look with Mom. "Are you sure?" Mom asks.

"I'd really like to meet him," Dad says.

I hide my face behind my hands and groan. "I'm just here to get changed," I plead, and they finally shuffle out of my room so I can continue panicking over my outfit. I'm glad that my parents are supportive, but the last thing I need is for them to scare him off before—well. Before I've had a chance to see where this all might go.

And I'm already nervous enough as it is.

I really didn't expect him to come up to the door and ring the bell and shake my parents' hands. It doesn't do much to make me feel less fluttery.

"You must be Danny," my mom says as she grins at him widely in a way that is so not subtle at all, and I just kind of want to disappear out of sheer embarrassment. "I've heard so much about you!"

"Hi, Mrs. Hanson," Danny says, then nods at my dad. "And Mr. Hanson. Nice to meet you."

"Nice to meet you, too," my dad assures him as he takes over the rather enthusiastic hand-shaking. "You boys going to see a movie?"

"Dad, I already told you that," I try to interfere, but Danny beams at him.

"Yes!"

"Oh, hey," my mom says. "Linus says you're Watson in the school play? We both can't wait to see it! We have tickets for tomorrow."

"I hope you like it," Danny says a little shyly. "I know I'm having fun with it. And Linus is a great Mr. Hudson. You could never tell he hasn't been onstage before."

"Oh, but he has," my dad chimes in. "Linus, have you forgotten?"

I just blink at him, a little lost, and my mom laughs.

"Oh, that's right. It was a preschool play! Some fairy tale, I think. Linus, you played a tree, don't you remember? We had to dress you up all in brown and green and you had that hat with the leaves on it? You were so proud of how well you could hold out your arms like branches for the whole scene—"

"Mom," I cut her off, blushing furiously. I really had forgotten about that. It's not like I can remember it well in the first place; I was four at the time.

"So you were a child actor. I had no idea." Danny bumps our shoulders together and my parents laugh with him, and even if this is a little embarrassing, their laughter makes me happy. I'm glad that they seem to get along, even if I can still see Dad hiding that camera behind his back.

My parents have known about me being gay for a long time now and they've always been fine with it in theory. And I know they love me. But they have never actually seen me act on it. They have never seen me with a boy. Because there has never been a boy to see me with until now.

But my mom seems to love him immediately and within a minute of them talking, it looks like my dad is about to adopt him on the spot.

We manage to get away eventually, without any photos being taken, and once in the car, I turn to him, shake my head. "What just happened back there?"

"Your parents are awesome," he answers happily.

"I didn't know you wanted to meet them."

"Oh! I'm sorry, should I not have? I mean, they seemed cool with you being—you know. Dating a boy and all that . . ."

"No, they're—that's not—it's fine," I assure him. "I just wasn't prepared for this."

"So we're okay?"

I nod. "We are always okay."

Even on a late Friday afternoon the small movie theater is never exactly crowded. We get seats in the back where no one can see us and I'm grateful for that; apparently my parents are absolutely okay with me going out with a boy, but I am still never quite sure what the rest of the world is going to think about it, and I don't want this night interrupted by people shouting mean things at us. I am determined to enjoy this, and so far, I am.

I manage to kind of focus on the movie even if I'm very aware the entire time that Danny is sitting next to me and that we're not here merely as friends and that I really have no clue what to do next.

If I were a slightly braver person, I might try to take his hand. But I'm afraid of my palms being sweaty and I'm even more afraid that he has maybe changed his mind about this and I'm going to make it awkward. So I sit in my seat and stare straight ahead and don't do anything. Every few minutes, I can feel him looking at me, though. I flicker my eyes back at him when I'm sure he has looked away and even in the dim lights of the movie theater he is still the cutest thing I have ever seen. Somehow he has made his hair extra spiky today and it is so adorable, I just want to touch it. But I don't. Luckily, I have more self-control than that.

Once the credits start rolling and the lights come back up, we walk out side by side and I can feel my levels of nervousness spiking, because as nerve-racking as this was already, now comes the part of the evening I have really been worried about. Now we have to sit over dinner and actually talk and I know that we have sat and talked a million times before. This is just different, okay?

Silence stretches between us as we walk out into the light of the foyer and I desperately try to think of something to say. But somehow, my mind is completely blank. Are there rules for appropriate topics you can talk about during a date? I'm torn between I have to be smart and witty and charming to win him over and just be yourself, he already asked you out, he obviously doesn't have a problem with the way your mind works! But seriously, all my brain comes up with as conversation prompters are random facts about the International Space Station and the documentary about humpback whales I saw the other day. My guess is that he probably doesn't want to talk about either of those things.

"Did you like the movie?" he asks.

I mentally kick myself because yes, that is a good way to start a conversation after just having seen a movie together! I could have thought of that and made an impression with my small-talk skills. But I guess the important thing is that we're talking at all.

"I did," I say, and it's true, it was nice. Even if I feel like I probably missed a lot because I was kind of focused on him sitting right there next to me the entire time. "What did you think?"

He shrugs, shoves his hands into his pockets, bumps our shoulders together. "I liked the company."

That makes me laugh. "You are ridiculous."

"Maybe. But I made you laugh, so I'm counting it as a win."

"I laugh all the time. Don't flatter yourself."

"You're so charming!" he says.

"I practiced in front of a mirror."

It's his turn to laugh and he nudges my arm again with his. "Now I am flattered that you went to all these lengths to prepare for our date tonight."

I tilt my head at him as we step out onto the street. "Who says I did it for you? Maybe that was all for the other boy I'm going on a date with after you drop me off at home."

"Well," he says determinedly. "Then I guess I have no choice but to keep you out as late as possible in order to prevent that from happening."

"What if I have a time machine?"

"Is it built into a DeLorean?"

I heave a sigh and shake my head at him. "Is there any other kind?"

And suddenly we are just talking, walking side by side to his car, and it's as easy and effortless as it always is. It makes me happy to realize that even with the circumstances of our social interaction somewhat changed, we can still get along easily enough. I'm still nervous. But this is also still Danny here with me, and I already know that he sort of likes me. It's mind-boggling and not something I can quite wrap my head around even now. But it still appears to be true and that makes me the luckiest guy in the world.

Dinner is at a small place not too far from the movie theater and since he called ahead and made a reservation, we get a table in the back that's a bit secluded from the rest of the room. I like that. Both the fact that he called ahead and the fact that not everyone can stare at us the entire time.

Conversation continues to flow easily enough even if he has to carry it pretty much alone for a few minutes once we are seated. The low lighting and soft music and the candle on the table and the single flower in a vase before us momentarily short-circuits my brain just a bit; the setting is undeniably romantic and if I had doubted even for a second before that this was not just two friends hanging out, I definitely have to believe it now: This is actually a date. I am actually on a date with the best and cutest and smartest guy I have ever met in my life. It's happening and it's not as good as I thought it would be—it's miles better! Because he's my friend and we like each other and it's easy whenever it's not paralyzingly frightening.

I've never been to this restaurant before because my family usually eats at home—both my parents love to cook. For a moment I'm nervous that I won't know anything on the menu and embarrass myself, but a quick glance assures me that I'm not completely out of my depth and my heart rate normalizes.

"I think I want pizza," Danny says.

I nod. "Pizza sounds good."

We order and once the waiter is gone, he props his chin up on one hand, blinks at me lazily across the table. "This is nice."

"Yeah," I breathe, clear my throat quickly. "It really is."

Even while we eat, I manage to not make a complete fool of myself. I don't spill anything, I don't knock over any glasses, I don't choke on my food. Not that I usually do these things a lot. I just get really clumsy when I'm nervous.

It's late by the time we leave the restaurant, but not that late. I don't have to be home for almost another two hours. My parents were generous with my curfew. And I don't want the night to end: I am having so much fun with him, and I'm not quite ready yet for my first-ever date to be over. But since I'm not quite sure how to say any of that or even if it would be okay to ask to spend a little more time together, I fall silent and just walk next to him in the direction of his car.

"Hey," he says after a long moment, and when I turn my head I find him already watching me.

"What?"

"Do you—I mean. I don't have to be home yet. Do you—?"

"No. Not for a while," I say.

"Would you like, um? It's cool if you want to go home, but if you don't have any other plans, we could—we could maybe talk? A bit more? Just—only if you want to. We could get some coffee or hot chocolate or whatever and . . ." He shrugs, bites his lip, and kicks up a little snow with his feet.

I lift my head and take in the scenery before me, the snow-covered sidewalks and icy street, the light from the streetlamps reflected soft and yellow off the shiny white surface of the snow. Thick flakes start falling again just at that moment and I turn my head up to greet them and smile and finally I have the best idea ever.

"Let's build a snow alien."

He blinks at me. "Is that like a snowman?"

I nod, bouncing a little on the heels of my feet with excitement. "It's exactly like a snowman, only you can get creative with it. Pointy ears, tentacles, whatever you like."

"That sounds great," he says. "Yes, let's do that!"

My parents are out on their own date night by now so I invite him back to my house and into my backyard, where we immediately set to work once I have retrieved two pairs of thick woolen gloves from inside. No need to freeze our fingers off, after all.

Together, we roll three huge snowballs and heave them on top of each other; the final result is almost as tall as I am myself and I'm already quite proud of our accomplishment. And then the fun part begins in which I form long pointy ears for our snowman to attach to either side of his head while Danny goes off in search of soft branches for arms. We give him eight arms. From the garden shed I retrieve the end of a leaf rake and we fix that to his chest as an armor plate. Because our snow alien is a superhero. I get a small plastic flowerpot from the cupboard on the porch that he gets as a snout, another soft twig becomes the mouth, and finally I run to get three round lumps of coal from the garage to use as eyes. Of course a snow alien has three eyes. Danny agrees with me.

Once we are done, we take a step back to admire our work. He looks absurd. He looks absolutely wonderful.

"I have to take a picture of this," Danny decides, tugging one glove off with his teeth to dig his phone from his jacket pocket, stepping back another foot to fit the entire glorious snow alien into his picture. He squints his eyes at the screen of his phone once the shutter has clicked, smiles. "Perfect."

"Can I see?" I want to know, and instead of turning the phone to show me, he presses our sides together, holding the screen so we can both watch it, his head tilted close to mine.

"Cute," I confirm, because I feel like I have to say something even if my heart is suddenly trying to hammer my ribs to pieces in my chest. It's cold out but he's close enough that I can feel how warm he is, and it's distracting. In a good way!

"We should take one of us, too," he says softly. "To commemorate this night."

"I, um, oh." I wince a little. I've just spent an hour running around in the snow and I know what that does to my skin; it's probably all red and splotchy and my hair is a mess and I'm not sure he really wants a picture of that.

"Come on," he says, and takes my gloved hand with his gloved hand, dragging me into the light of the porch lamp, which is quite bright if you stand right in the circle of light it projects.

"Are you sure?"

"I'll text you the picture. We need a memento!"

I'm absolutely certain I'll remember this night forever anyway, but I can't deny him anything. "If you really want a picture of me looking frozen solid," I joke.

He lifts an eyebrow, shifts me into position next to him. "What are you talking about—you look adorable!"

Before I can say anything else, he has slung an arm around my shoulders and I am being hugged from the side, and then his cheek is right there next to mine, his skin as cold as my own, but still the contact sends a shock of warmth through me. I hold my breath, do my best to smile as he holds his phone away from us, takes his picture.

I'm still not quite capable of speech as he checks how it turned out, stare at him with wide eyes as he grins widely at his screen.

"I'm having this framed," he says.

"Let me see that first," I insist.

He hands me his phone and I stare down at our two smiling faces and I—look really happy. Round-faced and with my cheeks and nose ridiculously red, but happy nonetheless.

"I like it," I say quietly.

He takes his phone back, slips it into his pocket, bites his lip as he lowers his eyes. "I like you."

"That's um. Good," I say, and gather all my courage. "Because I like you, too."

"Can I try something?" he asks, blinking up at me from under thick lashes.

"What?" I want to know.

"This" is all he says, and before I understand what is happening he has put both his hands on my cheeks, one gloved and one bare, and suddenly I am being kissed.

"Oh," I say, a little breathless when he pulls back a moment later.

He still has his hands on my face.

"Was that—was that all right?"

I swallow, think about it, manage to give a short, quick nod. My face feels warm even if it's still below freezing out here on the porch. "I was definitely not opposed to that. If that's what you mean."

"Then it was okay?"

"Yeah. Um. Yes. It was—"

"Can we do it again?"

I exhale heavily, feel my mouth curve into a smile. "Absolutely. If you want to. We can do that."

"I was hoping you'd say that," he whispers, grins, and then leans in again.

And no, I think as I finally muster the courage to wrap my arms around his back in a hug, I am definitely not opposed to this turn of events.

Chapter 57

Meg

I DON'T HAVE TO BE anywhere before later this afternoon for our last performance, so I actually take the time to sleep in on Saturday, exhausted after a long and emotionally draining week.

Mom is watching TV in the living room when I come downstairs; she's had a long week, too, and she's just sitting there wrapped in a robe and eating cereal from the box, giving me a bleary-eyed look when I enter the room.

"You look as awake as I feel," she says as a greeting.

I drop down next to her on the couch and let my head fall back against the backrest. "Ugh. Long week."

"I know."

I take the box from her to get a handful of cereal and check the TV screen while I chew. "Cartoons? How old are you?"

"Don't judge me. It's relaxing."

"I don't judge. Hey, no coffee?"

She sighs and shakes her head. "Too early to figure out how the machine works."

"Fine," I say. "I'll make some."

I get up and walk through to the kitchen, get the coffeemaker running, and then fish my phone out of my robe pocket to check my e-mail while I wait.

There's no new mail, but I do have a text, ten minutes old, and from Linus. I hold my breath, and suddenly my heart is pounding. I don't know what he could want, but we haven't really talked all week and I'm a little afraid that it won't be anything good.

The text simply says: *Good morning!*

I hesitate. Has he just texted the wrong contact? But what if he did mean me? Then it would be really rude not to text back and probably not help to mend fences between us. So I muster up all of my courage and text back: *Good morning to you too.*

I wait, the coffeemaker gurgling away next to me on the counter. It doesn't even take a minute before my phone beeps with a response.

Are you doing anything today?

Just the play, I write back. *Otherwise no, nothing.* This is good, right? That he asks?

Can we talk? he writes. *I think we need to.*

I'm not sure at all that I'm ready for this because it's still possible that all he wants is to tell me that he never wants to see me again. But yeah, I can't really take this uncertainty anymore.

Of course. Do you want to come over before the play?

I'll be there at three, he texts me. *Do you want me to bring cookies?*

I could almost cry with relief. I've missed him so much. And if he wants to bring cookies, then chances are that he's not coming over to end our friendship. I really hope that this is good news.

Chapter 58

Linus

WE HAVE OUR LAST PERFORMANCE today and I've never been less nervous about going onstage. I am, however, a little bit nervous about talking to Meg this afternoon. But there's no way around it; we simply need to have this conversation. And I don't want to wait any longer. Exciting things are happening in my life and I want to share them with my best friend.

I hope she's still my best friend!

Exams are over and the holidays are about to start so I don't have any studying to do, and no homework for once. Which means I have the morning completely to myself.

I text with Meg and then I have nothing to do for several hours. That's not really something that happens to me a lot.

Whenever I had nothing to do over the summer, I usually went to the coffee shop to catch a glimpse of Danny. I don't really have to do that anymore now, which is a thought that makes me almost laugh out loud because it still seems so unreal. I'm so surprised that this is something that actually happened to me. It's a good feeling, though.

And, now that I think about it, I still can go to the coffee shop to catch a glimpse of him anyway, can't I? Because it just so happens that he's working a half shift this morning.

"Mom?" I call into the living room as I'm walking down the hall to get my shoes. "I'm going out for a bit. I'll be back in half an hour. Can I have the car?"

"Sure," she calls back. "Where are you off to?"

"Just have a craving for some caramel macchiato," I explain.

I can hear her laughing. She knows why I really want to go to the coffee shop. Well, I can't blame her. I've been talking about nothing but Danny since last night.

I drive carefully because I hate driving in the snow, and when I pull up into the coffee shop's parking lot I can already see him standing there behind the counter. My heart jumps happily in my chest and I hurry to get out of the car, locking it behind me as I slip and slide my way across the icy walkway.

The way his face lights up when our eyes meet is all the reward I need for braving the snowy weather out there.

"Linus!" he says happily.

"Hi," I say back, and walk up to the counter. The shop is as good as empty, and his coworker is very politely ignoring us, smirking as if she knows exactly what's going on.

Well, and then she definitely knows what's going on as I reach the counter and Danny leans over it to quickly kiss me hello. "Good morning," he says softly.

I can't stop grinning. "It's a very good morning," I agree.

He touches my hand and I'm just about ready to faint with happiness. "Let me guess," he says. "Caramel macchiato?"

"You know me well."

"I think I'm starting to," he says, and looks very pleased about it.

I wait as he works on my drink and we chat about the performance later today and the party at Stella's house afterward. I'm excited about the party. Not only is it going to be my first party ever, I'm also going with my boyfriend. Ask me how much I never thought this would ever be my life.

Danny turns his back as he busies himself doing something to my drink that I can't see, and I take the time to quickly check my phone. I'm still a little worried that Meg will back out of meeting up with me later.

When Danny turns back to me and puts the coffee down in front of me, he looks kind of proud and a little nervous. "There you go. Especially made for you."

I look down at the steamed milk foam crowning the top of my coffee and I feel my eyes widen. "I didn't know you were into espresso art."

"Just a little something I've been experimenting with," he says, and blushes adorably.

I tilt my head at the picture drawn on my coffee. It's a smiley face with two long sticks on top of its head. "Thank you," I say. "This is so cute."

Danny lowers his eyes a little, the tips of his fingers on the counter nudging against mine. "It's supposed to be an alien. That's why he has those antennae on his head. It's lame, I know, but—"

"Oh my god," I gasp, and I just have to laugh now. No one has ever done anything like this for me before. "Thank you!"

"You like it?"

"I love it."

He takes my hand in his again and I hold on tight and can't look away. How did I get this lucky?

Chapter 59

I HAVE THE COFFEE READY by the time I see his mom's car pull into the driveway out the kitchen window, his short and sturdy frame emerging from the driver's side door.

He hugs me hello by the door and I take that as a good sign—he can't be too mad at me if he's still willing to hug me.

"Coffee?" I ask.

He rolls his eyes at me, hands me the box of cookies he brought. "Do you even have to ask?"

We settle in the living room, he on the couch and me on my mom's big, comfy armchair. I push the cookies toward him across the coffee table, then lean back and clear my throat.

"So."

"So," he echoes.

"I guess we should—talk?"

He nods. "I guess we should. Yes."

"I'm sorry," I say. "I know I owe you an apology. And I've wanted to talk to you all week, but I just didn't know how."

"Yes," he says. "Same here. I'm so sorry, Meg. I never meant to go behind your back. I wanted to tell you, but I didn't want to hurt you. That obviously didn't work out so well."

"It's okay," I promise. Because honestly, I just want this behind us.

"It's not," he argues. "I shouldn't have done it. Or at least—I should have told you. You have every right to be mad at me."

But suddenly, sitting here and drinking coffee together and seeing him look so serious and so sad and a little afraid, I just . . . don't have any anger left in me. I believe him when he says he didn't know how to tell me. And I know he would never have just ignored Sophia if she contacted him. That's just not something he could ever do. Linus has to be nice to everyone. "I'm not mad," I say. "But maybe you should be mad at me."

"For the drama club stuff?" He shakes his head. "I was, at first. But— you know, maybe you were right. Maybe taking risks is a good thing sometimes. And it kind of worked out well for me, in the end."

I lift my shoulders, opening and closing my mouth while I search for the right words. "It's not just that," I explain. "Well, it is, but it's more like—I was using you. I was deciding for you, I was making assumptions about what's best for you, and that's not okay. And for that I am really, deeply sorry. And all that stuff I said to you last Saturday—I didn't mean it. I'm so, so sorry."

"Thank you," he says. "It means a lot that you're saying that. And I know you were trying to be nice. And hey, after all, it's not like I'm not enjoying spending time with Danny!" He blushes furiously and lowers his eyes.

I sigh. I really just want to get the air cleared between us. This is important. I need him to understand how much I mean this. "I kept bailing on you. I promised we'd drive home together and disappeared. I ditched you during lunch. And all that stuff I said to you—I have no excuse. That was so not okay. You know I didn't mean it, right? I don't know what was wrong with me that day. A good friend wouldn't do that."

"Well, apparently they would," he disagrees. "Because you're my best friend, and you did do all of that."

"You know that's not what I mean."

"I was mad at you, it's true," he concedes. "But—I do know you, Meg. And I know you would never hurt me on purpose. You were going through a tough time."

"That's not an excuse."

"No. It's not. But you were pretty mad at me about the Sophia stuff," he points out. "I have no excuse for that, either."

"Well, I mean. Now we're even. That's good, right?"

"Yeah, I don't know about that." He drinks some coffee, frowns. "I know it seems that way, but do you think that's how friendship is really supposed to work? You hurt me, I hurt you back, and then we move on? Because that's not us, Meg. I don't want that to be us. And I don't want us to be even. I don't want us to need that. And I didn't talk to Sophia to get back at you for pushing me to talk to Danny. Because I know you didn't try setting me up with Danny to be mean to me, but also because I don't believe that hurting you back would fix anything if that had been the case."

"I definitely didn't want to be mean to you," I confirm. "Definitely not! I just—"

"You pretended to know my own life better than I did."

"Yes. But I didn't want to be condescending. And I didn't mean to go crazy. I don't know what happened. It seemed like a good idea at the time. A harmless distraction."

Linus nods thoughtfully. "And how do you feel now? Do you still want to be distracted?"

It seems to be a valid question and I take a moment to really think about it. It's like I've been carrying this weight of sadness around with me for so long, but . . . I think it's gotten lighter without me noticing. I still feel a little sad, but this sadness is about what happened with Linus, not about what happened with Sophia.

"I'm okay," I say, lifting a hand before he can interrupt. I know I've been using these words very liberally lately. "No, really. I am. I'm— I'm better. I'm just sorry that I hurt you. And I'm sorry about the way I dealt with being sad."

Linus smiles at me. "Look, you were right," he says. "It was harmless. Well, the drama club thing could have been seriously disastrous, but . . . you might have pushed me a bit more than was comfortable but I still didn't have to audition. It was my choice in the end. And I actually had fun. But the thing is, I don't think you did."

I shake my head. "I'm glad I joined drama club. I am. Even if I was pretty miserable for most of it. I think I would have been miserable either way, you know? That wasn't only the club's fault. And this way, at least good things happened for you, and I'm glad about that. And also, I'm still sorry. I only meant to help, I swear."

"So did I."

"We both just wanted to help each other out, huh?" I take a cookie, start picking out the chocolate chips. "We went about it in a really clumsy sort of way. And I was the one who went crazy. Not you."

"You did make me hang out with Danny more. And . . . well. Um. That was . . . good." He blushes again and bites his lip.

I think about it. "I guess—" I eat a chocolate chip and shrug at him. "I guess there is a really fine line between helping someone and sticking your nose where it doesn't belong."

"Seems that way." He grins at me over his coffee cup and I grin back.

"I promise to never do it again."

He puts down his mug, beams at me. "And I promise to be honest with you. Always."

"Okay."

"Speaking of honest—" He lowers his eyes again, and his smile is so wide he barely gets the next words out. "Danny and I, uh."

I sit up a little straighter. "What about Danny and you?"

"We . . ." He sighs, shrugs, laughs adorably. "He asked me out."

"Oh my god!" I bounce a little in my seat. "I knew it. Oh my god. This is so exciting! When are you going out with him?"

"In fact," he says, "we already did. Last night. We saw a movie and he took me to dinner, and, and . . ."

"And?" I prompt, leaning forward in my seat; I can barely contain my joy at hearing this. I was right all along!

Linus sucks in a breath, eyes finally flickering up to meet mine, and he looks so happy. "He kissed me."

I squeal loudly and jump from my seat to throw my arms around him in a tight hug, almost causing both of us to topple over onto the floor. "Finally! This is so great!"

He laughs and hugs me back, his face red like a fire truck when I pull back. "It's pretty great, yeah."

"You have a boyfriend," I say proudly.

He nods and smiles and puts both hands over his face. "I guess I do. I can't quite believe it yet."

"I can," I tell him, and I absolutely mean it.

Linus and I drive over to the school together and walk side by side to the auditorium. I'm really happy that we're at least doing this final performance as best friends. This is how it should have been the entire time.

We hug before I send him off to get ready with the rest of the actors while I go backstage to help Alyssa set things up for the first scene and check the lights and the props and get everything in order. Today, I'm enjoying this. More than I ever thought possible. It feels important. I'm contributing and I'm kind of even making new friends along the way.

"What's going on there?" Alyssa asks, suddenly appearing next to me and bumping our shoulders together conspiratorially, nodding toward the entryway where the actors are slowly trickling in for their obligatory show circle in which they always include us nonactors. Two of them are hanging back, however, hands linked between them, talking with their heads close together, big smiles on their faces. Danny and Linus.

"Oh," I say happily. "Yeah, that's apparently finally happening now."

"Oh thank god," Alyssa groans. "I was about to staple them together by the forehead until they stopped being stupid."

I nudge her arm with mine, grinning. "I thought you weren't sure about Danny."

She rolls her eyes. "I wasn't, until you brought it up. After that it took me about half an hour to notice it, too, and then I just felt stupid for not seeing it earlier. I'm glad they finally came to their senses."

"I know, right?" I say happily, and let her help me push the sofa on-stage so that the setting for the first scene is complete. I'm not about to reveal my dubious part in their matchmaking. I'm just glad that's all behind us now.

We join everyone else for the show circle as soon as we're done and then it's almost time—our final performance of our first-ever drama club play.

Our backstage team is a well-oiled machine by now and I actually get to observe quite a bit of the performance while I hand people their props and help Stella change her costume a few times. There's going to be a DVD of the production, but seeing it live is different—better, I think. Also, Linus is just great, and I'm quite sure no one except me sees it but I'm having a lot of fun observing the sneaky looks exchanged between Watson and Mr. Hudson. For me, it's the best part of this particular performance.

Chapter 60

Linus

THE LAST PERFORMANCE IS A lot of fun and goes really well and I'm definitely enjoying it more now that I've made up with Meg. I'm so glad that we're still friends.

I only spot Sophia in the crowd once the show is over and I'm leaving the auditorium to meet my parents out in the hall so they can hug me and go home before I leave for the after-party with everyone.

She's standing a little off to the side, already surrounded by various other drama club people who still know her from last year, and for just a second I hesitate. But she has already seen me and she looks as unsure as I feel and . . . I can't just walk away.

So I walk over, doing my best to not look too nervous.

"Linus," she calls out to me. "It's so good to see you."

"It's good to see you, too," I say, and let her hug me. "What are you doing here?"

"My exams were early so I'm home for Christmas vacation already. And . . . I just wanted to see the play."

"Oh. Did you like it?"

"It was awesome. You were great."

"Thank you!"

"And your guy is really cute, too."

"I, uh." I let out a nervous little laugh. "Yeah. He is. Um. He and I—we're—"

Her face lights up. "Wait, what? Really?"

I nod. "Really."

"I'm so happy for you," she exclaims, and hugs me again.

"Thanks."

"Uh," she hesitates. "I was—I was actually invited to the after-party just now. But . . . do you know where Meg is? I don't really want to go without making sure it's okay with her. This is your thing now; I don't want to make everything super awkward."

"Yeah, that's—" I look around, glad that she brought it up. "I don't know where she—oh, there she is," I say as I see her exiting the auditorium right at that moment. "Hold on—"

I hurry toward her but I can see from her face that she's already seen who I was just talking to. She looks . . . not angry, but definitely shocked.

"I didn't know she would be here," I say as soon as I reach her. "She just wanted to see the play."

"It's fine."

"I mean, she still has friends in the club and she wanted to see them, and—"

"Of course she did. I was actually kind of expecting her to show up eventually." She sighs.

"They invited her to the after-party," I say. "But she says she won't go if you don't want her to."

Meg looks at me, and she's pale but I recognize the determined look on her face. "No, she should come."

"Are you sure?"

"I don't want to spoil everyone's fun. She's their friend. She's allowed to hang out with them."

"Will you still come along, too?" I want to know. "Because I won't go if you won't. You're not going to hang out by yourself tonight."

"You're my favorite friend," she says, smiling at me. "I'm okay, Linus. Really. We can all go. It'll be fun. I won't even have to talk to her. There are enough people going, right? We can all just . . . stay respectfully away from each other."

I smile back at her and nod, and I'm not sure whether she's as fine as she says she is or just putting on a brave front, but all I can do is trust her judgment on this. "Okay. If you're sure."

"I am. Just—can you tell her? I don't want to—"

"Yes, of course," I promise. "I'll let her know. And then I just have to find my parents and then we can go, okay?"

"I'll find your parents for you and bring them over here," she offers. "They're probably with my mom anyway."

"Deal," I say, and walk back to Sophia to relay the message.

The party is at Stella's house and all the drama club kids are there. All of my new friends, and my best friend, and—drumroll, please—my boyfriend.

Because Danny is officially my boyfriend now, and it's a little too good to be true, but still. It is true. I have a boyfriend.

We will still study together and have coffee together and he will still drive me around in his battered old rust bucket that he calls a car.

But now he also holds my hand when we sit next to each other and he kisses me and he tells me I'm cute, which I'm still not used to hearing. I mean, it's only been a day. However, in that one day he has also managed to mention that I'm hot, which just made me laugh in his face, but hey, if he wants to think that, then I'm not complaining. Maybe I'll get used to the compliments eventually.

Tonight we're all sitting around Stella's parents' living room, having a *Star Wars* marathon (original trilogy), which apparently counts as an after-party, and there's pizza and cookies and tea and it's all very cozy and peaceful and so, so different than I imagined a party to be. I like it.

We don't all fit on the couch so we're scattered across the floor. I'm sitting with my back to the couch and I have a wonderful, kind, good-looking boy attached to me firmly with his arms around my middle and his head cushioned on my shoulder. I rest my cheek against his spiky hair, which he is wearing less spiky specifically for this occasion, and sigh happily.

Does life get any better than this?

"You suggested the movies, didn't you?" he whispers to me, and I turn my head to look down at him.

He still looks cute even in extreme close-up like this. "I might have," I tell him.

He grins and kisses me, says, "You're amazing," and cuddles back into my side.

I can't imagine a better way to celebrate.

Chapter 61

Meg

LINUS AND DANNY ARE ADORABLE together. I'm relieved that I was right about that and that they are both still talking to me. I know what I did was a little much, but hey, they're happy. I'm happy. We're all happy, and there is really nothing better than that.

"Does anyone want more popcorn?" Stella asks, lifting the bowl and waving it around the room.

"Sure," Katie says, grabbing for it. "Want me to make some? You have those bag things for the microwave, right?"

"I can do it," I volunteer, snatching the bowl from Stella before Katie can get it. I feel like I should contribute a bit to the evening if I really do want to be a part of this group.

"Thanks," Stella says. "Top drawer next to the fridge. Come get me if you can't figure out the microwave."

I wave at her and struggle to my feet; I'm sure I can figure out how the microwave works.

Feeling finally like a real part of this community, I make my way to the kitchen to get a new bag of popcorn. These people are awesome. And it doesn't even really matter that Sophia is here, I tell myself. She's staying out of my way, talking to her old friends, and if this is all I have to endure for the evening, I can absolutely do it, I can—

"Meg?" a voice behind me speaks up, a voice I haven't heard in months.

I swallow, turn slowly, not sure what I want to happen next. "Sophia. Hi."

"I thought. Um. Sorry if this is weird. I can leave. I just thought— I thought we could use a moment alone together."

"Um." I cross my arms as she steps farther into the kitchen and try to come up with something to say. "We have talked. Even though you were apparently talking to my best friend already at that point."

"Yeah. I'm really sorry about that. I was hoping we could have an actual conversation? About all of that?"

I can't keep myself from laughing out loud. "You dumped me, moved away, and then used Linus to—what, spy on me behind my back? And so far, I don't have an explanation for any of it. I have no clue what happened and you have made no effort to explain any of it to me. And—I don't know, Sophia. I thought—even if we're over, am I not at least worth an explanation?"

She stares down at her hands. Silence stretches for several moments before she lowers her head further, sighs. "You're right. I wasn't being fair to you. I wasn't being fair to either of us, but I should have—I could have explained. I could have talked to you, I—Meg, can we maybe step outside for a moment? I think we should—I'll explain. If that's what you want. Just, can we go somewhere no one will walk in on us?"

"We're at a party."

"I know. Sorry. I know. We can—let's talk some other time; we can—"

"No." The microwave dings behind me and I open it to snatch the bag out, reach for the bowl on the counter to refill it. "Let's talk now. I'll just bring this back to the others and then we can—I don't know, front porch?"

"Okay."

It's not a conversation I particularly want to have right now, but on the other hand, I'm not sure I'm going to be able to enjoy the rest of the night with this hanging over us. Better to just get it over and done with.

She meets me out on the front porch once I've handed the popcorn over to Malik, who was making grabby hands for it when I entered the living room. I mumbled something about having to make a quick phone call, just took a second to grin at Danny and Linus, who were holding hands and looking more at each other than at the screen, and then slipped out.

And there she is, sitting on the front steps, never taking her eyes off of me as I sit down next to her on the cold steps. This is really not the time of year to be sitting outside for too long.

"Okay," I say. "You wanted to talk. So talk."

She nods. "I made a mistake, Meg. I'm sorry. I screwed up. And I know I can't just—fix it. I know that's not how it works. But I want you to know—" She looks back up at me, and her face is serious. "I regretted it before I was even all the way out the door. You have to believe me."

"What did you regret? Breaking up with me?"

"Yes."

"Then why did you do it? I have tried and tried to understand it. For months now. And I still don't—I didn't even see it coming, you know?"

"I know. I—didn't, either. Does that sound crazy?"

"Yeah, it does. You were the one to dump me."

"It seemed like the best thing to do at the time. It wasn't—I didn't think it through. I just wanted what was best for the both of us."

"You mean you wanted what was best for you!"

"No!" She looks actually shocked. "If that had been the case, I would never have broken up with you! Never!"

"I can't really say that I understand this," I admit. "If you didn't do it for you, then—"

"I thought you'd be better off," she says quickly, then sighs, rubs a hand over her face. She looks tired. "Maybe that was stupid. But I just wanted—I just wanted you to be happy."

"That makes no sense. None. At all. Sorry."

"I know. And no matter what I say, it's going to sound like an excuse. I can't change that. But I want you to know that I regret it. For whatever that's worth. I wish I hadn't done it. I—" She closes her eyes, swallows. "I miss you."

"You wouldn't have to miss me if you hadn't dumped me."

"I know that. I know. But I'd still be away at college and . . . I thought it would be better this way."

"How did you think it was what I wanted?"

"I thought—" She shrugs. "I was going to move away and we'd be hours apart. There was no way we could still see each other all the time; it would all be so difficult."

"We had plans for that. We were going to alternate visits, every other weekend. And there's Skype. And texting. And e-mail. And phone calls. And next year I was going to join you in—"

"But that's the thing," she interrupts me. "You were going to give up all this time to talk to me and to spend time with me. We wouldn't just be able to do our homework together or nap together or just have a random hug in the third-floor corridor between classes. It would have taken so much time and effort."

"And I was absolutely willing to put in that time and effort. And you know that. I wanted to do it for you, for us, and it was only a year and then I'd have—"

"You were going to go to my college," she says. "Even that was determined by us being together. I was going to keep you from your studies and then you were going to follow me to my college. Which has a great arts department, but is that what you want? When you could be doing anything, Meg? Anything at all? It was only going to hold you back! Your strengths are not my strengths. And you weren't even going to try getting into all those amazing places that could teach you so much more?"

"If you had wanted me to pick a different college, why didn't you just say so?"

"It's not even about that. It's not about me wanting things. Because honestly? I wanted you to follow me. Of course I did! I couldn't stand the thought of a year apart. But the thought of making it five years or more? It killed me."

"So instead of separating us for a few years, you split us up for good."

"Everyone always says it's like ripping off a Band-Aid, right? Get it over with and then start recovering."

"Oh yeah? How is that working out for you?" I raise an eyebrow at her.

"I really messed everything up, didn't I?"

I nod. "Yes, you did. You should have talked to me about your concerns. Maybe we could have figured something out. Instead you just went ahead and made the decision for me."

"The same way you made the decision that Danny and Linus should be together?"

"Hey, that was different!"

"Was it, though?"

"I don't know. Maybe not. I really can't tell anymore. I don't know. But it worked out between them, didn't it?"

"I really do miss you, Meg."

And there it is, the thing I have been wanting to hear for months. And now that I have heard it, I'm just not sure what to do with it anymore. I'm not sure what it means. I miss her, too. There is no use denying that. I miss her every single day, so much I have to make an effort not to think about her every minute. But it's been a long few months since we last saw each other and a lot of things have changed.

"So where does that leave us?" I ask.

"Do you ever miss me?"

"Of course I do. I love you."

"I love you, too," she tells me, and it doesn't feel like it used to, to hear those words, just like it doesn't feel like it used to, to say those words. It used to make me so happy. But now I'm just not sure anymore what it even means.

"We can't just go back," I decide. "That's not—I don't want that."

"But we can't go back to not talking, either," she says. "I mean, we always seem to end up talking to each other again anyway."

"We could make a conscious effort," I suggest. "If we both agreed. I could delete your number and you could delete mine. I could block your e-mail. If we wanted to, we could establish complete radio silence. At least for a while. Or even for good, if that is what you wanted."

She pauses. "Is that what you want?"

"I asked you first."

"That's not fair."

"Yes, it is. You started this. You owe me this. Tell me what you want, and then we can go from there."

"I—" She wraps both hands around her knees, blinks down at the snow-covered ground. "I can't stand not talking to you. I don't think we can just disappear from each other's lives like this."

I honestly hadn't known what I wanted, but the relief I feel at her answer tells me that I probably had been hoping for something like this.

"So, we keep talking?"

"Are you okay with that?"

I don't know. I just don't know. But it seems better than any alternative. Because she's sitting there across from me and after everything that has happened, she is still the same Sophia I know so well. My Sophia. And I know that things have changed, but does that have to mean that everything has to be over?

"We could just—" I shrug. "We could just text and e-mail and chat. Maybe call each other. I don't know. We could try being friends. Would you like to try that?"

"I think I really would," she says. "If you would."

"It was my idea."

She smiles and bumps our shoulders together. "Thank you."

"That's what friends are for," I say, and . . . this is weird. It's weird sitting here with her and not wanting to kiss her. But maybe in time this can be our new thing. Meg and Sophia, best friends forever. Maybe we can actually make that work, at least. I like the thought.

"You know," she says, "that scene on *Buffy*? When Willow and Oz break up. And she says that stuff about how when she'll be old and blue-haired and turning a corner and he's there, she won't be surprised?"

"Do you think that could be us?" I say, leaning against her a little.

She stares at her knees, shrugs. "I'd like that. I just—I'd really like that."

"Me, too," I assure her, and I really do mean it. I know, deep down, that it's really over now. Only a few months late, but I guess we finally did have our breakup talk. And . . . I'm okay. I have a house full of friends waiting for me to get back to them. Which doesn't mean I won't miss her anymore. But, I don't even know why, I feel better now.

Back inside, she goes to rejoin her friends and I wink at Linus, who looks rather adorably flustered with Danny all cuddled up to him like that. I'm so happy for him.

I sit down in an empty space on the floor and can't really decide between focusing on the movie or joining the conversation going on next to me. It's Stella, Katie, and Alyssa discussing who's hotter, Han Solo or Princess Leia. I like hearing that Alyssa is rather vehemently arguing in favor of Carrie Fisher. I've had my suspicions about her for a while, but this makes me grin.

"Hey," she says, as if she'd been able to tell that I was just thinking about her.

"Huh?" I provide eloquently.

"I was just getting another soda. Do you want me to bring you anything?" she asks, and there's just something in the way she smiles at me.

I smile back and nod. "Oh, yeah, soda would be great. Thank you!"

"Coming right up," she says, and squeezes my shoulder a little as she gets up.

I can't stop smiling as I decide to join the conversation.

Chapter 62

Linus

I SCOOT OVER TO WHERE Meg is sitting when Danny goes to get us drinks. I saw her sneak outside with Sophia earlier, and she seems okay, but I just want to make sure.

"The movie was your choice, wasn't it?" she says as soon as I'm close enough.

I laugh. "I merely suggested it."

"This is really nice, though."

"It is. Um, so, you're having fun?"

She looks at me like she knows exactly what I'm doing and rolls her eyes a little. "I'm fine. I promise." She sounds sincere.

"You talked to her?"

"I did. It was—good."

"Good."

"Your boyfriend's gonna miss you," she points out, and grins.

I can't help but grin, too. My boyfriend. "He's gonna be back any second, he's just—"

Danny chooses that exact moment to come back, sitting down on the carpet next to me, and with him is Alyssa, who sits down in the empty spot next to Meg and hands her a paper cup.

"There you go," she says, and she has this really wide smile on her face and she's blushing a little and Meg makes eye contact with her, and . . .

I look over at Danny, who looks back at me, and I can tell that we're thinking the same thing. Instead of saying anything, he hands me my own paper cup.

"Thanks," I say.

He leans in and kisses me, right here in front of everyone, and I can feel my ears burning a little. "You're welcome," he says, and takes my hand.

Chapter 63

WE ALL TURN OUR ATTENTION back to the movie, fresh drinks in hand, surrounded by friends. It feels good. We accomplished something, all of us together. Not just putting on that play but also forming this group of people who get along well enough to want to keep hanging out once it's over.

Sophia smiles at me from across the room and I smile back at her. I can do that now. It feels okay to do that now.

Linus leans over to me, whispers, "Are you happy?"

I nod. "Yeah," I say. "I am."

"Good," he says, and I can tell from the way he holds himself, the way he leans back into Danny's side so comfortably, that he's having a really good time, too.

And to think that this school year started off so badly.

Countless books and movies keep promising that things will get better even when they seem hopeless. And you know what? I guess they're mostly right.

In any case, I'm having a good night. Sophia and I are over, but I still have all of this, all the people in this room.

And, I think, maybe now I'm finally ready to start something new with all of them by my side.

Chapter 64

Linus

IT'S THE FIRST DAY OF winter break and we're seriously behind on our *Star Trek* marathon. So I go over to Meg's house around lunchtime, bringing a box of cookies. She promised to order pizza.

"Hey," she greets when she opens the door, and she's even wearing her Starfleet Academy sweater, red hair pulled back into a ponytail. "Pizza should be here in half an hour, and Mom is at work all day so we have the living room to ourselves."

"Awesome." I hug her hello and then hurry to get inside and close the door behind us, because as pretty as all the snow is, it's really cold outside. "That means we can finally make a real dent in that rewatch list!"

"Yeah." She leads the way into the living room once I've toed my shoes off by the door. "It's about time, isn't it? At least if we want to finish before we start college."

I laugh. "Well, we have the rest of winter break, too."

She hops onto the couch and snatches the remote off the coffee table, tilts her head as she looks up at me. "True, but you'll be hanging out with Danny some of the time, right?"

I walk over and drop onto the couch next to her, lifting my shoulders in a shrug. "I guess," I say. "Some of the time. Yeah." I mean, he is my boyfriend. I'm looking forward to spending some alone time with him. But of course I'm gonna be hanging out with Meg, too.

"Good," she says. "After everything I've done for you two." She grins. "You better not be spending every afternoon on my couch after I put in all of that work. Hours and hours of it."

"I knew you were just trying to get rid of me," I tell her, pouting. "This is what I get in return for years of friendship."

"No. What you get is pizza," she says, pressing the button on the remote to start up the DVD menu. "I even ordered pineapple."

I shake my head. "Doesn't count. I brought cookies in exchange for that."

"No, the cookies are in exchange for the coffee," she says.

I look around, lifting my hands at her. "What coffee? I don't see any coffee."

"The coffee I'm going to make for us later if you behave now."

"Ha." I give her a challenging grin. "Are you actually saying right now that if I don't behave, you won't make coffee later? Because then you won't have any coffee, either. I don't think that's likely."

"Obviously I'm still going to make coffee," she says, and smiles at me. "But only for myself."

"You would never do that to me," I point out, and she laughs, leans over to bump our shoulders together.

"You're right," she says. "I would never do that to you."

Chapter 65

Meg

WE'VE FINISHED OUR PIZZA AND I've started a pot of coffee when my phone buzzes on the coffee table and I quickly pick it up while Linus is changing the DVD in the DVD player.

I unlock the screen and read my new text. "Alyssa wants to know if we want to go bowling with the rest of them tonight," I tell Linus.

He looks up at me and nods. "Yeah, I know. Danny texted me while you were in the kitchen. I was just going to ask you."

I raise both eyebrows at him. "Well? Do you want to go?"

He shrugs. "I don't know. I guess. Bowling's kind of fun."

"I've never really been," I admit, and just then my phone buzzes again with another text from Alyssa, who apparently really wants us to come along.

"Alyssa again?" Linus asks, and the smirk he's wearing is way too transparent.

"Yes," I say, and roll my eyes at him. "We're friends."

"Sure you are."

"Hey," I say. "Quit it with the meddling. I think we've established that it doesn't work for us."

He laughs and walks back over to the couch, sits down next to me. "Fine. You're right. Okay. So. Do you want to go bowling tonight?"

I nod. "Yeah. I think I do. If it's okay with you."

"It's very okay with me," he says. "I'm just gonna text Danny, okay?"

"Yeah, I should really text Alyssa, too," I say.

Alyssa has been texting on and off for the past few days and she's really nice—I think we're becoming really good friends. I like that thought. I'm kind of interested to see where it goes. Because . . . it might be going somewhere, and that thought no longer scares me. I guess I'm finally moving on, and it feels good.

"Okay," Linus says once he's done texting his boyfriend, and we put our phones down on the table side by side. "We have four more hours for our rewatch today. Let's do this!"

"Four more hours today, and then several dozen more over the rest of the break," I correct him.

"Well, of course." He nods. "And, oh, by the way, I was thinking. Once we're through with this one, let's take one weekend, all three *Lord of the Rings* movies, extended editions, and buckets full of sugar and coffee?"

I clap my hands I'm so excited about the idea. "That sounds amazing. Yes! I always wanted to do that!"

"Yay! Fantastic!"

I hesitate, but I just feel like I should ask. "We could—if you want to, we can invite the rest of the drama club people? Or just some of them?"

He seems to think about it for a second, then shakes his head. "Nah. This is kind of our thing, isn't it? We can go bowling with them afterward. We might need the exercise after sitting through all those movies."

I grin at him. "That sounds like a plan."

"We're good at planning," he says.

"Yeah," I say. "We're really good at that."

He bites his lip and I can tell he wants to say something else, so I don't start the episode just yet and patiently wait him out instead.

"Can I tell you something really sappy, and will you promise not to laugh at me if I do?" he finally asks.

I give him a look. "No. I'm absolutely going to laugh at you. But you can still tell me."

He huffs out a breath, then gives me an earnest smile. "I really missed you, Meg. Although right now, I'm desperately trying to remember why."

"Aw." I press one hand over my heart and blink at him. "You're right. That was incredibly sappy!"

"Okay, I know! Shut up."

"Absolutely not. Having lunch without me for a few weeks must have been so difficult for you! You can talk to me about it!"

"Don't be a jerk!" He grins a little crookedly. "You made me go bowling with a bunch of strangers all by myself!"

I gently hit his arm with the remote. "Yeah, but you got a boyfriend out of that! My sacrifice was so worth it!"

"Your sacrif—" He breaks off, shakes his head, and buries his face in his palms with a groan. "Forget it. I take it back. I didn't miss you at all. In fact, you skipping out on me all the time was a very welcome change!"

"No! You can't take it back," I inform him. "You missed me! You were sad and lonely without me!"

"I have no idea why I ever said anything like that."

"Well, I have no idea, either, but you did say it. It's out there now!"

He sighs and gives me a long, exasperated look, and it makes me laugh. He was always good at making me laugh. I lean over and give him a long hug from the side, and I know he understands what I'm trying to say.

"Yeah," he tells me, patting my elbow. "You're still my best friend, too."

I smile and briefly tighten my arms around his shoulders.

Yeah. He always does get what I'm trying to say.

Acknowledgments

Writing may seem like a solitary activity, but it's certainly taken a lot of people to make this story into a book.

First of all: Swoon Reads. Thank you so much for giving me this chance and for making my lifelong dream a reality. My editor Christine Barcellona is a superhero. If editing were a recognized superpower, she'd definitely need a cape. All of my thanks also go to Jean Feiwel, Lauren Scobell, Liz Dresner, Melinda Ackell, Raymond Ernesto Colón, Ashley Woodfolk, Kelsey Marrujo, Emily Settle, Teresa Ferraiolo, Emily Petrick, Janea Brachfeld, Kristie Radwilowicz, Claire Taylor, Kelly McGauley, and Helen Bray. This book wouldn't exist without you, and I'm pretty excited that it does exist, so you're all my heroes.

I'd also like to thank my family—my parents and grandparents, who put up with all of my stories when I was a kid, and my siblings, who at least pretended to not be too surprised when I told them I'd written a book.

I'm so lucky with my friends and beta readers. So many thanks first and foremost to Rachel Schaffer for always staying my friend even when I go into writing mode; she always manages to be interested in my novella-length e-mails, and even has enough patience left for brainstorming and reading my drafts. The same goes for Emily Murphy for all the comments and all the listening and all the support. Both of them put so many hours of help into this when they could have been reading finished books instead.

There's Beckie Laskey, who agreed to read this even though she knew some of my (much) earlier writing. Stephanie McKell, Claire Torrey, Amanda Brown, and Naomi Tajedler, who not only read all of this in various stages of done-ness but managed to cheer me up and keep me excited about writing and kept talking to me even though I do go kind of weird when I'm in the middle of a story. I also want to thank Sandy Hall for just the amount of encouragement I needed to try this in the first place; I might still be trying to work up the courage otherwise.

And then there are the friends, and there are the writing buddies and/or beta readers, who taught me so many things about writing or friendship or both over the years. Maria, Deirdre, Kes, Nicole, Caterina: I don't know if I ever would have gotten here at all if it hadn't been for all of you.

Also, anyone who's ever read any of my stuff and said nice things about it to me, encouraged me, and made me want to keep going: I'll be forever grateful to you for making me believe I could do this. To all of you: thank you!

Check out more books chosen for publication by readers like you.

DID YOU KNOW...

this book was picked by readers like you?

Join our book-obsessed community and help us discover awesome new writing talent.

1

Write it.
Share your original YA manuscript.

2

Read it.
Discover bright new bookish talent.

3

Share it.
Discuss, rate, and share your faves.

4

Love it.
Help us publish the books you love.

Share your own manuscript or dive between the pages at **swoonreads.com**